CRYSTALLINE SPACE

DARK STARS TRILOGY: BOOK 1

A K DUBOFF

Published by Dawnrunner Press
Cover Illustration by Vivid Covers

ISBN-10: 1954344163
ISBN-13: 978-1954344167
Copyright Registration Number: TXu002101391

0 9 8 7 6 5 4 3 2

Produced in the United States of America

TABLE OF CONTENTS

1

FLIRTING WITH DEATH was the perfect way to spend an afternoon.

My slim shadow stretched behind me as I paced along the brink of the cliff, squinting into the setting sun.

Next to me, Adrianne prepared to leap. She grinned from her perch at the edge.

"Just jump already," I urged while securing my pink hair into a braid past my shoulders.

"Relax, Elle. I'm getting in the zone." She stretched her arms wide and leaned forward, surrendering to the wind.

I peeked over the lip as she plummeted toward the depths of the sandstone canyon.

Adrianne's gleeful cheer echoed through the chasm as she fell. She kicked off an outcropping, launching herself into a cartwheel through the air, which she transitioned into a somersault. Every movement was fluid, reaching and twisting in ways I'd never be able to achieve myself.

While I watched her aerial acrobatics, I gripped my left shoulder in my right hand with subconscious envy—my reminder that showing off sometimes came with a price.

"Reset!" I called out to our friend Jiro when Adrianne was almost to the canyon floor.

"Loading," he confirmed behind me.

The air electrified, tingling my skin and pulsing in my ears. White light crept into the corners of my vision, accompanied by an intensifying hum. With a flash, my vision went black.

For a moment, I floated in nothingness. Then, the physical world resolved around me once more. The blackness receded into sunlight and my feet were again solidly on the rocky ground.

I was now standing in the same position I'd been minutes before when I made the reset point at the access terminal. Suspended inside the monument was a two-meter-tall crystal that glowed with a swirling blue inner light.

It was one of four monuments in the vicinity of our community, each connected to a larger crystalline network woven throughout the planet and surrounding worlds. The remarkable properties of the crystals made our play possible.

Every time someone touched one of the crystals, it would record the precise physical state within its zone at that moment—including the kinesthetic abilities, clothing, and hair style of each person, along with the general environmental configuration. The access panel on the monument could then be used to reset the surrounding landscape and our physical forms into one of the previously recorded states with our cognition intact. Out in the remote canyon where it was just us, we could reset as many times as we wanted since the action was restricted to each crystal monument's specific zone.

Adrianne beamed, exhilarated by her recent fall that now only existed in memory. "I needed that."

I let my good arm drop to my side and stepped back from the terminal. "Showoff."

"Let's see your moves." She smirked.

Despite being an unfair competition, I took the bait. "Watch and learn."

"Be quick," Jiro instructed, sweeping aside a lock of dark hair that had fallen in front of his almond eyes. "We need to get back."

He was right; it was almost dinnertime. As much as I dreamed about ways to prolong our last summer of freedom, even resetting the physical world didn't alter the underlying flow of time, only the physical state within the crystal's zone.

"Last one for the night." I jogged to the edge of the cliff and peered into the familiar canyon. It was at least one hundred meters to the bottom, but the shadows made the depth difficult to gauge. I beckoned Adrianne over. "Spot me."

We had learned the hard way to reset before hitting the bottom. Since we retained all of our memories after each physical reset, the splat at the end kind of put a damper on the thrill of freefall.

"I'm watching," she assured me.

I took a deep breath and raised my arms—my left only making it forty-five degrees from my side due to the permanent effects of a childhood injury. Even though I couldn't put on an aerial show as well as Adrianne, I could still fly.

A gust of wind crested the canyon and I leaned forward.

"Wait!" Jiro shouted.

Adrianne yanked me back by my braid.

"What's wrong?" I asked, regaining my balance. No sooner had I spoken than I saw the reason for his concern.

The crystal that normally exuded pleasant blue light now contained a dark cloud.

Jiro took a step away from the monument. "What's wrong with it?"

Adrianne and I cautiously approached. As I neared, the cloud took on more definition, as though individual black particulates were floating inside the prism.

"I have no idea," I murmured.

Nothing had ever disrupted the crystal before. Its existence was a given—as much as the sun rising and having chores.

"We should go," Adrianne stated as she backed toward the path leading to our town.

"Maybe it needs to recharge or something," Jiro suggested, following her.

"Yeah," I agreed, though I didn't believe it, and followed my longtime friends away from the canyon.

"Should we tell someone?" Adrianne asked. "I've never seen anything like that in one of the crystals."

"That would require explaining why we were out here," Jiro pointed out.

"That's *definitely* not going to happen." There was no way my mother would approve of me repeatedly jumping off a cliff in the adjacent zone while she prepared dinner back home. Especially after what had happened six years ago, this was the last place I wanted her to know I hung out. What she didn't know wouldn't worry her.

"If we're going to keep this to ourselves, then we should monitor it," Adrianne said.

"We could come back to check on the crystal tonight," I proposed. "If it looks good, maybe we could get in a night jump."

Adrianne beamed. "I *do* enjoy falling under the stars."

"Well, it's not like I have anywhere to be first thing in the morning," Jiro said with a devious sparkle in his eyes.

"Sneaking out for a night jump… it's like we're fourteen again." I chuckled.

"Only now we're better at not getting caught." Adrianne winked at me.

I smiled back. "22:00?"

"Works for me," Jiro agreed.

Adrianne nodded. "You know I'm in."

We picked our way through a field of boulders along our standard path. The rough terrain would be difficult for the uninitiated to navigate, but vaulting over rocks and sidestepping sticker bushes was second-nature to me.

I kept my gaze straight ahead as we crossed the border from the canyon crystal's zone to the domain of the town's crystal, trying to ignore the rock formation that had changed my life when I was twelve. My fall from the four-meter-tall boulder in the town's zone had dislocated my shoulder and broken my arm—a seemingly minor injury at first—but deeper tissue damage that knitted into scar tissue forever impaired my arm's mobility. By the time the doctors realized what had happened, it was too late to repair and the window for a town reset had long since passed.

As I'd come to grips with the injury and what it might mean for my future, I'd often fantasized about a universal-scale reset that wasn't limited by the rules governing our town. If everything everywhere could be reset, I could go back to how I was before the accident, just like everyone else would get a second chance. We could make things how they should be. Of course, that was impossible; one girl's minor injury wasn't worth disrupting our community, let alone the dozens of planets in the Hegemony's purview.

My mom always told me what was in the past was done; the only way was forward. I'd heard it so many times that part of me believed it, but deep down there was still lingering bitterness. Thanks to that one stupid mistake as a kid, I feared

I'd never be able to have the kind of future I'd dreamed about in the space force.

I suppressed the resentment welling in my chest. There was nothing I could do about it now.

Eventually, the trail became more defined, and we broke into a light jog. The sun was low in the sky by the time we reached pavement. I might be late for dinner, but not terribly.

The final path segment traced the upper ridge of the hills surrounding our town, Ochre. Stucco homes topped with solar panels were situated along meandering streets in the southern portion of the valley, and the administrative, commercial, and educational buildings occupied the north. A social square at the center of town was landscaped with mature trees, their sturdy branches distinct even from my distant vantage. The main crystal for our town at the center of the square cast a faint blue glow through the trees' shadows.

My family's house was toward the southeastern edge of town, so I'd made a shortcut trail down one of the slopes to facilitate easier access to the surrounding hills. "I'll see you tonight!" I called to Adrianne and Jiro as I dashed down my personal corridor toward home.

When I reached the bottom of the hill, I took a moment to dust myself off and smooth my hair. No need to call attention to the fact that I'd been running through bushes rather than focusing on preparations for my future.

I walked the rest of the way to the back entrance of my house. Light shone through the rear kitchen window, illuminating my path along the pavers bisecting my father's vegetable garden in the backyard.

The welcoming sight erased my apprehension about the strange cloud in the canyon crystal, but I tensed with the knowledge that these homeward treks were now numbered.

Without the adrenaline rush of a good cliff jump to clear my mind, my impending departure for the vocational academy crept into my thoughts. In a few weeks, playing in the canyon with my friends would be a distant memory. No more resets for fun—only the pressure of trying to get it right the first time.

Heart heavy, I opened the back door and braced for a berating about my tardy arrival.

"There you are!" my mother exclaimed from the kitchen when the screen door to the mud room clicked shut.

Scents of apple pie and steamed potatoes wafted toward me as I slipped off my shoes. "Sorry I'm late!"

I padded into the kitchen, my stomach letting out a low growl. Seated at the wooden table in the center of the room, my younger brother, Ben, was absorbed in a puzzle game on his tablet. At the counter along the back wall overlooking the garden, my mother was in the process of spooning freshly whipped potatoes into a blue serving bowl.

With the hope of stealing a taste, I headed for the counter, ruffling Ben's blond mop of hair as I passed by.

He batted away my hand with more force than normal; I guess at fourteen he was getting a little old for me to mess with him. "Mom said it's your turn to take out the trash," he mumbled without shifting his gaze from his tablet.

"The fish from last night is… lingering," my mother said, wrinkling her petite nose beneath evergreen eyes like my own.

"I'm on it." I pivoted on my heel and went back to the receptacle in the mud room.

As soon as the lid was cracked open, I understood the urgency of the request. Holding my breath, I slipped out the bag while jamming my feet back into my shoes, then sprinted around the side of the house to deposit the garbage into the central collector. When the bin was safely re-sealed, I took a deep breath. "I won't miss this—"

The chime in the town square pierced the quiet evening.

My pulse spiked as I ran back inside. "There isn't a town meeting tonight, is there?" I asked the moment I was through the kitchen door, shoes still on.

Ben had set down his tablet, and my father now stood in the archway between the kitchen and living room with his own tablet in hand. The worried glances passing between my parents confirmed my suspicion that the alarm wasn't for a scheduled event.

"Dinner can wait," my mother stated, wiping her hands on a dish towel. "Let's go."

"Any changes to log?" my father asked as the four of us headed through the living room toward the front door.

I shook my head since I hadn't made any purchases in the last three days that had yet to be recorded in the Hegemony's central database.

Ben groaned. "My game is new. Lemme back it up real quick." He darted back into the kitchen to his tablet.

The lines of worry on my father's forehead deepened as we waited. Unscheduled meetings were a rarity, and they almost never brought good news.

However, I tried to remain positive. After all, if something terrible had happened, we could fall back on the town's archive in the event of an accident more serious than a broken arm. Any inanimate objects would reset, too, so long as the raw materials were still within the crystal's zone and the object had been inside the zone during the previous check-in. Occasionally, handmade trinkets may be lost in our local resets, but it was worth the wellbeing of our town's inhabitants—especially since digital content was always secure on the Hegemony's offworld servers.

When Ben was finished backing up his game, we stepped out into the street along with the dozen other families on our block. The group of us hurried past the row of stucco houses as we headed toward the central square.

"Have you heard anything about the meeting?" my father asked one of our neighbors.

"No," he replied. "Interrupting dinner like this—must be important."

As we merged onto the main street into the heart of town, I kept an eye out for Adrianne and Jiro. In the back of my mind, I couldn't help but wonder if the unscheduled meeting had anything to do with the dark cloud we'd witnessed up in the canyon crystal.

My mother's hand brushed my back. "There's no need to be nervous."

"I'm not." But part of me *was* concerned. I could only remember three unscheduled meetings in my eighteen years of life; something must be seriously wrong.

"Not just about tonight," my mother continued in the tone she slipped into when she was channeling her day job as a therapist. "I've seen you reading over the course offerings at the Academy. You'll find something that's a good fit."

I stared down at my feet as I walked. "It all seems so…"

"Boring?" she completed for me.

"I was going to say 'mundane', but yeah."

She smiled and squeezed my right shoulder. "Knowing you, you'll find a way to make it interesting."

Maybe she was right, but nothing in the course catalog had piqued my interest in the slightest. The only path that sounded remotely appealing was becoming a Ranger in the Hegemony's space force, but I wasn't ready to tell my parents I was interested in applying to Tactical School. Even though I knew the Rangers would probably reject me because of my bum shoulder, I couldn't help dreaming about it. But, I needed to be realistic. And have options. To satisfy my parents and keep multiple paths open, I figured I'd try the vocational academy for one semester and then take it from there.

We arrived at the town square and found that most of Ochre's two thousand other residents had already congregated in the open plaza facing the crystal and its surrounding access terminal. Members of the crowd were shifting on their feet, eyes darting. Parents clutched their children tightly as urgent conversations buzzed throughout the square, speculating about the reason for the alarm.

The atmosphere was a stark contrast to our standard weekly assemblies, a special service where we would watch Mayor Therman touch the crystal to initiate a backup record for our community. Though he performed the task every day, watching the task was a weekly tradition; it gave us assurance that there was always a backup, specifically to ease our minds in situations such as this.

However, assurances only went so far.

"Dad, what's going on?" Ben asked with a quaver in his voice.

"Here's Mayor Therman," my father replied, his gaze fixed on the platform surrounding the crystal. "I'm sure he'll explain everything."

The elderly mayor approached the railing at the edge of the platform a meter above the paved square. He held up a frail hand, and the din of conversation faded to silence. "Thank you all for coming so quickly. We received a message from the Capital this evening about reports from the outer colonies related to a crystalline network malfunction."

Conversations reignited in the crowd, overpowering the

mayor's raspy voice.

"Quiet, please!" the city manager, Dilon, cut in. He held up his hands and waited for the townspeople to settle.

"As a precaution," the mayor continued, "the Hegemony has issued an order for us to perform a global reset. We will go back one month."

My parents each placed a reassuring hand on Ben's and my shoulders.

Local resets were common enough, but I'd only ever experienced one coordinated planet-scale reset before, when a transport shuttle exploded in a freak accident several years prior. We'd gone back three days to the previous check-in point that time. To go a whole month meant that something major must be going on.

"Just so long as I don't have to retake my final exams," I muttered in an attempt to break the tension.

"I'm sure the records have already been sent to the Academy, don't worry," my mother replied, missing my intended humor.

"Man, that's going to be a pain to reset all of the clocks," Ben added.

I wasn't sure if it was his own attempt at levity or genuine annoyance. Keeping track of *when* we were was always a challenge with any reset, by virtue of it being a rollback to a previous physical state rather than actual time travel. Anything outside the reset zone stayed the same, so we relied on the master clocks in the Capital for us to resync with the rest of society. We always made the town reset points for the same time of day to minimize confusion, but I couldn't remember where I may have been a month ago at the time of the reset point they intended to use.

Regardless of the logistic headache surrounding the reset,

my chest tightened as I thought about why the order was given in the first place. I feared the reset must have to do with the darkness in the canyon crystal—it was too big of a coincidence. That meant it was on other worlds, too.

With a renewed wave of alarm, I realized that I had touched the infected crystal moments before the darkness appeared. "Dad, I should have said something sooner, but—"

"Resetting," the mayor announced as he reached for the access terminal.

Before I could finish my warning, an electrical charge surged through the air and my ears buzzed. The world distorted around me into white light. Everything vanished into nothingness.

I floated in the darkness, drifting with no sense of self. I waited. And waited.

The reset was taking far too long—reality should be reforming by now. My consciousness wanted to panic, but I had no corporeal form to react.

Then, a physical world finally began to solidify at the edges of my vision. Except rather than the town square, I appeared to be in some sort of glass enclosure too brightly lit for me to see beyond its boundaries.

My eyes struggled to adjust to the dazzling light above me. A dark-haired man in a black uniform came into focus on the other side of the glass half a meter from my face.

"Are you a boy or a girl?" he asked me.

I blinked with confusion. At least, I think I blinked. Somehow I still didn't feel fully connected to myself. "A girl…" I said.

"What is your name?"

"Elle," I replied, more certain in my response this time. "Elle Hartmut."

A warm tingle ran through my limbs. As it passed, I was left with a renewed sense of my physical form.

Before I could look around to get my bearings, the man activated a holographic projection in front of me, depicting a sword, a shield, and a wand with a star on the end. "What is your strength?" he asked.

I evaluated the symbols. Was it a test?

The shield called to me initially, given my defensive attitude toward the whole situation. However, the wand was a much more alluring choice, almost certainly indicating magic. I was about to respond with that selection, but I caught myself. I'd always wanted to be strong—to regain the physical prowess I'd lost when I was injured. "The sword," I stated.

"Are you sure?" the man asked.

"Yes." Another tingling wave passed through my limbs and torso. My senses sharpened and I felt physically charged, ready to push myself to my limits.

"You are a fighter. Use your strength well," the man stated as he stepped back. The front half of the glass cylinder, which had a frosted band in the middle, swung open. "You're lucky you survived."

"What do you mean?" I stepped out of the chamber, unsteady on my feet. Looking down at myself, I realized I was wearing a white, form-fitting jumpsuit that was nothing like anything in my wardrobe. My pulse spiked. "Where am I? Where's my family?"

The middle-aged man strode across the sterile room to the side wall and touched a panel. With a mechanical whir, a section of the wall rolled down behind the smooth interior surface.

My breath caught as I stared out the newly exposed viewport. A planet—*my* planet—loomed before me, luminescent blue and brown set against a starscape. Dark tendrils were snaking through the atmosphere.

Panic constricted my chest. "What's going on?"

"Elle, I'm Commander Alastair Colren and you are aboard the *Evangiel*," he replied. "I represent the Hegemony. We have a mission for you."

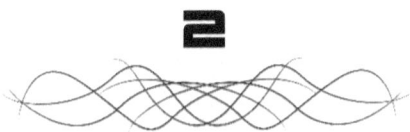

"HUH?" I WANTED to say something more articulate, but that was the best I had at the moment.

"Forgive me, this all must come as quite a shock." Commander Colren took a seat at a metal table near the viewport. He gestured to an acrylic chair across from him.

"You could say that." Dumbfounded, I stumbled toward the empty seat. I couldn't stop staring out the viewport at my home planet of Erusan. Was I really in space? I'd seen images and tried to imagine the view from a spaceship, but this... It didn't seem possible.

I took a shaky breath. "How did I get here?"

"I'll explain everything, don't worry," Colren replied.

"None of this makes any sense. What do you mean you have a mission for me? I'm no one."

Colren examined me with his piercing hazel eyes. "Had you recently come into contact with a crystal that exhibited a dark cloud?"

I struggled to think back to the events from a few hours before. "Yeah, I was hanging out with my friends outside of town, doing localized resets. We were just about to do another reset when we noticed it."

"In that moment, you were... altered," he explained.

I gaped at him. "What? How?"

"It's something like an immunity. You had a brief touch with the Darkness during the reset just prior, so when you encountered it again during the global reset, you were prepared to hang onto your sense of self."

My heart sank. "What about my friends? They touched the infected crystal, too."

"Unfortunately, we can only perform the extraction on one person at a time. You were the fortunate one," Colren replied.

"What about my family? My world?" Fear and worry clouded my mind. My parents, my brother, everyone who meant anything to me was still down there. They couldn't be gone.

The commander took a slow breath. "The world is suspended and its records are preserved in the Master Archive."

"Suspended? What in the stars does *that* mean?"

"It's a way of locking the records so they don't become corrupted. It's the best we can do once the Darkness infects a planet," he continued. "But you can help us do more."

I barked a nervous laugh. "Yeah. Right!" Either the last reset had messed with my head, or the man across from me was insane. I was leaning toward the former option; people didn't randomly wake up on spaceships. I had to be dreaming.

"Elle, I know this might seem like an elaborate prank, but I assure you it's not. You're special and we need you." The commander looked me square in the eyes—dead serious, as far as I could tell.

I inched back in my chair. "Whatever you think I am, I'm

not. I can't help you." The Hegemony needed scientists or heroic soldiers. Not me. As much as I aspired to be a Ranger, I knew it wouldn't happen. I was physically broken—and I certainly wasn't a genius.

The commander folded his hands on the table. "You're *exactly* who we need."

"I'm a kid."

He nodded. "The young do seem to be the most drawn during the extraction; there's a fearlessness in youth. I'd never discount someone because of age alone."

I still didn't believe any of it was real, but he certainly did. I figured if I heard him out, maybe that would end the insanity; all I wanted was to go back home and finish my summer vacation. I crossed my arms and leaned back in my seat, studying his expression for any tells that might reveal his true intentions. "What is it you want me to do?"

"We are assembling a team of others that have been extracted like you. Together, we hope that you'll be able to help us track down the cause for the spreading Darkness, and stop it. With your immunity, you'll be able to go places others can't."

Articulate speech failed me again. Me, stop the Darkness? Now he was *really* talking crazy. I laughed and shook my head with disbelief.

"It first appeared three months ago," Colren continued, undeterred. "Initially, we thought it was an isolated anomaly, but when it started to spread, we had to take action. We developed the extraction procedure to give us a means to fight back."

I wanted to dismiss his statements, but I was struck by the gravity of his tone. Maybe this wasn't a nightmare after all. If I really was on a Hegemony spaceship, and if my world was now uninhabitable, as he indicated, I had no idea where I could go.

My heart pounded in my chest. "I still don't understand how I got here. It doesn't seem possible."

"We have certain technology that's not exactly public knowledge," the commander replied. "Frankly, we don't know how it works, but it does."

I raised an eyebrow. "Magic?"

He chuckled. "You joke, but it may as well be."

Crazy or not, the thought of legitimate magic use caught my attention. I leaned forward with my elbows on the table. "What was that test you gave me when I first woke up?"

"The extraction procedure is for consciousness, but your physical manifestation is more fluid based on fragmented data stored in the crystalline network. Those questions were to bring your new body into focus and solidify your innate traits."

It was then that I noticed the long hair hanging down around my shoulders—not the faded pink dye job from minutes before on my homeworld, but bright fuchsia. And it didn't look like dye. "What the—?" I nearly leaped out of my chair.

As I tensed, I noticed that my left shoulder didn't feel tight in the way I was used to. I rolled it and then raised my arm, finding that I had full range of motion.

"Stars, I—" My chest constricted.

"This is you," Colren said. "The real you that you wanted to be."

"How did you...?"

Colren smiled with compassion. "Think of it like this: pretend your mind is like a digital file that we would back up on one of the central servers. The original computer used to create that file became corrupted. That file has now been downloaded into a new, better computer that was optimized to run that file. Likewise, your new body was bioprinted in that chamber to fit the ideals contained within your consciousness—built to your own specifications."

It still sounded like madness. I ran my fingers through the soft, fuchsia strands. "I guess I did have a few changes in mind."

"Whoever you were before, you still are. Now, you're just a different version of yourself."

I could barely breathe. Losing my world, my family, my friends. But gaining a whole, new body? It was too much to process. I wasn't broken anymore, yet I was separated from my loved ones and had no idea if I'd ever see them again. As much as I wanted to be healed, it wasn't a worthwhile trade.

I swallowed the lump in my throat. "And now I'm alone."

"Not alone," he hastily replied. "The others we've extracted have also found themselves to be faster and stronger than they were before."

"Others?" My heart skipped a beat, relief washing over me with the revelation that I wasn't the only one who'd been unexpectedly yanked from my home. If nothing else, we'd have that in common.

He nodded. "You have two companions so far, but we hope to be able to extract others. They have each manifested certain… abilities."

"Like what?"

Before he could answer, a thud sounded through the interior bulkhead, followed by a series of scuffles and another bang.

The commander sighed. "It would seem that one of your companions is experimenting again."

"That doesn't sound good."

"Oh, he's only getting used to his new body." Colren glanced at the wall. "Some of the transformations have been more substantial than others."

Not that I'd had a choice, but I was wondering more and more what I'd been pulled into. I cautiously eyed the side wall where the sound had come from. "May I meet them?"

"No sense in waiting." Colren rose from his chair and headed for the door on the wall opposite the viewport. "Try not to stare."

"At what?" I asked as I followed him.

"You'll see."

The door automatically slid to the side when we approached, revealing a steel-lined corridor. Struck with a blast of cooler air, I folded my arms to augment the insulation offered by the ruched white jumpsuit and followed Colren through the doorway. Holopanels and information displays integrated with the corridor walls hinted at a level of technological utilization that was far beyond anything in my day-to-day life back home, and I found myself awestruck by features that were probably commonplace for everyone else on the ship. The corridor curved gradually to the side in both directions, so it was impossible to see the ends. Doors lined both sides of the hall at irregular intervals, and we headed for one six meters to the right, adjacent to the room where I woke up.

Colren pressed his palm against a panel on the smooth wall. Following a beep, the door next to it slid open with a low hiss.

Scuffling sounds echoed out into the corridor, accompanied by the shout of a youthful male voice, "Relax, Toran! It's just the commander."

"And I have a new member for your group," Colren said as he stepped through the threshold.

Steeling myself, I peeked into the room.

Inside, Colren had stopped half a meter inside the door with his back to me, partially obstructing my view. To his left, I could make out the refined profile of a man in his early-twenties. His medium-brown hair was styled into a faux hawk and well-muscled arms flexed the fabric of his white jumpsuit.

The young man turned to face the door, training his captivating sky-blue eyes on me. "Why, hello there." He cracked a smile, brushing his index finger over a translucent crystal pendant hanging around his neck.

"Hi." I smiled back, hating that my cheeks suddenly felt flushed.

"This is Kaiden," Colren said, swiveling to face me. "He was the first we were able to retrieve."

Kaiden mimed tipping an invisible hat to me. "Pleasure to make your acquaintance."

"I'm Elle," I replied.

"Nice hair," a deep voice said from beyond the commander.

Then, I noticed the behemoth of a man who had been obscured from view when I first entered. Standing two meters tall and with the broadest shoulders I'd ever seen, the other man was a solid wall of muscle. The tattered top half of his white jumpsuit was tied around his waist.

"I rather like the new color," I responded to his flippant comment while I tried not to gawk at his exaggerated proportions.

"And this is Toran," Colren continued. "It's only been two days since we retrieved him."

"I've been hitting the gym pretty hard since then," Toran said with a grin.

I relaxed, seeing his good nature beneath the chiseled exterior. "I bet I could still beat you in a footrace."

"If there's anything left to run over," Kaiden interjected.

The dented floor and walls near Toran illustrated his point, which was underscored by a pile of twisted metal that appeared to be chair remains and perhaps a handful of shelving units.

Toran shrugged. "Don't knock it until you try it. Folding a chair or two is surprisingly empowering."

"I'll bet," Kaiden muttered under his breath.

I examined Toran. "Let me guess—you chose the shield, in the test when you were waking up."

Toran nodded.

"What about you?" I asked Kaiden.

"The wand, of course," he responded with a matter-of-fact tone like it was the most obvious choice in the world. "Didn't you?"

I shook my head. "No, the sword."

"Shame. You're missing out." A ball of sparkling white light appeared over the palm of Kaiden's outstretched right hand.

"Not in here!" Colren cut in.

The orb faded from his palm. "The demonstrations will have to wait for another time, I suppose."

"Like when you can't accidentally vent us into space by hurling a rogue fireball at the viewport." The commander smoothed his black uniform.

"I've gained a lot of control since then," Kaiden countered.

"All the same," Colren continued, "now that there are three of you—one from each discipline—we need to seal the Master Archive."

I glanced at the men's faces as they each nodded gravely. "Sorry, did I miss something?"

"The Darkness is advancing," Colren replied. "If we don't seal the Master Archive, it will be consumed and we'll have no means to reset the worlds after we stop the Darkness."

"Right, I figured out that much from context. But what was that about 'one from each discipline', and why us?"

"Oh, we're the divinely gifted almighty ones," Kaiden quipped. "They do like to skip over that part of the initiation briefing."

Colren groaned. "It's hardly that dramatic. You see, when the part of your consciousness that exists outside of spacetime was re-knitting with your new body, you were tapping into your most ancient genetic history—drawing on fragments scattered throughout the crystal backups from back in the time when the crystalline network was still forming. We know of a place that is believed to be the origin of the crystals, and there's a sanctuary around it to protect the Archive if ever there was a threat in the future. That sanctuary needs to be activated by three individuals embodying the tenets of ancient culture—strength, protection, and higher-self. By aligning with one of those tenets, you were imbued with the skills and predisposition to embody its ideals. Together, you can activate the safeguards around the Master Archive and buy us time while we figure out how to stop the Darkness for good."

I pursed my lips. "Nope, that does sound pretty dramatic."

Kaiden made a flourish of vindication with his hands.

"Regardless," Colren pressed on, "we need you. Sealing the Archive will be your first mission as a team, and it's imperative that you're successful."

Toran grunted. "No pressure."

I took a deep breath, my nerves fraying. "Okay, so we have some sort of ancient abilities now. But how does the sealing work? Are there any instructions?"

"No. That is for you to figure out," Colren replied. "I'm sure it will become clear when you arrive."

"Yeah… not buying it," I said. "This all still sounds crazy to me."

Kaiden laughed. "See, Toran? It's not just us saying so."

Our eyes locked for a moment, and the apprehension I'd been feeling since I woke up started to melt away. As bizarre as the situation was, others were facing the same set of impossible circumstances. I don't know if it was a byproduct of the extraction procedure or something else, but I felt at ease with Kaiden and Toran. I'd always been one to know within a few seconds of meeting someone if we'd get along or not, and I could tell that my two teammates were my kind of people.

"We can talk more once we reach our destination." Colren pulled out a communicator from his front pocket and made an entry. "There's no reason for us to linger here."

A moment later, a woman's voice came over the comm, "Jump in T-minus five minutes."

"Not again…" Kaiden murmured.

"Get strapped in," Colren instructed. " I need to get to my pod in Central Command." He rushed out of the room.

"We're about to do a spatial jump?" I asked, apprehension pitching my voice. Interstellar travel was common enough between the dozens of Hegemony systems, but I'd never left my home planet. I hadn't yet wrapped my head around being on a spaceship, let alone the notion of traveling through hyperspace to another system.

"Don't worry. It's every bit as disorienting as it sounds," Kaiden flashed me another grin and jogged toward the hallway door. "The pods are this way."

Hesitantly, I followed him with Toran close behind.

Kaiden led us down the corridor to one of the interior doors a dozen meters past the previous room. The chamber contained six oval pods arranged around a circular center console. An open transparent cover on each pod exposed an ergonomic couch within.

Without hesitation, Kaiden hurdled into the pod furthest from the door and began securing a harness. "Make sure the straps are tight."

"Very funny," Toran growled as he squeezed himself through the opening of a pod to the left of the door.

I jogged around to the pod on Kaiden's right so I could examine how he had buckled his harness. After making a quick mental note of the configuration, I reclined in my pod and began clipping the belts across myself. "Is all of this really necessary?"

"See what you think after the jump," Kaiden replied.

Just as I cinched up the last strap, the same announcer came over the comm again. "Jump in T-minus one minute."

"Good luck!" Kaiden called from next to me as the lids to our pods slid shut.

In the enclosed space, my heartbeat and breathing were almost deafening.

"Jump in T-minus thirty seconds," the announcer informed through a speaker inside the pod.

A static charge hummed in the pod, and I felt heavier—like I was being sucked against the seat.

At the ten-second mark, the announcer began a final countdown. "... Two... One."

Next thing I knew, my stomach was in my ears and my heart was at my feet. Reality elongated around me, then everything went black.

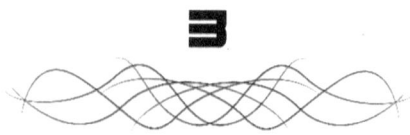

3

"ELLE. ELLE!" A voice roused me from the blackness.

My eyes shot open.

Kaiden was leaning over me, releasing my harness. "You passed out."

I groaned as I propped myself up on my elbows, realizing I was no longer strapped down. My head ached. "What just…?"

"Congratulations! You just completed your first spatial jump." Kaiden smiled down at me.

"I felt like I was being turned inside out."

"Yeah, good times."

I pressed the heel of my right hand to my temple. "I guess being strapped into the pods is a good idea, after all."

"I thought your opinion would come around," Kaiden replied, pushing back from my pod to give me some space.

"You'll get used to it," Toran's voice boomed from across the room. "Come on. We're being paged."

Still feeling like my stomach was lodged in my throat, I lurched out of the jump pod. "Where are we now?"

"That's a very good question," Kaiden replied as we exited

the room. "They haven't exactly been forthcoming with the logistics about our mission."

"I feel like I'm in a dream." The throbbing in my head was beginning to fade, but the physical sensation enforced that what I'd just been through was real.

Kaiden offered a sympathetic smile. "I'm still trying to get over that feeling myself."

"None of this makes sense," Toran said. "Colren's account of why we were chosen doesn't really explain it."

I scrunched up my nose. "Yeah, that whole thing about getting an 'immunity' from the Darkness? What is the Darkness, anyway?"

"The cloud appeared after an emergency reset where I was," Kaiden said. "I'd never seen anything like it—freaked everyone out."

"Yeah, same with me. My friends and I weren't sure if we should tell anyone."

"No one else saw it?" he asked. "I thought planets like yours had a crystal in the town square or something."

"We do, but that wasn't where it appeared. We were out by one in a canyon."

"A localized reset, then?"

I nodded. "We'd go up there to play around."

He raised an eyebrow. "Doing what, rock climbing?"

"We'd jump off a cliff."

His eyes widened. "I was not expecting you to say that."

I smiled coyly. "I have an adventurous side."

"I used to collect rocks!" Toran looked down at his hands and sighed. "There wasn't a lot to do on Dunlore."

I awkwardly patted his huge shoulder. "Something tells me we're going to have plenty of adventure coming up."

We took the corridor to a nearby lift, passing by two

groups of soldiers and a handful of solitary officers who cast us sidelong glances. I suspected that everyone on the ship knew who we were, at least in a general sense, and I found it odd that given our apparent importance we were expected to show ourselves around. Granted, it seemed like Kaiden had been given a proper tour and knew his way to the various locations of note; maybe they considered him our guide.

We entered the lift and rode it up two decks. I barely perceived any movement, unlike the elevators I was used to back home.

Kaiden must have noticed my awed expression, because he looked me over and chuckled. "It's just a lift, Elle."

"To you, maybe! I still can't get over the fact that I'm on a spaceship."

The door opened, and he smiled. "You haven't seen anything yet."

We stepped out and took a corridor to the left past a pod room and a weapons vault until it terminated at a door. Kaiden placed his hand on an adjacent panel. Rather than the door opening, a blue light blinked and a chime sounded.

"What's with the security?" I asked.

"This is the entry to Central Command," Kaiden replied. "I suspect they don't want people barging in right in the middle of a sensitive maneuver."

"I guess that makes sense. It just struck me as strange after they've left us to wander around on our own."

"They run the ship how they want it run," Toran said. "You know how boss people can be."

The door slid open, revealing Colren standing on the other side. "That's how us boss people are, huh?"

Toran turned bright red. "Sorry, sir, I didn't mean—"

The corners of Colren's lips curled up with amusement.

"All things considered, that's an appropriate title. You're not officially military soldiers, so I'm not your superior officer beyond my role as captain of this vessel."

I eyed him. "But we also don't have much of a choice about being here."

"That was one of the things I wanted to talk with you about," he replied. "Let's get settled in the conference room."

We followed him into the open area beyond the doorway. Central Command appeared to be a cross between an administrative operations center and the starships' bridges I'd seen depicted in media. I knew the technology existed, but I'd never witnessed it in person. Everyone around me seemed in their element, but I couldn't help doing numerous double-takes as I studied the room.

The area nearest the entry door was flanked by two crescent-shaped workstations equipped with monitors, a touch-surface desktop, and a number of holographic displays with complex readouts that may as well have been in another language. The four crew members working at the consoles glanced up at us as we passed by. Based on their tempered reactions, it seemed that they must have seen Toran in the past; if anything, my bright fuchsia hair drew more attention. Even as the workstations drew my eye, I was awestruck by the attention to detail in the blue and gray crew members' uniforms and their effortless use of the complex systems around them. I'd never thought of Erusan as being a backwater world, yet seeing the Hegemony ship, I realized just how much I'd missed out on.

Further into the bridge, a single command chair was surrounded by four additional consoles, all facing toward an expansive viewscreen spanning the curved forward wall. The domed ceiling above was inlaid with a ring of lights, and additional lighting around the baseboard of the perimeter illuminated the space to almost daylight levels. The starboard wall contained a row of a dozen pods like the one I'd used for the jump, though these were arranged vertically.

My eye was drawn to the front viewscreen by the glow of a purple-hued planet below. Despite the strange color, the cloud cover looked similar to my homeworld... except it was in another star system.

I was about to visit another planet.

Excitement welled in my chest despite the confusion and uncertainty swirling in my mind. Though the circumstances were far from ideal, this was the kind of adventure I'd fantasized about for as long as I could remember. I could be scared, or I could embrace it for what it was. This was my chance to prove myself. I didn't want to mess it up.

Colren led us to the left toward a separate conference room with seating for twelve. A transparent wall separated the room from the main bridge. As the commander passed through the entry door, he passed his hand over the wall and it altered to opaque off-white.

"Please, take a seat." He gestured to the near side of the table while walking around to sit in the center across from us.

I grabbed a chair to Kaiden's right while Toran sat to his left.

"So, the mission..." Kaiden said on our behalf.

"Right." Colren folded his hands on the tabletop. "This planet, Crystallis, holds the Master Archive. Only a handful of people in the upper echelon of the Hegemony know its location. It's imperative that this site be protected at any cost."

"And all we have to do is 'seal it'?" I asked, trying to get myself in the right frame of mind to embrace the bizarre scenario.

He nodded. "Yes, but I suspect that will be more complicated than it sounds. As we understand it, regular people aren't allowed to access the Archive. We know it's there, in the sense that we can see how everything around it behaves, but we can't get to the thing itself."

Toran tilted his head. "Like dark matter, only... not?"

"The technology behind the crystals predates our civilization by millennia. Though we don't understand how they operate, exactly, we do know that this world is the hub of their power. What little we have been able to glean from the world has spurred all our scientific advances—from our jump drives to the device that harnessed your hyperdimensional consciousness and the bioprinter that created these new bodies for you. If we have any hope of finding a solution to this Darkness infecting our worlds, the clues will be down there."

I crossed my arms. "And only we can access that tech, because we're the only ones who have been modified by it. I'm not sure if that makes sense or if it's insane."

"Convenient, if nothing else," Kaiden responded.

"Sounds like a safeguard to make sure outsiders can't get too much, too fast. Need to master one development in order to advance enough to get the next," Toran hypothesized.

Colren inclined his head. "Quite possibly."

"Okay, say we seal the Archive. Then what?" I asked.

The commander looked each of us in the eyes. "Then we figure out how to fight back."

"Not to be too self-deprecating here," Kaiden said, "but are we really the right people to take that on? Three untrained strangers, and you're pretty much tasking us with saving all of known civilization. I mean, c'mon."

"Yeah, I just graduated secondary school a month ago," I interjected. Opportunity or not, the realist in me recognized that I was in way over my head.

"It's not an ideal scenario, I know," Colren said. "We won't force you to do anything, but I'll lay out the case in as compelling a manner as I can. As of right now, we don't know what this Darkness is or where it came from. All that we *do* know is that you are the only three people to have encountered it on your worlds and made it out."

I raised my hand, and Colren inclined his head for me to speak. "I still don't understand the technology behind our bodies materializing here on the ship, but I'll ignore that for now. What I really want to know is how you knew to be at our worlds to have us 'download' at that time?"

He nodded and took a slow breath. "We're still getting our bearings, as well. The short version is that we have information regarding the Darkness' advance, and we have been waiting near the impacted worlds with the hope that we might be able to extract a few people."

Kaiden folded his hands on the desktop. "You keep glossing over a lot of details. I've been here for more than a week now, and you still won't explain anything about the Darkness or how you knew our abilities would manifest."

"There's not a simple answer to that besides all of the pieces falling into place," Colren stated.

"Well, we're listening." Kaiden tilted his head.

The Hedgeman representative leaned back in his chair. "Okay, well, for starters, there's more to the Master Archive than we typically discuss on public forums," he began. "We talk about the records being a documentation of what's already happened… but there are also records of events that haven't happened yet."

My heart skipped a beat. "Pardon?"

Next to me, Kaiden froze. "Do you mean…?"

Colren nodded. "We think that at some point there must have been a universal reset."

"Stars…" My stomach clenched. Some people had suggested a reset on that scale might be possible, but I never imagined that it may have already happened. "Is there any way to know for sure?"

"Unlike the interface consoles with the colonies, there aren't dates attached to the Master Archive—at least not using a code we yet understand," Colren continued. "The only reason we began to suspect the Archive records extend beyond real-time is because we noticed that certain branches of the records have blank spots corresponding with worlds getting consumed by the Darkness, and those blanks continue for some undetermined amount of time before resuming again."

"So, we beat this thing?" Toran asked.

The commander nodded. "We hope so."

Kaiden squinted. "Wait, you said that no regular people could go into the Archives, and we're the first modified people to have a chance of entering. How have you seen any of that?"

"Like I said, it's not straightforward. We can't get into the vault, but we can still observe parts of it."

"How?" Kaiden pressed.

"There are certain… relays, which enable us to access parts of the data contained within the crystals. We only know of four such devices—one of which is on this ship."

"And that's how you first got the tech for jump drives and the rest?" I asked.

Colren inclined his head. "That was almost two hundred years ago. The Hegemony uncovered the first device on one of the moons in orbit of the Capital world, and we've been following the breadcrumbs ever since. Though use of the crystals dates back to our people's earliest records and we've had the rudimentary control mechanisms we use today, it wasn't until the discovery of the interface device that we started to understand how the crystals work and where they may have come from."

I leaned forward. "Which is…?"

"We don't know," the commander admitted. "Whoever made them did it a long time ago using tech far more advanced than we can comprehend."

"I always thought the crystals themselves were natural formations," I said.

"Yeah, same," Kaiden murmured.

Toran tilted his head. "Meaning, these new abilities come from some kind of tech rather than magic?"

"It's not a clear distinction," Colren replied.

Kaiden smiled. "Whatever makes it possible, I'll take it."

"Says Mister Fireball," Toran ribbed.

"Hey, we all got to choose our skills." Kaiden shrugged.

Toran folded his arms, causing his biceps to bulge. "I regret nothing."

"Me either," I said, but I wasn't convinced. The idea of having magic-like abilities still called to me, but a lot of that may be due to not having had the chance to test out the new skills I *did* have.

"The question remains, will you help us?" Colren pressed.

I met his gaze. "I will."

Kaiden nodded after a slight pause. "Yes, I'll never shy away from a challenge."

"I'm in," Toran agreed

"Thank you." The commander looked genuinely relieved.

"Probably best not to thank us yet," Kaiden said. "We have no idea how to do what you're asking."

Colren nodded. "Willingness to try is the first step."

"Do we, like, take a shuttle down there, or…?" I prompted.

"Yes, acquire your gear and arm yourselves, then proceed to the hangar," the commander instructed.

"Is there someone to walk us through that, or—" I started to ask.

"I trust that you don't require supervision. Kaiden knows where to go to get everything you need. Dismissed." Colren marched back to the bridge.

"For being the universe's last, best hope, isn't it a little weird that he's turning us loose on the ship to do our own thing?" I whispered. "Shouldn't we have escorts, or something?"

Kaiden shrugged. "I was a little thrown off by that when I first got here, too. What I've realized is that it's safe here, and all of the control rooms are staffed. If we can't be trusted to fend for ourselves on the ship, we'd be hopeless planetside."

"True."

We filed out of the conference room back through the bridge to the corridor.

When we were alone in the hallway, Toran let out a long breath. "Also, for getting answers, why do I have even more questions now?"

Kaiden chuckled. "The feeling is mutual."

I shook my head. "This entire thing feels ridiculous. I mean, the tech that they're talking about here…"

"Saying it's from ancient aliens?" Toran sighed. "What are they going to tell us next?"

"Honestly, I'm kind of relieved," Kaiden said. "I've always liked the idea of magic—"

"I know we just met, but that was pretty obvious by the fact that you picked the wand," I interjected.

He rolled his eyes. "Well, yeah. But even liking it, it was

strange to think of something like a fireball materializing out of nothing. Though that explanation we got doesn't begin to explain how it's possible, it does at least indicate that someone at some time figured out how to make it work. That means there are rules, so it can be controlled."

I crossed my arms. "I hadn't thought about it that way."

"Yeah, I hadn't before, either," Kaiden admitted. "I got caught up in how fun it was to have the power at my fingertips, and then I realized that by not understanding it, I might eventually do something really bad. But if there's science behind it, there's also a pattern. If I can understand enough of the inner workings, I can maximize the abilities without losing control."

"I like the idea of you not accidently exploding a fireball on us," I said.

Toran nodded. "Yeah, start that studying ASAP... however you're supposed to go about doing that."

"Says the person who ruined all of the seating in what was supposed to be our lounge room." Kaiden raised an eyebrow at Toran.

"At least my practicing didn't involve lobbing balls of flaming energy at an exterior bulkhead."

I spread my hands flat at waist-level. "How about we just agree to no more magical attack spells on the spaceship?"

"Fine, so long as other practice doesn't involve destroying furniture we might not be able to replace," Kaiden replied.

"Okay," Toran agreed.

"Great." I smiled at them. "Now that we have some ground rules, I guess we should get down to that planet and figure out what we're supposed to do."

"You're forgetting something," Kaiden said.

"What's that?"

"You."

I tilted my head, brow furrowed. "What do you mean?"

"Seems like we should establish some guideline for using your abilities, too," he stated.

"Yeah, well, I don't actually know what those abilities *are* yet."

"You're supposed to have strength and fighting abilities, right?" Toran asked.

I eyed him. "Maybe, but you seem to have the strength thing covered."

"I think we're *all* stronger," Kaiden pointed out. "Toran was doing the chair-bending, but it looks like we'll also be able to take a beating."

I crossed my arms. "What other stuff?"

"Move fast, jump, strike, I dunno." Kaiden shrugged. "The only way to find out is to try."

"We already agreed no chair-bending, so Elle doesn't get to, either," Toran said.

"Fine, we'll figure out some other strength and agility tests when we get planetside," the other man agreed. "Really, I didn't start to figure out what I could do until I played around. The first few things just kind of came to me."

I grinned. "All right, then, I guess we should gear up."

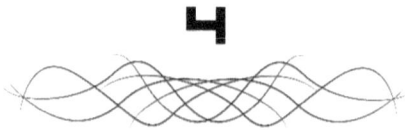

4

GETTING EQUIPMENT FOR a planetside mission wasn't as straightforward as it sounded in my head.

Following Kaiden's directions, the three of us took a lift down four decks to an area that was presented as 'the place where you get stuff'. Despite that description aligning with our present needs, I was immediately skeptical of us being able to get anything useful when Kaiden led us into an empty room.

"Take a wrong turn?" I asked.

He flashed a knowing smile. "This is it."

I looked around the plain space—approximately five meters square. "What am I missing?"

Toran sighed. "Don't we have enough to worry about without you messing with us?"

"There's nothing in here," I said. "I was hoping for a sword and some stylish armor, or something."

"Step onto the scanner," a female synthesized voice stated over hidden speakers.

I jumped with surprise as a ring of white lights a meter in diameter appeared in the center of the floor.

"Step into the scanner for equipment fitting," the voice said.

"Huh." Toran nodded. "I stand corrected."

"Colren mentioned the 3D printer when I first got here, but I haven't tried it out yet myself," Kaiden explained. "I guess it'll scan us and adapt any of its built-in patterns to our size."

Toran glared at him—a terrifying look from someone of his proportions. "You mean I could have had a shirt this whole time?"

Kaiden took a step backward. "I kind of thought you didn't want one."

"Nah, man, it's *cold*! The jumpsuit just didn't fit well."

I rolled my eyes. "Let's note this as an example of why open communication is important."

"My, you're a sage advisor for someone your age," Kaiden commented with a smirk.

"Hah!" I laughed. "No, my mom's a therapist. It rubs off."

He smiled. "I know how that goes... the moment you realize you're starting to become your parents."

"Oh, stars, don't remind me," Toran moaned. "Just wait until you get a little older and see it really start to come out."

I looked him over, realizing that it was impossible to get an accurate reading of his age—not to mention the fact that all of us were in different bodies than the ones we were born into. "How old are you?" I asked.

"Forty-two next month," Toran replied.

Kaiden tilted his head. "Really? I guess the transformation took off a few years."

Toran nodded. "I was also skinny and thirty centimeters shorter, so there's that." He laughed.

"And, Elle, you said you just graduated secondary school, right? So, you're... eighteen?" Kaiden asked.

I nodded. "A teenager with no life experience—I know, *exactly* who you want on the team tasked with saving the universe."

"Stars, I'm only twenty-two and I won't graduate from the Academy for another semester," Kaiden revealed. "Not exactly the image of experience over here, either."

"What were you studying?" I asked.

"Agriculture." He laughed. "How's that for useful in what we're doing?"

I raised an eyebrow. "Wouldn't have guessed that."

He shrugged. "My family hauled grain for a living, so I decided I'd rather be on the production end and get to stay put."

"I understand the appeal," Toran replied. "You traveled a lot as a kid?"

Kaiden nodded. "I was on Falstan II for an internship when all this went down, but I spent most of my childhood on a freighter."

My eyes widened. "Wow, that's…" I couldn't help but feel envious. The notion of being mobile all the time and getting to live in space was something I'd dreamed about since I was a kid.

He smiled. "Whatever you're thinking, it wasn't. A lot of crowded living quarters, bland food, and not nearly as dramatic a view as you'd imagine."

Annoyance over his nonchalantness lodged in my chest, but I let his words sink in for a few moments. He was being sincere, and I shouldn't fault him for that. Maybe traveling on a freighter *wasn't* everything I'd dreamed about. "I guess living in a small town isn't all bad," I said after a pause. "Having an orchard in the backyard is nice."

Kaiden got a wistful look in his eyes. "There were times I

would have done anything to have that."

"Same with me getting to travel around in space. I always wanted to go to Tactical School."

"Ah, the age-old desire to want what you don't have," Toran chimed in.

I swirled a length of my fuchsia hair around my index finger while looking over Toran's exaggerated physique. "I guess we're kind of walking personifications of that now, aren't we?"

Kaiden held up his hands as electricity crackled between his fingertips. "I have no complaints about the upgrades."

"What about you, Toran?" I questioned the other man. "Did you have a career and family before you were pulled here?"

He took a deep breath and looked down. "Yes, a wife and five-year-old daughter. I've been trying not to think about where they are right now."

A sharp pang struck my heart as emotion flitted across his face. I was worried about my own family, but they weren't reliant on me to keep them safe in a way a child needed parents. Toran couldn't do anything more to help his wife and daughter if he was frozen in suspended animation with them, but it was clear from his expression that he felt responsible for them all the same.

"They'll be fine," I tried to assure him.

"I was an engineer by trade, so I'm not one to sugarcoat facts," he replied. "I know we're in deep here. We can't measure what we don't know, and I haven't heard anything about our enemy that tells me what we're up against. Whatever happens, I'll be fighting for the well-being of my family. They're my universe."

I swallowed hard, wishing I had a more tangible person or

thing to fight for. I wanted my world back—my family, my friends, my last summer of being carefree. But, even after defeating the Darkness, I *still* wouldn't have those things; I'd be leaving home. However, just because my life would change regardless, that didn't mean others' lives were in transition. People like Toran deserved to be reunited with their loved ones, and if I could help make that happen, I needed to do everything I could to make it a reality. After all, I'd wanted to be a Ranger. Now that my body was healed, all I had to do was prove I was ready to put others before myself.

"We'll get them back, Toran," I said, more confident this time.

He softened, cracking a smile. "I don't think they'll recognize me."

I smiled back. "There's more to a person than how they look."

"That's assuming these new bodies are permanent," Kaiden pointed out.

"You also half your size back home?" I ribbed.

He smirked. "No, aside from the new magic, this is pretty much me. And you?"

I pointed at my fuchsia hair. "Not my natural shade."

Kaiden laughed. "Right."

"Aside from that, though," I looked myself over, "pretty close."

But I did *feel* different, even if my appearance only had minor cosmetic changes. I was energized in the way I always was right after a cliff jump—filled with a sense that I could tackle any challenge. My injury hadn't held me back from trying most things, but now that it wasn't pestering the back of my mind, it was like a weight had been lifted that I hadn't even realized was there.

I didn't want to admit it to the others, but I was actually excited to face off against an unknown enemy and to have the chance to use abilities that normally were fanciful dreams. I'd been given the opportunity to be a new version of myself unburdened by my past. It would be a genuine adventure.

"Whoever we were before, we have strangers counting on us now," Kaiden said, echoing my private thoughts.

"I'll give it my all," I said.

"Me too," Toran agreed.

Kaiden nodded. "Same. I don't know what that commitment means exactly, but the three of us are in this together."

I was silent for several seconds. "We're all kinda screwed, aren't we?"

"Probably, but *magic*." Kaiden waggled his fingers.

"I can't wait to get back home and loom over the guys who made fun of me in Physical Ed at school back in the day," Toran said.

"Just a touch petty," I commented.

Kaiden cast me a sidelong glance. "Don't pretend you're not thinking of all the ways you could show off now."

My thoughts flashed to Adrianne and her aerial acrobatics—such a frivolous activity under present circumstances, but more than a little part of me wanted to see how much I could out-maneuver her now. "Okay, maybe there are a few things I'd do myself. Not that I even rightly know what I *can* do now."

"Right! The equipment, and the mission." Kaiden pointed at the illuminated ring on the floor.

The computer had remained silent during our conversation, and I'd gotten so wrapped up in talking with my new associates that I'd almost forgotten why we had entered the room in the first place.

"Who goes first?" I asked.

"Congratulations for volunteering. Go on ahead." Kaiden flourished his hand.

I eyed the illuminated ring. "Any idea how this thing works?"

"Haven't a clue," Kaiden replied. "But it's unlikely to vaporize you."

"That makes me feel *way* better, thanks."

"Only way to test out the interface is to do it," Toran said. "We'll be right here."

Knowing now he was a parent back home, I could hear the measured patience and assurance in his tone. That little girl of his had a good dad, even if she wasn't old enough to know it yet.

"All right," I agreed, stepping into the ring.

The moment I was stationary inside, a pleasant chime sounded and a downlight bathed me in a white glow. A moment later, a holographic projection popped up at torso height, wrapping one hundred eighty degrees around me. The screen had multiple menu items, ranging from weapons to armor and other accessories.

"Welcome. Do you have a saved loadout profile?" the computer voice asked.

"No," I replied.

"Commencing new configuration."

A ring dropped down from a hidden recess in the ceiling, waving a light over me as it descended to the floor. It repeated the activity on the way up. When it returned to the ceiling, the holographic image around me changed to have a fine wireframe wrapping my body. I lifted one arm a few centimeters and found the wireframe moved with me.

"Make item selection," the computer prompted.

For lack of any other instruction, I reached out to interact with the holographic menu, first selecting the 'Armor' icon, since that seemed like the logical place to start; I figured I'd build up from there.

The icons for the other elements shifted upward and shrunk into a mini-ring while the primary menu area altered to display various submenus for armor. Ranging from street clothes to powered suits, it looked like I could pretty much have anything imaginable.

"Powered armor, guys?" I glanced over my shoulder at my two companions.

Kaiden shrugged. "Might be a little overkill, but may as well be prepared for anything."

I swiped my hand over the powered armor submenu.

The screen flashed red, accompanied by a harsh tone. "Insufficient privileges. Prerequisite training required," the computer stated.

I frowned. "Guess that's a no-go."

"Then why give the option in the first place?" Kaiden sighed.

Toran, who I was quickly discovering was the more pragmatic of the two, stroked his chin pensively. "I wonder what kind of training is required to qualify?"

"What are the prerequisites?" I asked the computer on his behalf.

"Melee weapon proficiency, light armor proficiency, medium armor proficiency, fifty recorded combat hours—"

"Stop." I held up my hand. "Okay, yeah, no powered armor for us."

"Yet," Kaiden said.

"Fifty hours of combat? Not happening anytime soon," I

pointed out.

He nodded. "Maybe we'll get there eventually."

That was kind of crazy to think about, but as shocking as the concept was, part of me was drawn to the idea. Essentially, it was beginning to look like I'd stumbled into being a Ranger without having to go through Tactical School.

I turned back to the holographic display, which had returned to its normal pale blue color. "Only display items that match my current clearance," I requested.

The screen reconfigured to show one-quarter of the previous options. At first glance, it looked like anything super fancy was out.

I flipped through the items, bringing up a preview image of each. "Street clothes, an awful onesie, hazsuits." I shook my head. "Once you see powered armor, it all seems kind of lame."

"Go back to those street clothes," Kaiden suggested. "I think I saw a note about ballistic ratings."

"Oh, really?" I scrolled back. Sure enough, the fabric was reinforced with ballistic-grade fibers to deflect projectiles, and a secondary treatment was designed to diffuse energy weapons fire or, presumably, magical attacks. "Okay, that's more intriguing than I initially thought," I admitted.

I narrowed the available designs to cuts most suited for a female figure. Though most of the outfits struck me as rather plain and boring, one coat jumped out at me. It was ankle-length, which would offer maximum protection, and a belt would allow it to be sealed in the front when needed. The garment came in a variety of colors, and I was initially drawn to the red. However, when I thought through the potential need to be stealthy while we were on our mission, I decided that plain black was the smarter option.

"I think I can work with this." I selected the coat, and the wireframe around me morphed to show the garment.

"Stylish," Kaiden commented.

"It suits you," Toran agreed.

I shrugged, and the coat moved with me. "Time to accessorize, I guess."

Next, I browsed through pants and selected a pair of black leggings to fit over my white base layer. I paired that with a pair of black knee-high combat boots with a purple accent trim that complemented my hair—no need to compromise on style while saving the universe—and a tactical belt from the same design group.

"That should cover it." I looked over my holographic outfit, pleased with how it had come together.

"Weapon," Kaiden prompted.

"Am I qualified to use anything?" I asked.

In response, the holographic display shifted to the weapons menu, which consisted of various swords and clubs. "No projectiles, then," I said. "Are the disciplines we picked literal, or…?"

"I think the icons for our disciplines are more symbolic," Kaiden said. "I draw power from my pendant, and a wand sounds really impractical. I'm thinking maybe a staff or something like that for myself."

The clubs struck me as a little too primitive, which left the bladed options. I looked over the menu. "Maybe a sabre? That's in the sword family."

Kaiden shrugged. "Get whatever you feel comfortable with. I doubt we'll need anything, anyway. I mean, we're just sealing the Archive, right?"

"Yeah, good point." I selected a sabre model with an electrified edge to enhance the sharpened metal. A representation of the weapon appeared in my hand and a scabbard for it at my waist. I waved the blade around. "This seems like it would be fun to use."

"Careful where you swing that when you get the real thing," Toran said with a smile.

"Confirm selections?" the computer prompted.

"Can you think of anything else I might need for now?" I asked my companions.

"Shirt?" Toran questioned.

"I don't know, I kind of like the look of the white suit under the black coat," I replied.

"Yeah, it works." Kaiden waved his hand. "Go for it."

"Confirm," I told the computer.

"Selection acknowledged. Processing." The main downlight in the ceiling and the lighted ring on the floor cut out. A moment later, a whirring sound started in the back wall of the room.

I stepped back toward the two men. "What's it doing?"

"Printing out the custom items, I imagine," Toran said.

"Step onto the scanner," the computer prompted.

"I guess we can get going on someone else while the first set prints," Kaiden said. "Go ahead, Toran."

The large man shook his head. "I don't believe that system is going to have many options for me. I'll watch over your shoulder while you go."

"All right." Kaiden stepped onto the platform and began going through the selection process.

After a few different configurations, Kaiden settled on an outfit consisting of a blue long-sleeve shirt, black pants, boots, and a black hooded cloak.

"A cloak? Really?" I razzed.

His sky-blue eyes seemed especially vibrant when contrast against the dark holographic hood framing his face. "You're envious, I can tell."

"It does offer better protection than your coat, Elle, with the hood up," Toran pointed out.

"Plus," Kaiden used one hand to draw the holographic representation of the cloak around his front, "stylish."

I rolled my eyes. "I really don't believe you were an agriculture major. You're way too dramatic."

"Never said I wasn't in theater."

"Now *that* I would believe."

A chime resonated through the chamber as the back wall slid open. My new garments were arranged on a rack, ready to wear.

I smiled. "That's service."

"Try it on," Kaiden encouraged.

I stepped around the scanner in the center of the room to access the rack. The pants fit well over the white suit I'd awoken in, and I slid on the boots and looped the tactical belt through the top of the pants. The belted coat fit almost like a cloak with sleeves, which seemed better suited for precise movements.

Finally, there was the sabre. I lifted it from its rack and slid it in its scabbard at my hip.

"I apologize in advance if I accidentally slice off one of your arms." I grinned at the two men while I walked back across the room.

"I can only hope sword fighting abilities come to you as naturally as magic spells did to Kaiden," Toran replied while Kaiden locked in his own selections.

"Well, if nothing else, the ensemble looks good," Kaiden commented while his gaze passed over me, lingering more than when we first met. "You've got a little..." He gently extracted some of my hair that was tucked inside my coat's collar and released it to fall down my back.

I tugged on some of the fuchsia hair hanging in front of me. "Thanks. It's a little longer than I'm used to."

"I like it." He met my gaze.

"Well," Toran cleared his throat, "time to get geared up myself." He lumbered into the center of the room.

Kaiden took a step back from me. "Yeah, mine should be ready any minute."

I crossed my arms and leaned against the wall while I waited for them to finish. While there was no denying Kaiden was my type, if I had to declare one, this was neither the time nor place to consider getting involved—or even to think about considering a possibility of something.

At least, not *yet*.

I caught myself. Things could get awkward and weird way too fast if I didn't divert from that line of thinking straight away. I wasn't in school anymore. I had more sense than that.

Setting aside the uninvited thoughts, I watched Toran try out clothing and armor options. He eventually settled on a new base layer and a set of lightweight, black scale armor that would accommodate his large frame, paired with a matching helmet and boots.

"If we ever have a chance to visit a city dressed like this, there is zero chance of anyone messing with us," I joked.

Toran confirmed his final selections then turned toward me. "I feel like we need a catchy team name."

"As cheesy as it sounds, I'm inclined to agree," Kaiden said.

"Yeah, I mean, if they want us to save the day, they better know who to thank," I agreed.

I evaluated our chosen outfits. "We're all wearing black. So, maybe something like 'Black Knights'?"

Kaiden scrunched up his nose. "The whole 'knights' thing might be a bit much."

"And 'black' feels a little… ominous," Toran said.

I ran through some synonyms in my head. "Something with 'defenders', maybe?"

"That's not bad. Or 'protectors' could work. How about a play on 'Space' or 'Void'?" Kaiden suggested.

"Or the Darkness," I added.

Toran thought for a moment. "How about 'Dark Protectors'?"

I shook my head. "That sounds like we're protecting the Darkness."

"Then, maybe 'Dark Sentinels'?" Toran suggested.

Kaiden lit up. "Yes."

I rolled the term around in my mind and mouthed it. It had a good ring to it, and the double meaning was a perfect bonus. "That will do very nicely."

KAIDEN HEFTED THE staff he'd selected to go with his new outfit. "I guess we should head down to the surface now?"

I raised an eyebrow. "I can't say I love the plan of running in there with no training or experience."

"What better way to *get* experience?"

"There's a lot wrong with that logic."

"I share Colren's concern about testing our abilities on this ship. Spacecraft are fragile," Toran jumped in. He was still adjusting the straps on his new black scale armor, which managed to make him look even more intimidating than he did walking around shirtless. Even though his gloved fists were his only weapon, I had no doubt that he'd be able to take out any opponent foolish enough to attack him.

"Fine," I agreed. "But I think we should experiment with our skills before we go into the Archive. There's no knowing what we may find in there."

"That works for me," Kaiden agreed. "Let's get ourselves a shuttle."

The hangar was on the same level as the room where we'd

gotten our equipment from the impressive 3D printer. We followed signage in the corridors to a set of double doors, which opened automatically as we approached.

The cavernous bay beyond contained several dozen fighters as well as four shuttle craft approximately twelve meters long, which appeared to have thick plating suitable for atmospheric entry. Gathered near the shuttles, a group of six workers dressed in blue coveralls were performing an inspection and making notes on tablets.

"Ah, hello!" a red-headed woman in the group called out. She jogged toward our approaching party.

"Hi," Kaiden replied. "Colren sent us. We're supposed to go down to the planet."

She nodded, bobbing her ponytail. "Commander Colren informed me about the mission. We have a shuttle prepped for you." The woman headed back toward the craft being inspected, then glanced over her shoulder at us. "I'm Chief Taminoret, by the way, but you can call me Tami—everyone does. I'm the lead technical specialist and run the maintenance team around here. If you need anything, just ask."

"Thanks," I replied. "What have you heard about us?"

Tami stopped and turned around. "We know we're up against something that has the leadership scared, and you're somehow connected to the solution. That's all we need to know."

"And it doesn't worry you that it's, you know, us?" I gestured at our clothes and primitive weapons.

She shrugged. "Heroes come from all backgrounds. If the commander trusts you, I do, too."

I wished I had as much faith in myself as she seemed to. "Thanks."

Tami resumed walking to the shuttle. "These craft have an

autopilot, so you won't need to do anything other than enter your destination."

"Good. I'm a little rusty," Kaiden said.

"You have piloting experience?" I asked him.

He smiled. "Can't grow up in the shipping business and not pick up a few skills."

"You'll be happy to know that the compensators in these are much more sophisticated than what you find in civilian tech," Tami told him. "You'll barely even feel the gs."

"That's a relief."

I frowned. "I wasn't thinking about space travel when I picked these clothes."

"You'll be fine," Tami said. "It looks like you have on a shipsuit underneath, so that will protect you."

"Oh, is that what these are?" I placed one hand on the white cloth covering my chest, which was one of the only parts of me where I hadn't added a second layer of clothing.

"They look thin, but they'll compress if the pressure changes and thermoregulate well," she explained. "It's a good thing to have on at all times."

I nodded. "Noted."

"So, your mission." Tami patted the shuttle's hull. "The nav computer is loaded with the coordinates for the Archive. No one else has been down there, so we can't say with any certainty how well the comms will work. Speaking of which…"

She motioned to one of the nearby workers, and he handed her a case containing three earpieces.

"Here are some comms for you," Tami said while distributing the earpieces to us. "Fair warning, there will be a—"

"Ow!" Kaiden exclaimed, gripped his right ear.

"—pinch when it implants," Tami finished. "It embeds

next to your ear canal and jawbone so it can pick up barely audible statements. Tap behind your ear for controls: one tap to open a general channel, double-tap to mute, hold to disconnect, slide to cycle to private channels."

Taking a deep breath, I placed the device in my left ear. As soon as it was inside, the entire left side of my face started to burn, radiating from a single point near my jaw that felt like a molten bug was burrowing inside.

The pain receded after fifteen seconds, and I rubbed the side of my face to massage the rest of the burning away. "Please tell me that was a one-time thing."

"Yes, you're all set now," Tami said. "The comms will also serve as a combat recorder, of sorts, to passively log your activities."

"Is that what connects to the equipment system and the prerequisites?" I asked.

She nodded. "The system will sync with the comm's log when you go in for an upgrade."

"Sounds straightforward enough," Kaiden commented.

Tami smiled. "We try to keep it simple. Any more questions?"

I looked at my companions. "Aside from what we're supposed to do when we get down there, and pretty much everything else about what's going on? Nope, I guess that covers it."

The mechanic frowned. "Sorry, I'm afraid I can't offer any additional insights."

"Rhetorical question," I replied.

"We'll figure it out," Kaiden told her.

Toran nodded. "Thank you for the comm. Who will the general channel connect to?"

"Central Command," Tami said, "but you'll find a private

channel for each of your team members, Commander Colren, and me here with the mechanical team."

I tapped behind my ear and then glided my hand downward. A synthesized voice similar to the computer in the equipment room stated names as I scrolled. I pressed the same place behind my ear and a low tone sounded, which I took to mean I'd closed out of the menu.

"All right, I guess we'll talk to you on the other side," Kaiden told her.

"Good luck." Tami placed her hand on a panel next to the shuttle's side hatch, and a door dropped open to form an entry ramp.

I followed Kaiden inside, with Toran close behind.

The opening led into a cozy common area with seating around a table and a galley. To the aft, a corridor had doors to either side and terminated in an airlock. Toward the nose of the craft, a corridor extended on the starboard side through the seating area, and next to the galley was a closed off room labeled as a lavatory.

"Homey," I said. The craft seemed entirely too small and vulnerable to travel on its own to a planet, extra hull plating or not.

"Are those bunk rooms?" Kaiden wondered aloud. He headed for the aft, seeming at home aboard the small vessel. He popped open the door on the port side, revealing a tiny room with a bunkbed. "Yep." He closed the door and checked the one across from it, which I couldn't see into from my vantage. "Same."

"I hope we don't have to spend the night in here," Toran said.

"Better than out in the open on an alien world," I countered. Another wave of nerves surged through me as it sunk in that I was on my way to another planet for the first time.

Toran nodded. "That's true."

With nervous anticipation, I wandered down the corridor toward the nose. Past the lavatory, the corridor opened into a compact bridge with two seats at the front and four additional seats at workstations around the back, each equipped with a flight harness. A broad viewport wrapped around the front of the bridge, offering a panoramic view of the hangar.

"No reason to delay," Kaiden said, coming up behind me. He took one of the front seats. "Want to co-pilot?" he asked me.

My heart skipped a beat. My first time on a shuttle and I'd get to co-pilot? "I'd love to, but I have no idea what to do."

"Don't worry. Just sit back and enjoy the ride." Kaiden's calm tone set me at ease.

"This is probably a bad time to tell you I hate flying," Toran grumbled as he entered the bridge through the corridor. His broad shoulders nearly brushed the side walls.

"Not ideal timing, no." Kaiden smiled back at him. "But if what Tami said is true, this won't be like any craft you've been on before." He pressed some physical controls on a front console, and a holographic overlay appeared on the console and over the front viewport.

Kaiden opened a navigation menu and located an entry for 'Master Archive'. "Ready to do this thing?" he asked us.

"Better go now before I change my mind," I replied.

"Let's get this over with," Toran moaned. He strapped into one of the chairs at the back, then closed his eyes.

I secured my own harness. "This will be the first planet I've been to other than my homeworld."

Kaiden glanced at me. "Really? Not even a trip offworld for

vacation?"

"No, my family was more the camping sort."

"I must have stopped by dozens of worlds at one point or another, but only set foot on a few. I guess after all of that travel growing up, that's why I wanted to settle down somewhere."

"Literally *put down roots*, eh?" I smirked.

He shook his head. "Ugh, I walked right into that one."

Behind me, Toran groaned. "Elle, that was terrible."

"Better get used to my wit and charm. I can do this all day!"

"So it begins…" Kaiden made a final entry on the front console, and the shuttle began gliding across the hangar toward an opening covered in an electrostatic shield.

Despite knowing it was ridiculous, I couldn't help holding my breath as we passed through. A wave of yellow, crackling light passed over the front viewport, and then we were in complete blackness. Pinpoints of light shone in the distance, but from my vantage, we may as well have been completely alone in the void.

The shuttle arced to the port side on its programmed path, bringing the *Evangiel* into view. The ship was larger than I'd realized—close to half a kilometer long and at least fifteen decks tall. Based on my research in preparation for applying to Tactical School, the ship appeared to be of a cruiser class, designed more for speed than battle. However, energy weapons and rail guns were tucked away in recesses around the hull, so it could certainly put up a fight, if needed.

As the shuttle passed by the *Evangiel*, the front viewport tinted to block out the sudden light shining from the system's star behind the purple-hued planet. Cloud cover made it impossible to see anything on the surface, especially on the night side.

The approach path took us to the leading edge of dawn. I

braced myself as the shuttle angled toward the atmosphere, causing a bright point of heat to appear at the nose of the vessel. I kept waiting for violent shaking or intense *g* forces to kick in, but there was barely any sensation of movement.

"What's taking so long to enter the atmosphere?" Toran asked behind me.

"We have." Kaiden stated. "We're at an elevation of eighty kilometers."

I peeked over my shoulder at the large man, and he had cracked an eye open. "Huh. I guess those compensators really *do* work."

"Nice ride, huh?" Kaiden kicked back in his seat with his hands behind his head. "I could almost take a nap."

"After we've done what we came here to do," I said. As much as I wanted to trust the autopilot, I really didn't like the idea of the only person on the craft with significant flying experience dozing off.

"I'm joking," he assured me. "I'm way too worried about what we're going to find down there to relax."

I was, too. The further we descended, the more my stomach tightened. I still couldn't make out anything of the landscape below, and my mind kept going to all of the ancient, mythical monsters that might be waiting for us.

A shudder wracked the shuttle. The console turned red and a warning claxon echoed in the bridge.

My heart leaped into my throat. "What happened?"

"I don't know." Kaiden's hands raced over the controls. "Shit! That's very bad."

"What?" Toran demanded from the back seat.

"The compensators are out and the guidance system lost its target. It's flying blind."

Concern added a quaver to Toran's deep voice, "Where are

we going?"

"I don't know! I wasn't in control." Kaiden swept his hand over the front console and pushed a map overlay onto the front viewport. He pointed to a blinking point on the map. "This looks like where we're supposed to go."

"Okay, then let's go there," I said.

Kaiden motioned out the viewport. "Yeah, except I have no idea where *we* are *now*."

I knew next to nothing about ship controls, but even I could tell that the digital altimeter and GPS readouts were jumping all over the place.

"We should pull up," I suggested, trying to stay calm despite my racing heart. "If the positioning works from the upper atmosphere, we can eyeball it from above and take an approach."

"Won't help," he replied. "We're already on the entry path I would have taken when flying us in manually. If we're going to land this, we need to stay the course."

"Might get a signal again at a lower altitude," Toran said while gripping the armrests of his seat. "There's a blind spot like this when entering Dunlore."

"Let's hope," Kaiden murmured. "I think we're somewhere around ten kilometers up now. There could be mountains."

"Great." I tightened the straps on my harness and gripped the armrests. This really wasn't how or when I wanted to die. I pressed the comm activation point behind my ear, and it chirped. "Central Command, we've lost our nav lock."

Silence.

"Central Command," Toran said behind me. After a pause, he sighed. "Nothing. Whatever broke the lock and knocked out the compensators must be messing with the comms, too."

"At least we were headed in the right direction," Kaiden

said. He pulled the manual yoke toward him, which had been locked at the base of the control console. The shuddering subsided a little as he leveled off.

"I wish these clouds would break," he muttered.

"Try the docking guidance system," Toran suggested. "The sensors use lasers to verify distances."

"Not sure what kind of range that will get us, but better than being blind." Kaiden located the appropriate system and activated it. "See if you can pull up the readings, Elle."

I grabbed the holographic of the data and dragged it toward me. It presently showed a schematic of the shuttle with a green border around it, but there were no other indicators. The menu offered no clues, but then I spotted a 'Settings' option. Flipping through that, I noticed an option for 'Show actual distances'; that sounded promising.

As soon as I selected the setting, numbers appeared around the edges of the shuttle schematic. Behind and above only showed an infinity symbol, but to the forward starboard corner one number was counting down fast.

"Turn to port!" I shouted.

A rock face parted through the clouds two hundred meters ahead. The shuttle banked hard to port, and my harness dug into my shoulders.

Kaiden swore under his breath as he fought to get a new trajectory that would take us around the slope. "That was way too close."

"This isn't detailed, but it's something." I moved the schematic showing the distances back to the center display so Kaiden could see it while flying.

He glanced between the distances on the schematic and the map of the original course, which was floating at the top of the view. "We need to set down and get our bearings. I have no idea where we are."

"Any option that involves not dying is good with me," I said.

Kaiden kept an eye on the proximity readings until he found a path where the front and sides were clear and only the distance below was counting down.

Finally, at an altitude of one kilometer, the cloud cover thinned and we got our first look at the planet's landscape. There was almost no vegetation or signs of water, with bizarre dark rock formations stretching as far as I could see. A mountain range towered in the distance, and the land dropped away other places into what I assumed were canyons. The path in front of us appeared to be fairly flat and free of potential hazards, but the shuttle bucked against strong winds.

"That lighter patch up ahead looks like a good landing spot?" he asked no one in particular while fighting to keep the shuttle level as the winds swirled around us.

"Sure," I said, willing to agree to anything just to be back on solid ground.

The shuttle descended the remaining distance. As we neared the ground, I saw that the topography was more varied than I'd initially thought, with some of the seemingly smooth areas actually being boulder fields that reminded me of my home.

Kaiden selected a patch of gravel and set the shuttle down. With a relieved sigh, he shut off the engine, and the holographic overlay faded from the controls. "Yay! We didn't die."

"Good flying," I told him.

"I do what I can."

"Well, this mission is off to a *great* start." I unbuckled my harness, my heartrate returning to normal. I pressed behind my ear to try the comms again. "Central Command?" Like before, there was no reply. "Okay, so we're on our own."

"Figured." Kaiden sighed. "Good thinking on the docking sensors, Toran. Do you have piloting experience, too?"

The large man shook his head. "A little, but control systems were a required course as an engineering student. Glad I was paying attention in class!"

"Thank the stars for that," I murmured. Even if we were out of communication with the main ship, I felt much better knowing my companions had experience to offer.

Toran smiled for a moment, then it faded. "So, how do we identify our position?"

"I was trying to figure that out," Kaiden said while he pushed back from the console. "We might need to take the shuttle up and circle around. I'm not crazy about hanging out at a low altitude beneath the clouds with those strong winds, though."

"What do we know about where we were going?" I asked.

Toran brought up the map from the original navigation plot using the console next to his seat. "It appears to be at the base of a valley between three peaks."

"That kind of formation should be easy to identify from the ground, provided the peaks aren't too hidden in the clouds," Kaiden said.

With a clear course of action at hand, I jumped up from my seat. "Let's head out!"

Toran frowned. "You might be a little too enthusiastic, given the situation."

"First time on another planet, what can I say?"

"All right, lead the way," Kaiden said.

"Have your weapon handy," Toran cautioned. "We don't know what may be out there."

I kept my hand on my sword hilt as we exited the bridge into the common room. "Wait, the air is safe, right?"

"Pretty sure they wouldn't have sent us down here without suits if we couldn't breathe," Kaiden pointed out.

"Clearly they don't know everything about this place," I countered.

Toran checked a panel next to the door. "Oxygen levels and temperature look okay."

"Good enough for me." Kaiden released the door lock.

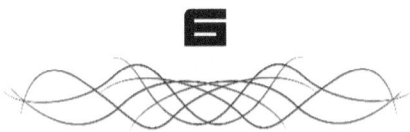

THE SEAL RELEASED with a hiss, and the hatch swung outward to form a ramp down.

A gust of warm air ruffled my hair, carrying an aroma of dirt and iron. "Something doesn't feel right about this place."

"Definitely not the most hospitable." Kaiden motioned toward the hatch. "Do the honors, Elle."

I peeked outside. Everything in the monotone landscape had a matte appearance in the diffused light; only the gravel beneath us had the slightest degree of sparkle. I'd always pictured other worlds to be vibrant and filled with strange plants, but the landscape around me was closer to a barren wasteland. I cautiously walked down the ramp, my excitement turning to nerves at the prospect of venturing out into the unknown.

I finished my descent and took my first steps on an alien world. An exhilarating tingle passed through as the sparkly gravel crunched underfoot. I grinned up at my companions. "I'm officially an interstellar traveler."

Kaiden smiled back and descended the ramp. "Congratulations!"

I crouched to get a better look at the strange ground covering. "Is this crushed crystal?"

Kaiden bent down next to me and scooped up some of the gravel into his palm. "Huh. I think it is."

Toran joined us on the ground, surveying the area. "This formation looks like too perfect a circle to be natural. Do you think it may be the result of weapons fire?"

Kaiden frowned. "Anything is possible. Who knows the last time someone may have been around this planet. It could be from a battle a millennium ago."

"Kind of crazy to think about." I stood up and scanned the horizon for any sign of the three peaks we were looking for.

"Maybe that battle is what prompted the ancient civilization to make the sanctuary around the Master Archive, in case another conflict happened," Kaiden hypothesized.

"I could see that," I agreed. "And that would explain why the Master Archive is hidden in the first place."

"The power to control records of the past and potentially see the future. That seems very valuable," Toran murmured.

"Do you think it's true—about the Archive having a record of events that haven't happened yet?" I asked.

Kaiden shrugged. "It sounds a little crazy, but having my consciousness downloaded into a bioprinted body also sounds mad."

"I won't discount anything unless I see compelling evidence to disregard it," Toran stated. "The last few days have changed my views on what I previously thought were certainties."

"Yeah, I know what you mean." I nudged the gravel with the toe of my boot; now that I was on the world, it didn't seem very foreign at all. "Yesterday, the most important question on my mind was what classes I should take my first term at the Academy."

"A week ago, I was taking soil samples as part of a new fertilizer study." Kaiden laughed. "Stars, what happened to us?"

Toran shook his head. "I believe this is what's meant when it's said that someone's life has been turned upside down."

"It certainly feels that way," I muttered. The thrill of adventure I'd sensed on the shuttle was fading quickly now that I was on a barren world with little direction about how to complete our vague mission.

Kaiden straightened. "Hey, are those the peaks?" He pointed to the east.

I jogged over to him so I could follow the sightline of his arm. Just shy of the horizon, a collection of mountains rose from the surrounding landscape and disappeared into the cloud cover, with three peaks standing out as a slightly different shade of gray from the rest.

"That could be it," I said. "I wish we could see the top."

"Nothing we can do about that. These clouds aren't going anywhere," Kaiden replied.

"I can't tell from here if the shade is different," I continued. "If it is, it might indicate a different material and why those peaks were called out as landmarks on the map."

Kaiden nodded. "Maybe if we could get a different angle it would show up differently."

"My thoughts exactly."

Most of the area around us was flat, but to the south there was a low hill with several boulders near the top. "Maybe up there—" Before I'd finished my statement, Toran broke into a run toward the hill. "Where are you going?" I shouted after him.

"I want to see if I can lift that rock!" he called back.

"Is he serious?" I muttered.

Kaiden shrugged. "We *did* want to get in some practice with our abilities."

"Yeah, that was before we crash-landed and—"

"Elle, just go with it. Trust me, you'll go crazy if you try to control this situation. Consider yourself at the mercy of the universe's will, and you'll have a much better time."

I stared at him, blinking slowly.

Kaiden grinned. "Race you to the top!" He took off full-speed after Toran.

I bolted after him, despite my better judgment about running headlong into the unknown. Reckless or not, I wasn't about to let someone beat me in a footrace; running was one thing my shoulder injury hadn't taken from me.

It only took a dozen strides for me to overtake Kaiden and his brief head start. I surged ahead, amazed at how effortlessly my legs pumped across the ground. Even though I'd considered myself in good shape back home, it was clear that my new body was even more tuned for athletics. I wasn't winded in the slightest from the run up the hill, and my pulse was barely above normal. It was freeing in a way I'd never experienced before, like I'd found a calling I'd never known to look for.

At the top of the rise, Toran was sizing up a meter-tall boulder.

I slowed to a jog and came to rest next to him. "Moving on from chair-bending to rock-lifting, huh?" I asked.

He chuckled. "You're not the least bit curious if I can lift it?"

I smirked. "Didn't say that."

Kaiden made it to the summit. "Damn, you're speedy, Elle!"

"You challenged the wrong opponent if you expected to win," I gloated.

He bristled. "Well, can you do this?"

Flames licked the end of his staff, swelling into a spherical blaze. When the orb reached the size of his head, Kaiden discharged it toward a boulder forty meters from our location. The orb exploded on impact, enveloping the tan rock in flames before it died out. A charred circle marred the stone where it had born the blunt of the assault.

I pursed my lips. "Impressive."

Kaiden looked rather pleased with himself. "That's the biggest one yet."

"And *this* is why we agreed not to practice on the ship," Toran stated. He wrapped his arms around the boulder. "Now, let's see..." His fingertips found suitable grip points, and heaved the massive rock upward, releasing a cloud of dust.

"Hey, look at that!" Kaiden raised his eyebrows as Toran stood upright with the rock.

I smiled with excitement. "Stars!"

Toran beamed, though his face was red from the exertion. "Can't wait to see what else I—"

A growl behind me broke the quiet of the landscape.

Toran dropped the boulder, his expression changing from jovial to serious in an instant.

Every muscle in my body tensed, poised for action. As if driven by instinct, I drew my sabre. The electrified edge of the steel blade glowed blue in the soft purple light. I pivoted on the ball of my foot to face whatever had made the sound.

A four-legged creature crept from the shadow between two boulders ten meters from us. Standing ninety centimeters tall at the shoulder, it had a spiked ridge down its back, which transitioned into a barbed tail, and its talon-like feet sported fifteen-centimeter claws. Three yellow eyes were recessed in a thick skull, and its jaws parted to reveal jagged teeth.

Next to me, Kaiden had leveled his staff toward the creature, and Toran's hands were now clenched into fists wrapped in his knuckle guards.

"How are we going to handle this?" I asked in a low voice. It didn't thrill me that my first brush with an alien creature might be a fight—especially considering that I hadn't yet had a chance to test my own abilities.

"It might just be guarding a nest," Toran said.

Kaiden shrugged. "Or it wants to eat us."

The stone lizard stepped forward and hissed. Two more creatures appeared in nearby crevasses, and then a fourth emerged to my right.

I swallowed. "I think we're on the menu."

"All right, so maybe backing away and leaving it alone isn't an option," Toran concluded.

"Kaiden, you want to magic these things away?" I questioned.

"I have no idea how much damage a blast will do against these things, but I'll try." He gripped the crystal around his neck in his left hand and pointed his staff at the stone lizard to my right. The staff began to glow with blue light, and then an energy orb shot from the end toward the creature.

Blue electricity danced across the stone lizard's skin as the blast connected. It shrieked and took a step back, but its three eyes narrowed with what appeared to be renewed focus.

The stone lizard in the middle right took the opportunity to rush forward, snapping at my leg.

I pulled my coat around me to block it, and it only got a mouth full of fabric. I kicked it as hard as I could.

The creature slid backward a meter from the force of the

blow, then returned to the offensive line with the others.

"I already don't like these things." I raised my sword with both hands and charged for the same creature on the right that Kaiden had attacked. A meter from the target, I slashed at an angle to slice it at the base of the neck.

The blade carved through the armored flesh, spewing dark purple blood. With a sickening gurgle, it dropped to the ground, dead.

I stood in stunned silence. I'd never killed anything bigger than an insect before. But it had attacked me—a wild creature intent on killing. I buried the impulse to feel remorse for taking a life. I had a job to do, and that would mean cutting down anything that barred my way.

While I was frozen in reflection, Toran charged the second creature, which had attacked me moments before. He punched downward on the top of its head with his armored knuckled. A sharp *crack* echoed around the boulders as his fist impacted.

The creature staggered back but remained standing.

Toran jumped clear just in time for Kaiden to lob a fireball from his staff toward the wounded stone lizard. The flames enveloped the creature. It shrieked as it fell into a burned pile on the ground.

"Fire works better on these things, it seems," Kaiden commented.

"Yes, do more of that!" I shouted while running toward the third creature with my sword.

I mirrored my first attack, swiping downward at an angle toward the stone lizard's neck. However, it dodged my attack at the final moment and lunged for my ankle. The powerful jaws wrapped around my boot and it shook its head.

The thick material on the boot shaft managed to keep the fangs from breaking through, but the violent thrashing of the creature's head was enough to throw me off-balance. I hit the ground hard on my back, my limbs spread to my sides. Fortunately, I hadn't lost my grip on my sword, but I had no leverage from that angle.

The fourth creature lunged for my throat. I tried to swing my sword up, but the stone lizard was moving too fast. I braced for the bite.

A fireball flew past my head and struck the creature in the face a mere thirty centimeters away.

I squeezed my eyes closed against the light from the blast. Heat burned my face, like I'd just stuck my head into an oven.

The heat subsided after a second, leaving the creature stunned and blinded.

I took the opportunity to bolt upright, stabbing my sabre into the side of its neck. The blade pierced several centimeters in, and I twisted.

Dark purple blood oozed from the wound, and I withdrew the blade as the stone lizard collapsed into a lifeless pile on the ground.

Toran dashed toward the remaining stone lizard, a fist raised above his head. He struck the side of the creature's skull, crushing it between his fist and one of the boulders. The stone lizard fell to the ground, blood trickling from its smashed jaw.

Kaiden slowly released a breath. "Okay, so that just happened."

Toran took two deep, rapid breaths. "That felt weird, right?"

I scrambled to my feet. "If by 'weird' you mean way too natural for never having done those things before, then yeah. Very, very weird."

Kaiden examined the corpses of the creatures. "I can't decide if I should feel bad about killing them."

"I was wondering the same thing," I admitted. "I mean, they *did* attack us."

"We have a mission to complete, they got in the way," Toran said.

I nodded. "I imagine they won't be the last things to try to stop us."

"Almost certainly not." Kaiden rested his staff on the ground. "I think this staff amplifies my abilities somehow—or makes them easier to channel."

"Yeah, those fireballs are pretty awesome." I grinned.

He smiled back. "It was kind of nice to let loose against a specific target."

"And for not having a weapon, those fists did a lot of damage," I commented.

Toran inspected his knuckle guard. "I did what I had to do to keep us safe."

"Yeah, thanks for the help back there," I said to them. "I thought I was done for when that one took me down."

"We need to work as a team. For a first go-around, I think that went well," Kaiden replied.

"I think so, too," I agreed. "I guess now I have some sense of what I can do."

He nodded. "See? Hands-on learning is quite informative."

I raised an eyebrow. "Yeah, that was never up for debate. I just thought it might be nice to practice, you know, where things weren't trying to kill us."

"Weren't you the one who couldn't wait to get off the shuttle?"

"I… That's beside the point. *I* didn't go running off toward the rocks with the vicious lizard things."

"The possibility of their presence was not something I had considered," Toran admitted.

"Doesn't matter. It all worked out." I cleaned my blade on one of dead creature's hides and then sheathed the sabre.

Kaiden cast me a playful sidelong glance. "All part of going with the flow."

I took a deep breath. "*Anyway*, I believe we were about to get a look at those mountain peaks."

"Right." Kaiden walked over toward a boulder with a relatively flat top. "This looks like it would make a good vantage point."

There didn't appear to be a good way up around the smooth sides, and no lower rocks were close enough to climb. "Could I get a boost?" I asked Toran.

"Of course." He cupped his hands for me to step in, then easily hoisted my legs to his shoulder height while I used my hands to stabilize me on the rock. The boulder curved to a manageable angle at that level, and I was able to scramble the rest of the way to the top.

I stood up and surveyed the surrounding landscape from the new vantage. The fifty meter elevation gain from our shuttle's landing position didn't reveal any deep secrets, but the different angle did confirm that the three peaks in the distance were a distinctly different shade than the surrounding mountains, and the configuration was remarkably similar to the map we were working from.

"I think that those mountains *are* our target," I called down to my companions.

"Great, but how do we get there?" Kaiden replied. "We'll need to go over the pass, but we'll be flying blind through the clouds."

"I believe we have answered the great mystery about why no one ever comes here," Toran stated.

"Super welcoming place, isn't it?" I slid down the side of

the boulder and Toran caught me, lowering me the rest of the way to the ground. I dusted myself off. "Back to the shuttle? Maybe a path through will reveal itself closer to the mountains."

"Guess we don't have another choice," Kaiden agreed.

We jogged down the hill back to the shuttle and returned to our seats on the bridge. The target mountain range was behind us based on our landing orientation, so Kaiden powered up the shuttle and rotated it to face the direction we needed to go. Strong winds wracked the craft as soon as we were a hundred meters off the ground.

Kaiden fought the controls to hold it steady. "We'll need to fly with the proximity sensors and naked eye."

"I'm on it," I said, getting the display configured for him like I had before. The overlay appeared on the front viewport.

I cinched my harness tighter as the shaking from the wind intensified closer to the mountains. The foothills sloped upward into the clouds, leaving no clue as to the best way into the valley we hoped was waiting for us on the other side.

"Maybe up through there?" I suggested, pointing toward one of the hill slopes that was slightly more gradual than the others.

"Worth a shot." Kaiden directed the craft toward it, keeping a distance of approximately two hundred meters from the ground as it angled upward.

The hillside eventually intersected with another, barely visible at the edge of what we could make out through the thick clouds. However, paired with the proximity readings, it was just enough to make our way through a pass between the mountain peaks.

As if a veil had been lifted, the clouds parted on the other side, revealing a valley dotted with crystal spires.

I sucked in a breath. "Wow."

"You can say that again." Kaiden's jaw slacked. "Some of those have to be a hundred meters tall."

"I had no idea crystals could get that big," I murmured.

"I suspect many of the things we'll find on this world don't exist elsewhere," Toran said.

"Good point."

I tore my gaze from the amazing formations beneath us to look upward. The clouds were as thick above us as elsewhere, but they stayed above the interior edge of the peaks almost like there was an invisible dome keeping them out.

The winds had also vanished as soon as we broke through the clouds, allowing Kaiden to relax at the controls. He followed my gaze upward. "There's something different about this place, that's for sure."

"A good sign we're where we're supposed to be," I said.

He nodded. "But where is the Archive entrance itself?"

I hadn't a clue what to suggest. The valley had to be at least two kilometers in diameter at its widest point, and there were so many formations around the landscape that there was no clear target.

"Might just have to walk around until we find it." I glanced over at Kaiden to gauge his reaction to the statement, and I noticed the crystal pendant around his neck was glowing the way it did when he was casting a spell. "Uh, Kaiden... your necklace."

He looked down at his chest. "Stars! When did it start doing that?"

"I don't know. I just noticed it."

"What's going on?" Toran asked, unable to see from his vantage.

"My pendant is glowing," Kaiden explained.

"Curious," the large man mused.

I looked at him over my shoulder. "Have a theory, or...?"

"Where did that crystal shard come from?" Toran asked.

"It appeared with me in the bioprinter," Kaiden revealed. "It was strung around my neck, just like this."

"Well, you've indicated it's part of whatever gives you magical abilities. If that power is all connected, then maybe it's responding to this place," Toran conjectured.

"I guess that makes sense," Kaiden said. He looped the shuttle around as it approached the far edge of the valley.

At the furthest point in the arc, I noticed that the light in the crystal dimmed. "Hey, what if it grows brighter the closer it is to the power source?" I suggested.

"Keep an eye on it. I'll take us around to see what it does."

I watched the light intensity as Kaiden circled the shuttle through the valley. After completing a circuit, it was clear the light was brighter in one specific area near a particularly large crystal with two smaller crystals forming an irregular 'V' at its base. On the first pass, I'd thought the crystals had broken and fallen that way naturally, but I was starting to suspect that it marked an entrance.

"That's gotta be it," I said, pointing to the location.

"All right, let me set us down."

Kaiden found a relatively flat spot with enough clearance between the other formations to accommodate the shuttle, and he landed.

I unstrapped my harness as the holographic overlays deactivated. "What do you think we'll find inside?"

"Hopefully, a clearly labeled button for 'Seal Archive' and a pile of gold for our trouble," Kaiden said with a grin.

I laughed. "That would be pretty spectacular."

"As nice as that would be, I suspect there will be a trial,"

Toran said in a serious tone. "Colren said that someone from each of the three disciplines was required to seal the Archive, so we'll likely each have to do something."

"Yeah, I was worried that might be the case." I frowned.

Kaiden rose from his seat. "No sense worrying about it until we get inside and know exactly what to do."

"You're right. Only one way to find out." I followed him toward the common room.

"We just have to work together, like we did in the fight," Toran said while following me.

I smiled over my shoulder at him. "We're old pros now. We've got this."

They chuckled even though the statement was ridiculous. I had no clear sense for how long I had been unconscious during the jump earlier in the day, but I suspected that only a few hours had passed since I was in the canyon on Erusan with my friends. I was used to physical changes happening around me due to resets, but there was always consistency in what was happening. To be thrust into a new environment with people I didn't know was nothing short of disorienting. At least we were united by the experience of having no idea what was going on.

We exited the shuttle to find that the ground underfoot had a similar sparkle to the gravel near our previous landing site, but there were also distinct chunks of crystal here.

Kaiden's pendant was almost blindingly bright as he bent down to pick up a piece. Curiously, the fragments on the ground didn't seem to react to the presence of his crystal at all. "These feel different," he said.

I grabbed a crystal chunk from the ground myself. "What do you mean?"

"It's like there's a current running through mine, but these are just a plain piece of mineral," Kaiden explained. "Can you sense it?" He held out the pendant dangling from the chain around his neck.

I wrapped my hand around the crystal and tried to focus on it. There was a warmth to the stone—more than a product of being carried next to his chest. "Yeah, there is something."

"May I?" Toran asked.

I released the pendant, and Toran took it in his hand. "Hmm. Doesn't seem particularly different to me, but I'll take your word for it." He let it go.

Kaiden shrugged. "Maybe there are different types of crystals?"

I dropped the inert crystal I'd picked up, then looked over at the crystals framing the opening. "We won't get any answers standing around out here."

"All right, let's do it." Kaiden trudged toward what we hoped was the entrance to the Archive.

The terrain was broken up by clumps of crystal amid rocks and boulders of various sizes. Some of the formations towered twenty meters above us, and others barely cleared the top of my head. The dark stones were similar to those where we'd encountered the stone lizards, so I kept my hand on the hilt of my sheathed sabre just in case.

The final stretch of terrain was only a slight incline, but the gravel and crystal shards underfoot shifted with every step. I slid down almost as much ground as I gained with each stride. After several unsuccessful attempts, I took a running start and loped up the hill as quickly as I could. To my relief, the strategy worked. I found solid footing at the top of the slope.

I grinned down at my companions. "What's taking you guys so long?"

Kaiden sighed. "Very funny." He stepped back and then took a running start like I had, clearing the patch of scree in a dozen rapid strides.

Toran followed suit. "That shouldn't have been the most difficult thing we've done today."

I chuckled. "The day isn't over yet!"

The flat landing outside the entrance was only four meters deep, so I had to crane my neck to look at the top of the two crystals framing the entrance. Each was approximately ten meters tall, with flat faces near their pointed tops arranged so they held each other in place against the base of the one-hundred-meter-tall crystal behind them.

Standing at the entrance, I could now tell that the path inside hugged the outside edge of that mammoth vertical crystal, with the glass-like surface on the left and dark, rough rock on the right for as far as I could see into the dim cave mouth.

"I was expecting something more high-tech," I commented.

"Me too. 'Archive' sounds more like a datacenter, not a cave," Kaiden agreed.

Toran strode through the opening, undeterred. "No telling what's inside."

I followed him in. The temperature immediately dropped by five degrees.

"I don't suppose anyone brought a light?" Toran asked. "I didn't think to grab a flashlight from the ship."

"Me either," I realized. With the image of a datacenter in my head, illumination needs weren't even a consideration.

"No worries." Kaiden followed us in. The glow of his pendant cast a pool of soft blue light around him. He then extended his right hand, and a larger orb appeared in his palm.

I raised my eyebrows. "Neat trick."

"See? Not all fireballs and blasting stuff."

"Lead the way." Toran motioned for Kaiden to go ahead.

The light cast from the orb was just bright enough to illuminate the cave's ceiling eight meters overhead. Shadows seemed to absorb the light, but the crystal wall to the left shined with extra brilliance, though none of its glow extended beyond the crystal's face.

Past the entry archway, the cavern sloped downward as it spiraled around the massive central crystal, gradually narrowing until the tunnel was six meters wide and five tall. One hundred fifty meters in, the glow from Kaiden's hand hit what appeared to be a back stone wall. A single two-meter-tall crystal column stood at the center of a domed chamber at the terminus, with the wall of crystal still to our left.

"That's it?" I frowned.

Kaiden's brow knit. "No, there has to be more here."

The three of us approached the opaque, white column. As we neared, I discovered that the back wall wasn't as featureless as I'd assumed from the distance. There were three symbols carved into the stone wall, each inlaid with crystal: a sword, a wand, and a shield.

"Those look familiar." I pointed at the symbols.

"Sure do," Kaiden agreed.

Toran scrutinized the freestanding crystal column. "I believe there's writing carved on here."

I walked over next to him to take a look. There were definitely markings in the crystal, but the language didn't look familiar to me. "No clue what that says."

Kaiden joined us. "Huh. I think that's Laeric."

I'd never seen the ancient root language in print before, but I'd heard about it in my writing composition classes in school. "You know it?"

He winced. "Not *exactly*. A lot of the biology terms from

my agro classes have Laeric roots. I took one semester of the language years ago as a foundation course, but that's…" He shook his head.

"It's a lot more than I can offer," I said.

Toran sighed. "I'm afraid my studies were more focused on numbers than words."

"What we need is a camera so we can run it through the translator in the shuttle's computer," I said.

"Didn't think to bring one of those, either," Toran said.

"Yeah, and I'm guessing it's not one of those things that's randomly in the emergency supplies." I sighed. "Okay, so this has been a good learning experience about *other* gear we should get."

"The little things you don't think about," Kaiden muttered. He pursed his lips as he examined the column. "Some of this *is* familiar. Like, this word here, comes up in plant genetics talking about the… original, or iconic, standard for a species. I believe the literal translation is something along the lines of 'artifact'."

I raised an eyebrow. "Any idea what that means?"

"No. But I also see mentions of 'three' and 'open'," he said. "Could be referencing us."

"Perhaps we each need to touch the symbol associated with our discipline?" Toran suggested.

"Makes sense to me." I returned to the back wall and touched the carved sword symbol with my right hand.

Kaiden and Toran each touched their respective symbols.

I waited. After ten seconds of nothing, I scowled. "Is there some sort of secret incantation, maybe?"

"If that's the case, it could be anything." Kaiden looked around the chamber. "Open Archive?"

We waited another five seconds with no avail.

Kaiden tried again, "Access Master Archi—"

"This is pointless," Toran interrupted. "No designer would make it so people had to guess random phrases. We're missing something."

Kaiden groaned. "You think?"

I thought for a moment. "That center monument might be instructions. What if the 'artifacts' it's talking about are actual *objects*? Like, ancient relics or something."

Toran frowned. "Meaning we might need to gather those objects—whatever they may be—in order to access the Master Archive?"

Kaiden sighed. "Well, that's going to be a problem."

7

I WANDERED OVER to the column in the center of the chamber. "How do we figure out what and where the artifacts are, if that is what this is indicating?"

"There's more here, but I can't read it," Kaiden said returning to the monument. "Maybe it's instructions for how to find them."

"We need a copy of this." I ran my fingertips over the crystal's surface. The text was carved, leaving a recess for each stroke. "And it doesn't have to be a picture. What about a rubbing?"

Kaiden's face lit up. "Good thinking! We just need a sheet of something thin and smooth."

"What about a writing implement?" Toran asked. "I haven't seen anything non-digital since I arrived on the *Evangiel*."

"Charcoal?" I suggested.

Kaiden grinned. "All I hear is an excuse to burn something with a fireball."

"Let's go raid the shuttle and see what we can find." I

jogged up the shallow incline of the tunnel.

Upon exiting the cave, Kaiden extinguished his light orb, and we skidded down the scree to get back to our shuttle.

Finding a suitable material for our needs was tricky. I'd hoped that maybe we *would* find a camera or something else to snap a shot of the carving, but the only devices capable of capturing an image were integrated with the ship and would be too difficult to remove. That left the alternative plan of a rubbing, but we needed a sheet of thin paper or something similar that would be able to pick up the fine lines of the carved text.

I considered the bed sheets on the bunk, but they were too thick. The only other thin-ish materials were sheets for emergency patching, but those had no give to get a relief imprint. Even the materials in the lavatory came up short.

"There *has* to be a way to duplicate that image aside from re-drawing it," I said, staring at the scavenged supplies strewn around the common room.

"Might just have to go back to the *Evangiel* to get a camera and come back," Kaiden said.

"No, we just need to get creative." My eye was drawn to the patching supplies. "Maybe we've been thinking about this the wrong way."

"What's the other option?" Toran asked.

I grabbed the sheet of patching material. "I was originally thinking we could take a relief rubbing, but what if we take a negative instead?"

"Ah, yes!" Toran nodded. "Paint something on the face of the column and use it like a stamp on the sheet."

"Exactly."

Kaiden drooped. "So, no more fireballs."

"Not right now."

He sighed. "Oh well." He eyed the items on the floor. "That black sealant could work for the paint."

I smiled. "I think we're back in business."

We grabbed the supplies, including a flashlight, and scrambled back up the hill to the cavern. I took the sealant so Kaiden could light our way, and Toran carried the piece of sheeting.

Once we were back at the crystal column, I had a pang of regret. "Is it wrong of us to deface monument like this?"

"There won't be anything left of it if we can't protect it, and we can't protect it if we can't get inside the Archive," Kaiden pointed out. He switched from the light orb in his hand to the flashlight; the new illumination didn't fill the cavern as well, but he'd need both hands free.

"Sealant can be removed," Toran said. "When we come back with the artifacts, we'll make it good as new."

I nodded. "Okay."

The sealant painted on easily using an applicator at the top of the can. I coated the front of the column, careful not to get any of the material in the carved grooves of the letters. When the area containing text was completely coated, Toran and Kaiden lifted the sheet into place. Toran held it steady against the column's face while Kaiden carefully smoothed his hands over it to make sure it made consistent contact. They then pulled it straight back to avoid smudging the imprint.

I breathed a sigh of relief as soon as I saw the result. The characters had crisp lines at their edges surrounded by the black sealant. The contrast wasn't great with the black against dull gray, but a little digital manipulation of the scan and the computer on the *Evangiel* could sort out the translation for us.

Kaiden nodded with satisfaction as he looked over our handiwork. "For not planning any of this, that went surprisingly well."

"If the universe-saving doesn't go well, I think the Dark Sentinels have a future as archaeologists," I joked.

"Always smart to foster multiple career prospects." Kaiden smiled.

Toran seemed disinterested in the joking as he grabbed hold of the sheeting. "This will take time to set completely. We should get back to the shuttle."

I took one last look around the cavern. "All right. We'll be back."

Toran carried the sheet out while I took the sealant and Kaiden restored his light orb.

We set a brisk pace, anxious to get back to the *Evangiel* and learn what the engraving said. When we reached the shuttle, we secured the sheet on the floor in the common room and then took our seats on the bridge.

"Everyone is going to be really disappointed when they find out we haven't accomplished anything," I said while I strapped in.

Kaiden powered up the shuttle. "We did do *something*. I mean, we have more information than we did before."

"Even Colren admitted that this wouldn't be straightforward," Toran added. "I imagine they were prepared for us to return having not completed the task."

I nodded. "All the same, you always *hope* you're wrong and that everything will go smoothly."

"That's true."

"At least we're bringing back something with us," Kaiden said.

"That's true—it's something tangible," I agreed. "They won't be able to accuse us of flying around and not trying before we came back."

Kaiden laughed. "I'd really hope they wouldn't do that."

I shrugged. "These military guys, you never know. 'If you're still breathing, you didn't try hard enough!'"

Toran snorted behind me. "And you still wanted to go to Tactical School?"

"Well, yeah. Because… spaceships."

"I guess things are working out pretty well for you now, then," he replied, a touch of bitterness in his tone.

"Believe me, this is *not* how I expected my summer vacation to go." I looked over my shoulder at him. "I don't want you to think I'm taking this situation lightly. I may joke around, but that's how I deal with stress."

"I got that impression," he murmured.

I softened. "Hey, I get that you're worried about your family. I am, too."

"It's sinking in now," Toran continued. "Colren had been telling us all we had to do was wait until we extracted someone who picked Strength, and then we could seal the Archive and go back to our lives. Maybe we'd play a role in stopping the Darkness, whatever it is, but our only certain task was to protect the Master Archive. Now, we know that sealing it isn't an easy afternoon activity. And if *this* is complicated, you can bet the rest of it will be, too. I don't know when I'll be able to see my family again, or if we'll even be able to seal the Archive while there's anything left to save."

"Thinking about the worst case scenario isn't going to help us," Kaiden said while he lifted the shuttle off the ground. "We can freak out if the text from the column doesn't give us any clues, but I'm going to count today as forward progress until I know otherwise."

I nodded. "Yes, we need to stay positive. Everyone will be safe in suspended animation until this gets sorted out." I needed to believe it was true for my own sake—for my loved ones back home.

Then it struck me, too. I had no idea where my home was relative to our present location. Down on this alien world, for all I knew, we could be the only three people left in existence.

I shook off the feeling and buried the thoughts in the back of my mind. The here and now is what mattered. Worrying about things that were beyond my control would only distract me. Even if it came off as aloof to Toran, we all had to cope with the situation in our own ways.

The shuttle rose up in the center of the valley until it was enveloped in clouds. Turbulent winds shook the craft as soon the valley was out of sight.

"Enough of this." Kaiden angled the craft upward and initiated the control sequence to launch it into space.

The initial acceleration without the compensators pinned me against the back of my seat. After a minute of feeling too heavy to lift my hand, the pressure began to subside.

The control console chirped.

Kaiden chuckled. "Sure, *now* we have a navigation lock." He changed the destination to the *Evangiel*, and the autopilot took over. The shuttle glided toward the larger ship in orbit of the purple planet. He tapped behind his ear. "*Evangiel*, this is Shuttle 1 returning from the surface."

"We read you, Shuttle 1. This is Central Command," a woman said on the shuttle's central comm. "Proceed to debrief with Commander Colren upon arrival."

The docking assist display that had saved us appeared on the front screen as we made the final approach. With barely more than a bump, the shuttle touched down on the landing platform and then passed through the golden electrostatic field. Workers ran over to receive the craft as it returned to its parking space inside the hanger, and the engine wound down.

"We probably shouldn't say anything about what we found down there until we've talked with Colren," I suggested.

"Agreed," Toran said.

"Should be an interesting debrief." Kaiden unstrapped his harness and stood up.

I rose from my own seat. "On the bright side of things, we got in a fight and are now two minutes closer to meeting the prerequisites for powered armor."

Kaiden laughed. "Seriously, that's what you're thinking around right now?"

"Hey, it's related to the mission!"

Toran groaned. "I'll get the sheet with the inscription."

Kaiden released the side hatch to drop the exit ramp, and I followed him down while Toran brought up the rear with the piece of sheeting.

"Sorry it's kind of a mess in there," I said to Tami when she approached. "We, uh, needed to improvise. And, the inertial compensators are out."

"Also, a portable camera would be super helpful," Kaiden added.

She squinted at us and tilted her head. "What in the stars did you do down there?"

"Impromptu archaeology," I replied, then followed Kaiden toward the exit.

"We're starting out with such a good impression with the maintenance team." Toran shook his head.

"I don't remember where anything in there goes. Better they put it back how it's supposed to be," Kaiden replied.

"I think we should make ourselves a travel bag with all the random stuff we might need," I suggested.

Kaiden raised his staff. "Yes."

"It may be difficult to anticipate everything, but I think that's a very good idea," Toran concurred.

We exited the hangar and took the lift up to the level with Central Command. We were buzzed in at the main door.

Colren greeted us from the center of the bridge. "We weren't expecting you so soon." His eyes narrowed when he saw Toran carrying the piece of sheeting. "What's that?"

"That requires some explanation," Kaiden said.

The four of us got situated in the conference room.

Kaiden folded his hands on the tabletop. "First off, I saw nothing on Crystallis that would prevent a regular person from setting foot on it. The cloud cover is a hindrance, but once at a lower elevation, it's more or less like any other world."

The commander frowned. "I was told it was impossible."

"Well, either we missed something, or your information was inaccurate," Toran replied. "Lore and legend can have a way of twisting the truth."

"What *did* you find down there?" Colren prompted.

We took turns explaining the events that had occurred since our departure for the planet. The commander sat quietly while we recounted the details, and he became visibly more engaged when we got to the part about the valley and the cavern entrance.

"Now, it *does* appear that only people with specialized skills can access the Archive," Kaiden explained. "However, it might not be the people alone. My Laeric is rusty, but I think there's mention of three artifacts."

Toran placed the piece of sheeting, which had dried, on the table.

Colren's face paled. "I was afraid you were going to say that."

My eyes widened. "You knew about this?"

"Like you said, legend and lore… it's difficult to know what's accurate." The commander sighed. "Let's hope these are instructions."

He tapped on the tabletop and made an entry. A moment later, a beam of light projected from the ceiling passed over the piece of sheeting. To my right, a black rectangle two meters in diameter appeared in the center of the previously blank wall. The black was soon replaced by a scanned image of the sheet.

"Now to find out what it says…" Colren murmured, making additional entries.

The image of the screen flipped to its mirror image, and the contrast adjusted so the dark gray lettering stood out from the surrounding black sealant residue. White outlines appeared over the letters, and an overlay of blue text appeared above the original.

"It's indeed Laeric," Colren said.

The opening text read:

> *Those who seek knowledge must be willing to work as one. Three must come together with their artifacts of power. What was done is not fated to always be. Join as one to seize destiny.*

Beneath the cryptic phrase were three additional blocks of text containing a string of numbers. The first was labeled as *Valor*, the second as *Spirit*, and the third as *Protection*.

Colren tilted his head. "Hmm. Apparently, we didn't get the translation right before."

"Spirit doesn't sound as fun as Magic," Kaiden said.

Toran looked thoughtful. "I rather like Protection."

"Valor has more of a ring to it than Strength," I said.

"Regardless of the preferred translation of the discipline

names," Colren continued, "there remains the matter of acquiring these artifacts and how they will be used."

"What are the numbers?" I asked.

"Need to run an analysis," the commander replied. He selected the three number blocks and instructed the computer to evaluate the sequences. After ten seconds, blue text appeared on the screen with the numbers arranged in a different format. "They're coordinates."

Kaiden nodded. "Makes sense, given the context."

"Coordinates to what?" Toran asked.

"We'll have to map them," Colren responded, his fingers already moving over the tabletop. He removed the imprinted sheet and leaned it against the side wall.

A hologram of a star map appeared above the table. Three red dots lit up.

"Looks like planets," Kaiden observed.

"They're far apart. We'll need to jump to get a closer look at each," Colren stated.

My stomach turned over. "Great."

"Which one would you like to investigate first?" he asked.

"I'd vote for going after the Spirit artifact, since Kaiden has a better handle on his abilities than us at the moment," I suggested.

Toran frowned. "I've been practicing, too."

Kaiden's gaze flitted between us. "Considering we have no idea what kind of challenge we'll face, a physical or defensive type engagement might be more straightforward than one involving magic."

I nodded. "That's a good point."

"So, me first?" Toran asked.

"Sounds good," I replied.

"Okay, I'll arrange the jump to those coordinates. Stand

by." The commander rose from the table and gave us a parting nod.

My chest constricted. "Ugh, I'm not looking forward to more jumps."

"They get easier," Kaiden assured me. "You may even stay conscious long enough this time to experience the sensation of your heart being at your feet."

"I think that's right around the time I blacked out last time."

He smiled. "Ah, then you still have the joy of tasting blue and seeing the sound waves."

I crossed my arms. "That sounds more like a bad drug trip."

Kaiden shrugged. "They like to leave the synesthesia out of the travel brochures."

I scowled. "No wonder they always put civilians under while in transit."

Toran nodded. "But, *we* need to be alert the moment we arrive. Five minutes to get our bearings rather than two hours of grogginess while working off the sedatives."

"I dunno, I could go for a nap right around now," I said.

Kaiden grinned. "Nonsense! That's what stims are for."

"Ten minutes until jump," a woman announced over the intercom.

I sighed and followed my companions toward the door. "Fantastic."

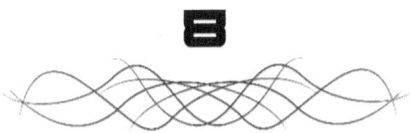

I WISHED I hadn't stayed conscious during the jump, but I did.

Kaiden's irreverent description didn't do the real thing justice. The initial transition into hyperspace was definitely the worst, when all sense of physical order evaporated, but the remaining duration of the jump warped what little remained of my sense of reality. As I heard colors and tasted sounds, the only constant was my heartbeat—though it was occasionally in my feet and other times in my chest where it should be. I focused on the rhythm and tried to relax.

I had no definitive sense of time passage while in hyperspace, but eventually the synesthesia subsided and the pressure holding me against the bottom of the pod lessened.

A chime sounded over the speaker in the pod, then the synthesized voice of the ship's computer stated, "Jump complete."

The seal on my pod released with a hiss.

Shaking slightly, I released my harness and pushed up the pod's lid.

Kaiden sat up in the pod next to me, wearing only his shipsuit base layer. "Hey! You made it."

I smiled back weakly. "I'm a quick study, I guess."

Toran squeezed out of his pod. "I'm with Elle: jumps are terrible."

"Better than spending years in transit." Kaiden exited his pod and started donning his outer clothes.

I hauled myself up, bracing on the edge of the pod while my senses settled. "It's still better than sitting through one of my old chemistry teacher's lectures."

Kaiden raised an eyebrow. "That bad a class, huh?"

"He liked to use the analogy that chemistry was the literature of molecules, and would proceed to explain chemical reactions as though it was a bizarre love triangle."

Toran and Kaiden blinked, then burst out laughing.

"I don't know what you're talking about. That class sounds *amazing*!" Kaiden exclaimed.

"Oh, it was, the *first* year. Yes, the joys of living in a small town when you get the same teacher multiple times. And it was all fine, until he was the teacher assigned to teach Sex Ed, and those analogies reversed."

The two guys completely lost it. Kaiden dropped his staff on the deck he was laughing so hard, and Toran had to lean against his pod, doubled over. Whether they genuinely found it that amusing or they just needed to release some of the tension from the events over the past few hours, I was happy to see them unwind.

I casually got dressed while I waited for them to regain some semblance of composure.

"So, anyway," I said when their faces were less red, "just remember that valence electrons are promiscuous temptresses."

The two men continued snickering while they finished getting dressed.

"Thanks, Elle, I needed that," Toran said while securing the final clasps on his armor.

I gave a little curtsy. "Happy to be of service."

"We should assemble our goodie bag of random helpful things," Kaiden suggested.

"Good call." I crossed my arms. "Where do we do that?"

"Tami?" Toran suggested.

I nodded. "She did say she'd help out with anything we need."

"That was *before* we trashed her shuttle," Kaiden pointed out.

"Well, we wouldn't have needed to rip everything apart if we had a bag like that in the first place, so…" I faded out.

Kaiden bowed his head. "Tami it is."

We returned to the hangar five decks below. Though we considered calling over the comms to make the request, it seemed more polite to go in person so we could apologize again for the mess.

Not surprisingly, Tami didn't look pleased to see us.

"You're back. What can I do for you?" she asked with the forced friendly tone of a disgruntled service worker.

"Hey, hope it wasn't too much trouble to clean up the mess on the shuttle. Sorry about that," I said, feeling it best to address the issue before asking for a favor. "We had a situation."

We explained the circumstances to Tami, and her demeanor softened as soon as she realized what we'd been up against.

"That was a creative solution," she said when we finished. "I'm glad you were able to work it out."

"Yeah, us too," I replied. "We were hoping to stock up so

we don't find ourselves in a tough spot like that again."

"Camera, rope, tape, and paper, for starters," Kaiden said.

"Tactical accessory pack, basically." Tami nodded. "We can definitely set you up. Are you heading out again already?"

I looked to my companions. "Not sure, exactly."

"I guess we need to figure out where on the planet to go," Toran said.

"All right," the mechanic said. "If you'd like to finish planning, I'll gather some materials for you."

Kaiden nodded. "That would be great, thank you. We'll call down when we're getting ready to head out."

"Sounds good." Tami turned back to her work.

"Well, that went a lot better than I feared it might," I whispered while we walked out of the hangar.

"Nah, people in her position are used to picking up after people who make way bigger messes than we did—like getting ships blown up," Toran said.

"I guess that's true."

Kaiden glanced over his shoulder to make sure no one was nearby. "So, about the Protection artifact… how are we supposed to find it? Coordinates to a planet aren't specific enough to find an item."

"Colren didn't seem concerned," I said.

"Well, Colren also has a crew to manage and bosses to report to." Kaiden directed us to the side of the hallway and stopped. "As long as the ship is moving, it looks like we're making progress. And as soon as he sends us down to a planet, it's on *us* to deliver, not him."

I scowled. "You think he brought us here only to dump us off and hope for the best?"

"I wouldn't put it past him. You've seen how much he dodges direct questions."

"My hope was that he'd warm up after we produced something, which we did."

"A copy of some text off of a crystal column?" Kaiden scoffed. "Sure, it's not *nothing*, but the guy has been tasked with stopping the Darkness. Yeah, a thing they just called 'the Darkness' because no one knows what it is. I've been involved in this for a week, but the Hegemony has known about it for three months. If they've been working on a solution for that long and have turned to *us* for a solution, they're all kinds of desperate. You better bet he'd do something like turn us loose on a planet and hope for the best."

My stomach dropped. "Stars! You think it's really that bad?"

"I had my suspicions, but I thought maybe I was being paranoid. Based on how he reacted when we brought in that duplicate, though… I think I'd greatly underestimated the situation."

"All right, no more joking." I hugged myself.

"No, please do," Toran said. "I shouldn't have tried to stop you before. We need to stay sharp, and the best way to do that is by not getting wound too tightly."

Kaiden massaged between his eyes. "I really wanted this whole thing to be overblown theatrics—the Hegemony following some ancient lore because they thought it would play well in the ratings, while they actually have a real plan going and we're a distraction. Now, I'm starting to think we *are* the plan."

"Yeah, we said 'we should go here' and a jump was scheduled within minutes," Toran said. "People in Colren's position don't take orders from people like us under normal circumstances."

I sighed. "Guys, what have we gotten ourselves into?"

"We didn't get ourselves into anything. The trouble found us," Toran said.

"How'd you come in contact with an infected crystal, anyway?" I asked him.

"I was doing maintenance on a crystal interface console."

"Wait, you know how those things work?"

"The interface, yes," he confirmed. "Like I said, I'm an engineer by trade."

I turned to Kaiden. "What about you?"

"There was a crystal in one of the fields I was monitoring for my internship research. I used it for check-ins since it was the most convenient to get to."

"So, it was everyday life. It really *was* random," I said.

"Unless there's some validity to Colren's statement that the reality we're living in now was part of a universal reset no one remembers," Toran pointed out.

"Is that possible?"

"At this point, I'm willing to believe anything is possible," Kaiden replied. "But even if it is, it doesn't change what we're up against now and what we have to do. They're looking to us for answers."

"Our part isn't going to be finished when we seal the Archive, is it?" I asked.

Kaiden shook his head. "That's looking less likely the more I learn."

"I meant it when I said I'd do whatever it takes," Toran said.

"Me too," I murmured. "Even though it's on us to solve, we're the lucky ones. We're here—not trapped in a suspended state of nothingness."

Toran shook his head. "I hope they don't know where they are or what's happened."

I hoped so, too. The few seconds I was floating in nothingness before I materialized on the *Evangiel* were some of the most terrifying moments of my life. I can't imagine what it would do to a person to have that stretch on for hours, let alone months. "No sense worrying about things we can't control, as my mom always used to tell me," I said, trying to stay positive. "Let's just focus on getting them out of there."

He nodded. "Right."

"The question remains, how do we find the artifacts on these worlds?" questioned Kaiden.

"Well, we know your pendant reacts with the magical energy, right? Maybe we can use that somehow," I suggested.

He didn't look convinced. "That was within a couple hundred meters. Searching an entire planet is a completely different scale."

"There has to be some way, though, right? There must be a signal or something we could scan for," I insisted.

"You know, you might be on to something with that," Toran said slowly. "I had a bunch of equipment I'd carry with me for the interface console maintenance, of course, and some of the electronics would go haywire if they got too close to the crystal. I think it's safe to assume they do put off a measurable energy signature, but I can't say from how far away it could be detected."

I shrugged. "Sounds worth investigating."

Kaiden nodded. "I'll vote for anything that saves us from aimlessly wandering hostile continents looking for clues."

"I'll talk with the comm tech and see if we can figure something out," Toran offered.

"In the meantime, I don't suppose I could take a break? I really wasn't joking about that nap," I said. "It was dinnertime when I materialized up here—not that that has bearing on the new body, necessarily… I dunno."

"Yeah, now that you mention it, I'm starving," Kaiden said. "Why don't we grab a quick meal and then we'll get you some sleeping quarters?"

"Sounds good. Toran?"

He shook his head. "I'll eat while I work. I'll reach out when I have something."

"Okay, good luck," Kaiden bid as he led me toward the lift.

We walked several meters down the corridor in silence.

Kaiden glanced over this shoulder and stopped; we were alone. "How are you holding up?" he asked.

"Keeping the freak-outs at bay, so pretty good." I forced a smile.

"I can still barely wrap my head around any of this."

"You seem like you know what you're doing."

He chuckled. "Then I'm faking it well. This is so far beyond anything I would have done in my normal life."

"You seem pretty outgoing."

He shook his head. "I used to keep to myself—as soon as I wasn't trapped on a freighter forced to be around the same eight people all the time. Joking is your coping mechanism, trying to take everything in stride is mine."

There were moments when I'd thought Kaiden was maybe putting on an act, but I'd always assumed it was to show off in the way I'd seen people do in school when they were hoping to gain a measure of social notoriety. Talking with him now, however, I started to second-guess those impressions. "It's not a bad attitude to have," I replied after a pause. "I could have benefitted from that philosophy at other times in my life."

"It's weird," Kaiden mused. "When I woke up here, it was like a switch flipped. I'd always been the shy, nerdy guy who watched everyone else have all the fun, but I never knew how to get in on the action. I mean, have you ever known an agriculture major to be the life of a party? They called me 'plant guy', for stars' sake!"

I winced. "Not the best nickname."

"Other people had worse. But I was far from popular, and I was certainly never in a position to be the center of attention. To go from that to then suddenly have magical abilities and be *important*? I guess it went to my head. Now, though, seeing what deep shit we're in, I mostly just want to go back to being the anonymous guy collecting plant samples."

"Like it or not, we're no longer the people we used to be," I murmured.

"The more that sinks in, the more I'm not sure who I want to be going forward."

I was struck by the sincerity of Kaiden's statement. Any façade he may have put on before was gone. This was the real him, and he was just as scared and confused as me about our uncertain future. It was more than just our mission—we'd been reborn and offered the chance to become the people we'd always aspired to be. Our new selves were there for the taking. Except, it wasn't easy to let go of the parts of our pasts preventing us from completing that transition.

"I'm not sure who I want to be, either," I admitted.

His sky-blue eyes met mine, deep with a wisdom beyond his years. "I think you do. You just need to realize there's nothing holding you back now."

"Same for you."

Kaiden tore his gaze away. "Everything was so certain two weeks ago."

"Adapt and move forward, right?" I smiled.

He smiled back after a moment. "Yeah, I guess so."

We continued our stroll toward the lift and called it.

When we stepped inside, I leaned against the back wall. "I can understand why you adopted your new life philosophy. I can't imagine what it would have been like being the first to wake up here."

"Yeah, it was... disorienting, to say the least."

"You must have thought Colren was out of his mind when he told you what happened."

He laughed. "I did. It wasn't until Toran showed up that I started to think maybe there was some truth to it."

"Did you see the Darkness?" I asked him somberly. "In the crystal, I mean."

"Yes." He looked down. "That's the only reason I didn't take one of the shuttles and leave right away."

"What do you think it is?"

"Something unlike anything else we've seen before. My fear is that it's as ancient as the crystals themselves, and if we don't understand the tech we use, then how are we supposed to understand the alien tech attacking us?"

"Well, the Master Archive might have some answers."

"I hope so. And I hope Toran can come up with an artifact detector, or whatever might give us some direction."

I caught his gaze. "Hey, we'll figure this out."

He shook his head and laughed. "Elle, you are being *way* too calm about all of this."

"I may be young and inexperienced, but I've been through enough to know that losing my cool doesn't improve anything. I spent a lot of time being angry at the universe, and all it did was expend energy I could have spent working toward an actual solution."

"What were you angry about?" Kaiden asked as the lift doors opened.

I hadn't intended to bring up anything about my past, but

I couldn't very well backpedal. "I used to do some reckless things with my friends," I explained while he led me toward the Mess. "We'd hang out in the hills above our town and do flips off of boulders and stuff. We were kids, so we thought the world revolved around us. If anything went wrong, there was always a reset to make it right.

"Then, one day, I fell and broke my arm, and I learned that the universe *didn't* revolve around me. I was twelve and should have known better by then. Anyway, it didn't heal right, so I could only raise my left arm up to here," I demonstrated the range of motion, "and there went my dreams of being a Ranger or anything else that would keep me away from a normal desk job."

He gave me a sympathetic nod. "For what it's worth, the central worlds have some pretty great medical tech these days. I bet they would have been able to fix you up."

"Maybe. But to a girl in a small town on an outer colony world, I didn't feel like I had options. I spent the better part of a year afterward moping that they didn't take the injury more seriously when it first happened, but really I was upset with myself for taking stupid risks."

"So, you started jumping off cliffs instead?"

I laughed. "I didn't say I was good at learning from my mistakes."

We reached the Mess entrance and Kaiden stopped outside the door. He was silent for several seconds. "I can understand how that injury on your homeworld changed a lot of things for you, but it doesn't define your future anymore."

"I know, and I'm grateful for that, despite the rather large caveat that the fate of our civilization is partially in my hands."

"Everything has a price."

"But, come on!" I held up my hands to mime a scale.

"Shoulder injury. Interplanetary savior. The universe might be asking for a bit much here."

"In all fairness, you *did* get more than just your shoulder fixed. I mean, the pink hair had to cost at least two planets' worth of saving."

"I think I might also be a centimeter or two taller, so that's probably another four planets right there."

"It adds up fast. You might have gotten the Interplanetary Savior-level upgrade package after all."

"Damn! I'm locked in now." I snapped my fingers.

"Better make the most of it."

"I do have new friends to keep me company. It could be a lot worse."

"Admittedly, things got a lot better when you showed up—" Kaiden cut himself off and looked at the rubberized floor. "We should get food so you can have that nap."

I placed my hand on my stomach. "Yes! I'm starving. Fighting stone lizard-things apparently works up an appetite."

We stepped forward and the doors to the Mess parted, revealing a rectangular room with seating for seventy people at tables of various sizes. The starboard bulkhead sported broad viewports running the length of the room, and the port side had a buffet line and bar.

"Fancy," I commented.

"Don't let it fool you. They serve military gruel at its finest."

We grabbed trays and browsed the buffet line. I got an assortment of items to sample, most of which were more difficult to identify than I would have liked.

The tables were relatively empty, being an irregular hour for a meal, so we were able to get seats at a four-top by one of the viewports. Though the planet wasn't visible, there was a picturesque view of two moons.

I dug into my meal. After one bite, my shoulders slumped. "All right, I see what you mean."

"Yeah, even as an agro major, I have no idea what this green stuff is."

"I'm just going to pretend its arugula and call it good."

He nodded. "Can't argue with that plan."

We ate mostly in silence, only making the occasional comment about missing fresh produce from our respective homeworlds. It was nice to find we could be comfortable sitting together without saying anything; I'd found some people always had to keep a conversation going or they'd get nervous and weird. That was something I'd always valued in Adrianne and Jiro back home—hanging out at the cliff on a sunny afternoon quietly enjoying the view. I hoped the meal was a sign I'd be able to have a similar rapport with Kaiden as we got to know each other better.

My eyelids were heavy by the time we finished eating. After bussing our table, Kaiden showed me the residential area one deck below, near our jump pod room and the bioprinter.

"It's not much," Kaiden said as we approached, "but you do get your own room."

"That's good. I'm not used to sharing."

"Only child?" he asked.

"No, younger brother." A sharp twinge struck my heart as I thought about him and the rest of my family.

"I have two older brothers, myself. Fortunately, they took an interest in the family business so I wasn't forced in that direction, too."

I released a long breath. "Being the oldest does come with a lot of expectations."

"Just wait until you get to tell your parents this story."

"They'll flip—and that's only based on what's happened so far. I can't imagine what it'll be like by the end."

"We'll find out soon enough." Kaiden gestured to one of the doors. "This one will be you."

I placed my hand on the panel next to the door, and the door slid open. Inside, the chamber contained a single bed, wardrobe, and wash facilities behind a partition.

"Not bad," I said.

"I'll be next door if you need anything. Or, comms." He pointed to his ear.

I smiled. "Thanks."

He glanced at his own door. "All right, sleep well. See you in a few hours."

"See you then. I'm looking forward to seeing what Toran comes up with."

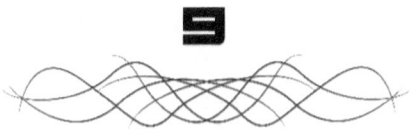

I DRUMMED MY fingers on the tabletop, regretting my agreement to get out of bed.

"You really think this will work?" I asked Toran.

"It's all guesstimated science. There's no way to be certain," he admitted.

"Only one way to find out." Kaiden removed the crystal pendant from around his neck and handed it to the other man, per the proposed plan.

While Kaiden and I had slept for the past five hours, Toran had been hard at work with one of Central Command's communication specialists in the same common room where I'd been introduced to my two companions, though it now contained replacement chairs and Toran's sculpture of twisted metal had been removed.

Toran had supposedly figured out a way to scan for the unique energy signature emitted by items with magical properties. His explanation for how the detection system worked sounded straightforward enough, but we hadn't had a great track record of things going according to plan. The result of his efforts with the communication tech was a device the size of a dinner plate, which has a cradle to serve as the interface with Kaiden's crystal. Based on what Toran had explained, the device would read the energy signature from the crystal and then amplify and broadcast it using the *Evangiel*'s communication and sensor suite.

Though Toran had explained the science behind it, I was more interested in the results.

"Here it goes…" Toran placed the crystal in the device on the table in front of us.

As soon as the crystal pendant was in the cradle, a soft hum filled the air. I was drawn to the tone, though I had no direct way to interact with it. I imagined a current of energy flowing through me, and the sense of it filled my mind.

On the table, the device emitted a soft blue glow, though the crystal itself remained unchanged.

"Hmm, interesting," Toran said.

"What's happening?" Kaiden asked. There was a hint of concern in his tone, which I attributed to his crystal being used in the experimental activity.

"The good news is that the device is working how I hoped," Toran explained. "The less good news is that we're getting multiple hits on the planet."

I frowned. "So, we still don't know where the artifact is?"

"No, but this narrows it down a lot," he said.

Kaiden pursed his lips in apparent thought. "What might also resonate with this tone?"

"Likely crystals."

"And how similar are those crystals to each other?" Kaiden asked.

"You know—they come in all sizes," Toran replied.

"But what about their resonance, or whatever? Is there a

unique signature?"

Toran perked up. "I see where you're going with this."

He made some entries on the touch-surface tabletop, and a list of numeric values appeared. "Okay, these are all of the hits we got on the planet. Let's run an analysis to find their similarities and differences." He made another entry.

The items in the list shifted to the left and additional columns appeared—some numerals, and others showing a waveform. Segments of the waveforms and secondary lines within them were highlighted in different colors.

Toran pointed to one. "Okay, it looks like this green line is the common thread in all of them. The waveform depicted with the purple line appears in all but four of the samples, though its amplitude changes."

"Maybe that has something to do with the crystals of different sizes—larger the crystal, larger the amplitude?" I suggested, somewhat amazed that anything from my physics class had stuck with me.

"Could be," Toran agreed.

"Hasn't the Hegemony studied all of this?" Kaiden asked. "You'd think there'd be documentation of the crystals' properties."

"Yes, their research is why this analysis has taken seconds rather than days. I've cross-referenced our readings with the metadata," replied Toran. "This is different, though—none of those researchers had access to the kind of crystal that you have. I don't know what makes it different, exactly, but it's throwing off some weird readings that don't match anything on the record."

My brow knit. "Do any of the readings on the surface have those same weirdnesses?" Well, at least I'd been able to ask one question while sounding like I knew what I was talking about.

Toran continued to examine the data. "That's what I'm trying to figure out. It's difficult to gauge because the sensors aren't designed to measure this sort of thing. I think they're missing some of the nuances."

Kaiden leaned on the desktop. "You mentioned that the purple line is missing in four of the samples. That may be significant."

"Yes, I was thinking that, too." Toran's eyes narrowed as he scanned over the details about those four data points. "There's definitely something different about these. It's possible they're not recording crystals at all."

"One might be the artifact," I said.

Toran nodded. "Perhaps."

"Well, it's only four sites, right?" Kaiden said. "That's a whole lot less to search than an entire planet. Why don't we just do a fly-by and check it out?"

"Sounds good to me. They're all on the same continent, so we don't even have to circle the globe."

I smiled. "Even better."

Kaiden tapped behind his ear. "Commander, we have targets on the planet." He explained what we'd found and the plan to perform a visual assessment. Within a minute, we had confirmation to proceed.

I called down to Tami to give her a heads up about our imminent departure, and we proceeded to the hangar.

"I can't wait to see what the artifact is," I said.

"I'm not holding my breath for anything wondrous," Toran replied.

"It's gotta be ancient though, right?" I said. "These things probably date back to when the crystalline network was created."

"I'm certainly intrigued. I mean, as of a day ago, I didn't

even know the crystals *were* created, so any items developed by those same designers must be pretty powerful."

"True. If nothing else, it will have unique properties—though that doesn't mean it will be useful."

"Hey, as long as it gets the Archive open, it doesn't matter what else it does or doesn't do," I pointed out.

Kaiden held up his index finger. "Excellent point."

We arrived at the hangar and found Tami waiting for us by the shuttle with a backpack resting on the deck.

"We have everything ready for you," she said. "Shuttle is put back together, and I have some extra supplies for you." She hoisted the backpack from her feet and held it outward.

Toran took it from her like it was a feather. "Thank you."

"I threw in a couple of extra things I thought might come in handy—med supplies, emergency rations, fire starter, thermal blankets. You never know."

"I've got the fire starting handled," Kaiden said with a grin, holding up his index finger with a flame on its tip.

"But if you're unconscious, we're screwed," I countered. "Thank you, Tami. We'll try not to tear it apart again this time around."

She flashed a weary smile. "If you do, we'll just put it back together again."

After an exchange of well wishes and reiterated thanks, we boarded the shuttle and assumed our seats on the bridge. Kaiden initiated the startup sequence, and we began taxiing toward the electrostatic shield.

"Fingers crossed that the weather on this planet cooperates," I said.

Our shuttle glided out of the hangar and followed its automated course to the first location Toran had identified on the planet.

Kaiden remained much more attentive than he had at the beginning of the previous voyage—not surprising, given what had happened last time. However, his concerns proved unwarranted as we descended through the atmosphere toward the target.

The cloud cover was light, especially in contrast to the last planet, and I took in the view of the landscape on the approach. All the land as far as I could see in every direction was green, broken only by the occasional body of water. The terrain was predominantly rolling hills, though several mountain ranges towered in the distance. At least three-quarters of the visible land was forested. I couldn't make out the type of trees at altitude, but the canopy was thick enough that I had no idea what secrets the forests may contain; a hidden tomb for an ancient artifact wasn't out of the question.

"We're coming up on the first location," Kaiden announced.

I followed the line displayed on the front viewport's holographic overlay. It appeared to lead to one of the green hills in a treeless area, indistinguishable from the others around it.

"I don't see anything there," I said.

"Yeah, I don't, either." Kaiden frowned.

"This was the strongest of the anomalous signals, so it seemed to be the most likely location," Toran reported from behind me.

"Should I set us down?" Kaiden asked. He checked his pendant and it was glowing, but only slightly.

"Circle us around. Let's see if any landmark jumps out," Toran suggested.

Kaiden took over manual control of the shuttle and performed three circles of the target area.

I kept an eye on the ground with each pass, looking for anything that might explain the energy readings. As far as I could tell, it was only hills, forest, and a field—no different from the landscape for kilometers in every direction.

"Another cave?" Kaiden proposed.

Toran shrugged. "Perhaps, but that could take a long time to identify. Let's see if the other locations have anything obvious, and we can circle back to here if we come up short."

"I like that plan," I said.

Kaiden switched back over to the automated flight path, setting the second location as the destination.

The landscape transitioned into mountains and then open grasslands as the hundreds of kilometers zoomed by beneath us. The greens yellowed the further northeast we went, and eventually turned to a warm golden hue.

"This reminds me of where I was doing my internship on Falstan II," Kaiden commented.

I scrunched my nose. "It's a little... plain."

"Flat, rock-hard soil, and little precipitation—the perfect environment for testing experimental strains of grain to support new colonies trying to become self-sustaining in the border worlds," he replied.

"Ah, yes. That makes sense."

After four hundred kilometers, the shuttle slowed and descended toward a crystal monolith rising from the flat landscape.

"Okay, now *that's* something worth investigating," Kaiden said after confirming that his pendant was glowing in its presence.

"Agreed, set it down," Toran said.

Kaiden piloted the shuttle to twenty meters from the crystal. It came to rest on the ground with a slight bump.

"Investigating time!" I jumped up from my seat. If I was going to be the 'new me' and commit myself to the mission at hand, I needed to get psyched up.

"I can't match that enthusiasm. Lead the way." Kaiden flourished his hand.

I smiled. "I figured I should compensate for the lack of scenery. I mean, the last place was in a hidden valley with giant crystals and stuff. This is… grass."

Toran followed me into the common room. "Not very riveting, is it?"

"It would be a *lot* more interesting if we found an artifact buried at the base of the crystal," I said.

The large man chuckled. "I appreciate your dedication to finding the redeeming qualities of the location."

I shrugged. "Hey, with the size of the task in front of us, I figure we should focus on the little things."

"And that includes, 'Ooo, we saw a pretty thing'?" Kaiden asked.

"Was that an objection?"

"No…"

I nodded. "Good, then there's no harm in appreciating the sights. After all, we're out to save these worlds—I think it's worth knowing exactly what it is we're fighting for."

"Protecting my home was already enough motivation," Toran said.

"For me, too, but Elle's right—this isn't just about us," Kaiden said.

Toran released the hatch seal, dropping the ramp. "I know."

We filed out of the shuttle and jogged the twenty meters to the crystal monument. The ground was firm underfoot, and the amber, knee-high grass crunched with each step.

The monument was different than what I was used to back on Erusan. Rather than an enclosure and a high-tech interface panel, this four-meter-tall crystal only had three stone columns placed around it.

"Okay... what do we do?" I placed my hands on my hips.

"Excellent question." Kaiden crossed his arms. "Toran? This is the Protection artifact, so I imagine you'll have to be the one to retrieve it."

Toran lumbered toward the central crystal and reached out toward it. The crystal's soft blue glow intensified as his hand neared, but there was no other change. He made contact.

An electric shock radiated from the crystal and arced to the three columns. The stones shuddered, then rotated ninety degrees to the right.

My eyes widened. "Okay, that was something."

Kaiden looked around. "Is there a door, or...?"

Toran frowned. "I don't understand."

I circled the crystal, looking for any clue. It was only unremarkable grass beside the monument. "I've got nothing, guys."

"Neither do I," Kaiden said.

Toran took a deep breath. "Why don't we inspect the other locations? This might not be the first one, or perhaps one of those has a clue."

Kaiden nodded. "All right."

We returned to the shuttle. As we took off, I kept an eye out the viewport to see if there was any change to the surrounding landscape, but nothing was visible from the air, either.

The next location was to the south. Grasslands became sub-tropical forests as we continued southward. The elevation increased, and eventually we arrived at a plateau surrounded by lush jungle. Like the previous site, there was a solitary crystal with three stone columns arranged in a triangle around it.

Kaiden set the shuttle down near the crystal at the center of the plateau.

"Any bets on if this one does the same thing?" I asked.

Kaiden shook his head. "I'm not taking that bet. The answer is too obvious."

Toran rose from his seat. "Let's find out if you're right."

We jogged down the shuttle's ramp and approached the monument. Kaiden and I kept our distance while Toran walked up to it with his hand outstretched. Again, the crystal's glow intensified as he approached, and then electricity arced out to the columns when he touched it. The columns each turned ninety degrees.

I titled my head while staring at the configuration. "Is it just me, or is the layout of those stone columns relative to the crystal remarkably similar to the placement of these monuments and that first site we checked out?"

"It is," Kaiden agreed.

"We should go to the fourth site and then return to the first," Toran said.

I pointed over my shoulder with my thumb. "Back to the shuttle."

We repeated the process of activating the crystal at the final site, which was in the mountains to the west.

As we flew back toward the first site in the rolling hills, I held my breath that there would be an obvious change to the landscape that would indicate we'd done the right thing. Unfortunately, it looked the same.

"Kaiden shook his head. "I don't get it."

"I never suspected it would be easy," Toran said. He caught himself. "Well, I *hoped* it would be, but I didn't figure that would be the case."

"And just think, after we do this, we get to do it two more times on different planets!" I threw up my hands with mock excitement.

Kaiden sighed. "Except, it will probably be something completely different, because it would be way too straightforward to, you know, let us just do the thing."

"We need to demonstrate worth," Toran said. "I believe the point is to show our commitment to the disciplines we chose."

"What might Protection embody?" I asked.

"I have no idea."

"Well, looks like we'll need to do some wandering, after all." Kaiden set down the shuttle in a relatively flat area in the dip between two hills. There were few trees in the surrounding kilometer, but a dense forest ringed the site in a crescent shape to the west and north.

"We're a little southeast of the signal's epicenter, but this looked like the best landing site in the vicinity," he stated.

"It will be fine." Toran grabbed our backpack of emergency supplies and led the way off the shuttle.

The ground was spongier here, almost like walking on padded carpet. Vibrant green grass grew to my knees in most places, with some patches nearly waist-height. The numerous hills made it impossible to see more than fifty meters in any direction while at the low points, so we stopped at each crest to survey our surroundings.

"Ugh, there could be something one ridge over and we'd never know," I groaned after we'd been wandering aimlessly for half an hour.

"Are you sure your discipline isn't 'patience', not 'protection'?" Kaiden joked.

"A solution will present itself," Toran stated, but anxiety

added a quaver to his voice. More than any of us, he bore the self-imposed weight of responsibility to look after his family. His very transformation from a small-statured man to his present hulking proportions spoke to his commitment to care for them. To him, I imagined this search for the Protection artifact was more than just finding an item—it was a tangible representation of his duty to defend his loved ones.

"Yeah, just have to keep looking." I wanted to say something more flippant, but I could tell he was already on edge. I didn't envy what it must feel like to know my child was in danger.

I followed Toran down the hillside to one of the more open areas we'd encountered. The grassy plain transitioned into forest a hundred meters away, and a high ridge was ahead of us to the northeast. A gentle breeze rustled the grass as we walked. Aside from our own footprints and the wind, the world was eerily quiet. Eventually, though, a new sound was carried on the breeze—a series of low thuds.

I came to attention, not sure if it was only in my head. Listening intently, trying to identify the source of the sound. I determined it was coming from the direction we were headed—and it was getting louder. The ground rumbled underfoot.

I froze. "Uh, guys... What is that?"

THE HAIRS ON the back of my neck stood up. Whatever was on the other side of the ridge was closing fast on our position.

Tremors shook the ground—a steady rhythm I feared was footsteps.

My concerns were confirmed a moment later when a stone face appeared over the crest of the hill. It looked as though its features had been carved into a boulder, with deep eyes, a shallow nose, and cracked lips molded in an expressionless line. Flecks of moss provided green and brown contrast, creating the illusion of a patch beard and hair on top of its head. As it lumbered up the far side of the hill, broad shoulders with the same stone-like appearance came into view, followed by a deep chest.

I didn't wait to see the rest of it. "Run!"

Pivoting toward the tree line, I broke into a full-on sprint with Toran and Kaiden to my right.

"Where did it come from?" Kaiden shouted while we ran.

I kept my attention on the ground in front of me. "No idea. And I don't want to find out if it has friends!"

We were almost to the trees—just another dozen meters to go.

"Gah!"

Kaiden stumble at my side, apparently having tripped over something hidden in the knee-high grass. Toran caught his shoulder to keep him from falling.

"Thanks." Kaiden found his footing and continued moving forward.

Toran, however, stopped.

I slowed. "What are you doing?" I called back over my shoulder.

"I think this creature is what we're looking for." He pointed toward Kaiden's chest.

The crystal was glowing vibrant blue, like it had on Crystallis when we found the valley containing the Archive.

I stopped and turned around. "No way!"

"*That's* the thing emitting the signal?" Kaiden stared with a slack jaw at the rock titan pursuing us. "What are we supposed to do with it?"

"I believe that's for me to figure out." Toran clenched his fists and squared off against the approaching giant. "I'm here for the Protection artifact!" he bellowed.

The giant halted. It was even larger than I'd estimated, standing nine meters tall with rock forearms the size of Toran. "Prove your worth," it boomed.

"How?" I asked no one in particular.

The giant clapped its massive hands, then crouched down and pounded its palms against the ground. The force shook the land underfoot, and the rumbling continued to intensify. It was soon shaking so much I had difficulty keeping my footing. Just when I was wondering if it would ever stop, new forms emerged from the ground, swelling under the grass and soil.

I stumbled backward. "What the…?"

The first creature emerged—a stone golem reminiscent of the rock titan, only two meters tall. The others broke through with a spray of soil and the shaking stopped. Six of them surrounded us; all had their fists raised, ready for a fight.

I drew my sabre. "Do we have to take out all of those things?"

Kaiden conjured an orb of electrical energy on the end of his staff. "I think we're about to find out."

Toran made the first move. He ran toward the nearest golem five meters away, raising his right hand on the final approach. His fist connected with the side of the golem's head

The creature roared in a deep, raspy voice. It swung at Toran with its club-like arm, catching him in the center of his chest.

Toran groaned and staggered back but managed to stay on his feet. Without hesitation, he drove his left first upward to uppercut the golem.

Before I could see its reaction, the wind was knocked out of me and I found myself face-down in the grass. I quickly rolled onto my back, annoyed with myself that I'd been distracted by a single engagement while completely ignoring my own surroundings. I wasn't surprised to look up at two golems standing over me.

"Hey, guys!" I greeted the creatures while slicing my sword toward their heads.

The two golems blocked the slash with their forearms, then drove their other fists down as a counterattack.

I rolled free just in time, then leaped to my feet. "That's how you want to be, huh?"

I attacked and parried, the golems using their arms to swing and stab as they circled me.

My responses to their attacks came to me as a clear vision a moment before I acted. Without thinking, I spun and ducked, occasionally thrusting or slashing my sword when an opening presented itself. I hadn't ever trained in that type of combat, but it was a part of me now like I'd been practicing for my whole life. I was strong, precise, agile—the way I'd always dreamed of being. Through whatever process had re-formed me on the *Evangiel*, I had also been imbued with muscle memory to make the most of my new body. And I loved it.

Unfortunately, those skills weren't going to win the fight with my current foes. Despite repeatedly landing clean blows on the golems with the electrified edge of my sabre, I wasn't making a scratch. I needed a new strategy.

I risked a look around to locate my companions. Toran was out of my field of vision, but I spotted Kaiden seven meters away to my right front. He was engaged with one golem of his own, and a pile of mud rested on matted grass nearby.

"Did you take one out?" I shouted to him.

"Yeah, the energy orbs eventually did the trick," he replied, lobbing another crackling ball at the golem near him.

"My sword is useless." I kicked one of my golems away as it got too close, then blocked a swing from the other. "This is getting old."

"Almost... done... here..." Kaiden said in between rapid-fire orbs cast from his staff.

The golem lunged for him in what appeared to be a last-resort move, and Kaiden thrust his staff forward at the same moment another energy orb released. The staff entered the golem's chest. The creature disintegrated into a pile of mud.

I had no time to offer congratulations before the two golems attacking me decided to try a new move. One reached out to hug me, and the other dropped down and tried to curl itself around my legs.

It was a brilliant move, I had to admit. They must have realized that Kaiden's weapon was a genuine threat, so, by entwining themselves around me, they could gain some measure of safety, assuming he wouldn't be willing to fire on his comrade.

I wasn't about to go down without a fight.

I lifted my right leg in time to keep it out of the bottom golem's grasp, and then pinched my outside leg against the golem's back. The top golem had pinned my arms against my sides, but I hadn't lost my grip on my sword. I thrust the blade into the ground to use it as a pivot point, then kicked upward with my right leg as hard as I could. The force was enough to loosen the bottom golem's grip on my boot, and I got free.

The top golem still had me wrapped in a vise-like embrace, however, and it tightened its grip around my chest, forcing the air from my lungs.

An electrical shock coursed through me, and the golem's grip loosened. Without hesitation, I ducked from its grasp and leaped free. I ran five meters away.

In the corner of my vision, Kaiden was advancing with his staff leveled on the golem. Another orb blasted from the end of the weapon.

I took a deep breath, flexing my bruised ribs.

"You okay?" he asked while stepping sideways toward me.

"Yeah, thanks." I repositioned so we'd be standing abreast when he reached my position. While I'd normally not like the idea of someone hurtling magical attacks in my direction, it was clear Kaiden had banked on the fact that it took numerous blasts to bring down a golem, so the creature would absorb most of the attack and leave me unscathed. Fortunately, he had been right.

Despite the number of blasts required, those magical attacks *did* have a measurable impact on the golem, while my sword did nothing. "Hey, do you think you could charge my sword?" I questioned when he was by my side.

Kaiden kept firing toward the golems. "What?"

"I saw what happened when you took out the last one—the end of your staff was electrified and it pierced its chest," I explained. "My sword isn't breaking the surface, but maybe…"

"We can try," Kaiden said. He paused his assault for a moment, touching the end of the staff to my sabre's blade. Electric sparks danced across the metal. "Huh. I think that actually worked."

I grinned. "Nice!"

"Might not last long. Get swinging!"

While he focused on the golem that had grabbed my chest, I refocused on the bottom one that had gone after my feet. It had since stood up and appeared to be sizing up another attack.

I made my move, racing forward for a strike center mass. To distract it, I pretended to be swinging for its neck, but I brought my shoulder back at the last second and switched to a stabbing motion. My electrified blade plunged into the creature's chest. A roar turned to a gurgle as the golem dissolved into a muddy mound.

I wiped my forehead with the back of my hand. "That was ridiculous."

Kaiden lowered his staff. "Where's Toran?"

I spun around to search for our other companion. After three seconds, I spotted him engaged with a golem twenty meters away.

We ran in his direction. After going no more than five strides, one of Toran's fists struck the golem in its chest, and the creature disintegrated. He must have already taken care of the other one, as I didn't see any golems remaining.

"Was that it? Was that the test?" I asked.

Kaiden shook his head. "I don't know. There's still that." He gestured at the rock titan looming over us.

The massive creature stood motionless, watching us with its expressionless eyes.

I released a long breath. There was no way we could take on something that big, considering how much trouble the little golems had given us. We'd taken out its minions; that seemed like a reasonably rigorous challenge.

"Is that the proof you needed?" Toran shouted to the giant.

In response, the giant clapped its hands together, then pounded its palms against the ground. Following the tremble from the initial impact, the shaking intensified, and the ground once again swelled upward until half a dozen new golems burst through the soil.

My jaw dropped. "You *have* to be kidding!"

11

"I AM *NOT* doing all of that again," Kaiden groaned.

Toran stared up at the rock titan. "We've been going about this wrong. We need to go after the giant itself."

I pointed up at it. "That? How are we supposed to take on *that*? It's huge!"

"I don't know, but we'll figure out something." He ran toward its foot.

"He pretends to be rational, but he's out of his mind!" I objected.

"We can't let him go in alone," Kaiden said. "Don't get crushed."

Dumbstruck, I ran after them. "What kind of advice is that?"

"Sorry, it's all I've got."

I looked down at my sword; the electrical charge had dissipated. If the blade had been ineffective against the golems, it was laughable against the rock titan. "Do the thing to my sword again," I requested.

Kaiden touched his staff to my blade while we kept moving

forward, slowing just enough to minimize the bounce in our strides. The blade lit up with electrical energy once again.

"Thanks. Be careful," I told him.

"You too."

We bolted in separate directions, with Kaiden heading to the giant's right while I joined Toran on the left to go after it with physical attacks. I knew the clock was ticking with the charge on my blade.

The giant was entirely stone, from what I could see, so there weren't vulnerable parts of it like there would be with flesh. Its proportions were alien to my eye, with arms that hung down to its knees, short legs, and a rounded torso. I didn't know how we could possibly disable or kill a stone creature, but I figured the best way to start was to knock it down.

So, I went for its foot. After all, I figure that stubbing my toe always made *me* want to sit down, so having a sword jammed into a heel probably wouldn't feel great, either… assuming the creature *could* feel anything.

The foot more closely resembled a flat-ish boulder than anything in my anatomical frame of reference. I ran up to it and slashed with my sword. The electrified blade sliced into the stone, but the giant seemed completely unfazed. I drew my weapon back and stabbed it at the point where an ankle bone would be on a person. Again, no effect.

"This isn't working!"

Next to me, Toran was pummeling his fists into the back of the giant's calf. "Persistence."

I didn't buy it. At the rate we were going, the giant might be injured enough to fall sometime in the next century—if it didn't get annoyed and step on us first.

We'd need a more aggressive approach. I only stood to approximately the middle of the giant's calf, and its ankle was close to the height of my waist. I'd need to get higher if I was going to access a part of the rock titan that might be more susceptible to real damage.

The giant lifting up its left foot to take a slow step. I took the opportunity, jumping onto the top of the foot.

"Elle!" Toran called, but I ignored him. This was my chance to prove to myself that I had what it took to be a part of the bigger fight unfolding around me.

I held out my hands to either side to keep myself steady as the giant raised its foot. The creature's forearm was angled at forty-five degrees above me to my left; it was the closest thing to a ramp I'd ever get to access its head. Keeping one arm outstretched for balance, I quickly sheathed my sword. The rock titan was about to complete its step, and I needed to make my move at apex of its stride.

I leaped, spreading my arms as I flew toward its wrist—the only point with a small enough circumference to give me a chance of hanging on. My chest slammed against the stone, almost knocking the wind out of me as I landed on an awkward angle half on top of the giant's hand. I searched with my fingertips for any semblance of a handhold. My left hand came up empty, but I was able to lock in my right hand. Fortunately, my left leg had hooked over the top of the wrist, so I was able to hold myself in place while I continued to search for a proper grip for my left fingers.

The giant raised its hand, blurring the world around me. My stomach lurched from the sudden motion, but I managed to lock in my grip.

A second later, the giant flicked its wrist in an attempt to shake me off. I held on with all my might, realizing that I hadn't thought through my plan very well—or, at all.

My fingertips burned as I clung to the stone. I started to

slip.

The shaking subsided. I may only have a moment to act.

"Elle!" Toran called from below. I look down and saw him holding up a length of rope from the bag Tami had prepared for us.

I shifted my weight to straddle the giant's wrist, freeing my hands. Toran chucked the rope bundle up to me, keeping hold of one end in his hands. I caught the rope and then dashed up the top side of the giant's arm toward its shoulder.

I'd only made it as far as the creature's elbow when its other hand swooped in to brush me off. There was no doubt in my mind I'd be crushed between the two stone surfaces.

With no other option, I rolled off the far side of the arm, still gripping the rope with Toran holding the other end. The rope caught in the stone groove between the creature's forearm and elbow. I dangled five meters high in the air, not sure if I should climb back up or descend.

"We've got it, come on!" Toran shouted. He was waving for me to descend.

I slid down the rope. My palms burned, forcing me to loosen my grip. I couldn't control my fall at the end, and I landed hard, rolling to the side.

"Grab the rope!" Toran instructed.

I leaped to my feet and managed to get a hold on the rope before the giant yanked it away. I pulled down my coat sleeves to cover the raw palms of my hand, and then tightened my grip.

A sudden roar behind me almost made me drop it again. One of the six new golems was lumbering toward me.

"Ugh, those things are still here?" I backed away from it, wishing I could sprout another set of hands to hold my sword.

Toran ran toward me while keeping his end of the rope taut on the giant's arm. He circled his rope above me; the two lengths crossed behind the creature's arm and cinched tight, unlikely to slip off.

"This way," he said, dashing behind the rock titan to outpace the pursuing golem.

We kept the rope taut as we looped around the back side of the giant. I wasn't sure exactly what Toran had planned, but he had the look in his eyes of someone with a vision.

The plan started to become clear as we rounded the creature's right side. The rope was now angled across the giant's back from where it was wrapped around the left elbow. Unfortunately, there were also five golems waiting for us, who had encircled Kaiden.

"What are you doing?" he questioned us while blasting an electrical ball at one of the golems.

"Taking this thing down," Toran replied. He cut across the giant's front, jumping over its right foot and then the left.

I followed him as closely as I could, glancing to my side to see that Kaiden had halted his energy ball hurling and was backing away from the giant and the golems while keeping an eye on what we were doing.

We rounded the giant's left ankle, coming full circle with the loop.

"Kaiden!" Toran called.

The other man ran over to us, glancing over his shoulder to make sure the golems couldn't reach him.

"Hurry," Toran urged.

We bundled the two ends of the rope together and continued the circuit around the giant's back for a second pass, taking us dangerously close to the group of golems. At the giant's right side, the three of us lined up with Toran at the head of the group. Together, we leaned back and pulled as hard as we could.

The rope cinched tighter, keeping the giant from being able to lift its feet. We didn't have the strength to draw the creature's legs together and knock it off balance, but it was enough to distract it. The other golems didn't seem to like us getting the upper hand; they made a run for us.

"Stand clear! Going to rope one," Toran instructed.

I didn't know what he meant until I saw him duck one of the golems' attacks, then roll and loop it from behind with the rope. He deftly circled it, pinning the creature's hands against its sides.

The golem shrieked, then ran away as it tried to get free from the tie. However, this only drew the rope tighter around the giant. The remaining golems weren't fooled as easily, and they lunged for us.

"If there's another stage to the plan, we should do it now!" I shouted over the golems' roars, drawing my sword once more; the electric charge had long since worn off, but I could at least use it to block attacks.

"I'll handle them," Toran said in a calm, even tone.

His hands clenched into fists and he charged toward the golems. He barreled into the throng, landing a firm blow on each golem as he ran past. Something had changed in his offense, though there was no external alteration in appearance. The calm confidence he exhibited moments before had morphed into an aura of determination.

As he raced toward the enemies with his fists drawn back, his eyes narrowed and he set his jaw.

The blows connected two at a time, plowing through the golems and knocking them backward and to the side. Before the first two creatures had fallen halfway down, they had already begun disintegrating. He struck the next two, and they toppled aside, and in one motion he finished off the remaining golem nearby.

With its arms bound, the rock titan was unable to summon more. The one bound to the end of the rope continued to struggle, tightening the hold around the giant.

Toran rounded on the enormous rock beast. "What more must I do to prove myself?"

The rock titan made no verbal response. It looked down at me and nodded, the gaze of its dark eyes burrowing into me. Then, it fell forward—directly for us.

Kaiden and Toran ran to the side.

I was frozen; I knew I had to get out of the way, but it felt like my feet had been rooted to the ground.

"Elle, move!" Toran shouted.

A shadow passed over me as the giant tipped over toward where I was standing.

I willed myself to move, but my feet wouldn't obey. There wouldn't be time to escape.

Toran dash toward me in the final moments before the giant would crush me, towering over me to face the falling giant.

I braced for the impact.

A deafening crack of colliding rocks overwhelmed my senses. The light blocked out around me as the giant reached the ground. Only, I wasn't crushed. Toran and I were still standing, and we were surrounded by a mound of soil. A smaller mound to my left stood where I had last seen the final golem.

Heart pounding in my ears, I brushed the dirt off my hair and shoulders. "What happened?"

Toran shook his head. "I don't know. I held up my hands over you, and it fell apart the moment it touched me."

Kaiden ran over to us, gathering his cloak in his hands so

it didn't drag in the wet soil. "Are you all right?"

"Yeah," I replied.

Toran frowned. "That wasn't how I expected that to go. I thought the giant would give us the artifact if we defeated it."

Kaiden was silent for several seconds. "Maybe defeating it wasn't the point. The discipline is Protection, right? You put yourself in harm's way in an attempt to save Elle, and that's when it dissolved."

"Hmm." Toran nodded. "Perhaps, but what about the artifact?"

"I don't know. Maybe it's not a literal 'thing' but rather achieving a certain state of mind?" Kaiden suggested.

I scrunched up my nose. "That doesn't seem right, given our experience on Crystallis."

"We assumed it must be an item when we looked at the translation, but there also wasn't anything in the chamber to indicate a place to insert a physical thing," he countered.

Toran brushed himself off. "We should look around. Perhaps something new has appeared in the landscape. That giant came from somewhere."

We hopped over the piles of soil in the battlefield and cleaned ourselves up as best we could. After checking the mound of the former giant to make sure it hadn't had an item inside it, we decided to go back toward the hills in the direction the rock titan had come from.

We crested two ridges on our trek northeast. The first was identical to the dozens of other rises we had traversed since leaving the shuttle, but at the brow of the second, the landscape changed. In the place that appeared to be a former hill, there was now an open maw of moist soil, presumably the place where the giant had been birthed. At its center was a crystal monument similar to the others we had visited on the planet, only twice the size.

Every crystal I had seen in my lifetime was opaque white that glowed with a soft blue inner light. Aside from the Darkness, there was never anything inside the crystals. This one, however, was different. Suspended within the crystal, three meters from the ground, was a dark object; I couldn't make out what it was, exactly, from this distance.

"Was this here before?" Kaiden asked.

I shook my head. "We flew right over this area with the shuttle. It must have been covered up until the giant was formed."

Toran's gaze was fixed on the object inside the crystal. "I imagine that must be the artifact."

"A reasonable guess," I concurred.

Without another word, Toran loped down the hillside toward the eight-meter-tall crystal. Unlike the other crystals on the world, this one didn't have any secondary stones ringing it. The base was more than two meters wide, placing the object inside deep in the crystal. As we approached, the object took on more definition, and I realized that it was actually two items placed next to each other—a set of gauntlets.

Toran surveyed the crystal. "If those gauntlets are the artifact, how am I supposed to get them out?"

"Try touching it," I suggested. "The others activated when you did."

Tentatively, Toran reached out to place his right palm on the crystal's smooth side.

The inner, blue glow intensified until I needed to close my eyes to slits. With a sudden burst, the crystal shattered into a fine dust. The gauntlets within floated gently to the ground.

Toran stood in stunned silence for a moment, then reached down to pick them up. As his fingers brushed the gauntlets, a golden wave of light radiated from them and enveloped him. It only lasted for a second, but when it faded, a contented smile was on Toran's lips and he had a brightness in his eyes where there had only been concern and sadness before.

"I think we found the magical item," I quipped.

"Indeed." Toran slipped the backpack off of his shoulders, setting it on the ground, and rested the gauntlets on top. He removed his knuckle guards and placed them inside the bag, then gently picked up the gauntlets.

The gloves didn't look large enough to accommodate his hands to my eye, yet they slid on with no trouble. Once in place, they moved and flexed more like a second skin than armor. Predominantly black, the gloves were adorned with golden accents and lines of ornate scripture, which appeared to be in the same Laeric language as the crystal monument on Crystallis.

"One down, two to go," Kaiden said.

"How do you feel?" I asked Toran.

He examined his hands as he rotated his wrists front to back. "Different, but I can't quite explain how." He thought for a moment. "You know that moment when you first woke up on the *Evangiel*, and you selected your discipline? It's like that—imbued with a new sense of power, only more intense."

Kaiden smiled. "I have a feeling you just became even more badass."

The other man shrugged. "I can't say I was anything special before."

"You one-hit those rock things. I think that counts for something," I said.

"I suppose I did."

"Plus, you saved me," I added. "Thank you. I should have said that earlier."

"Of course, Elle. We're a team. We're in this together." Toran smiled warmly.

"Well, I guess we got what we came for, right?" Kaiden asked.

"I believe so," Toran replied.

Kaiden nodded. "Then we should head back. We still have two more artifacts to pick up, and who knows what that will entail."

We turned to head up the hill toward the shuttle.

"Which one should we go after next?" I asked.

"I still think the Spirit artifact might be the most complicated," Kaiden said. "Yeah, I've *technically* practiced more than the two of you, but I've only had these powers for a week. I'm by no means an expert."

I nodded. "Mine then?"

"Are you okay with that?"

"Sure," I told him. "I mean, we all helped with this, even though Toran ended it. I know I won't be going into it alone."

"Of course, we'll have your back," he assured me.

"Okay, then Strength—er, Valor—artifact it is!" I grinned. I'd survived this engagement, so now it was time to prove myself as a capable leader in my own challenge.

We returned to the shuttle and Kaiden piloted it back to the *Evangiel*. When we had docked, Tami seemed pleased to see that we hadn't ripped apart the vessel's interior again, and she was especially happy to hear that the rope in our new supply kit had come in handy. Since we'd left the previous length on the planet, as it had been mostly buried in the soil when the giant disintegrated, she provided a new bundle to replace it.

With Toran sporting the new gauntlets, we took the lift to Central Command to give Colren our report.

"Good, you're back," the commander said as soon as we were buzzed through the door to the *Evangiel*'s bridge.

"We got the artifact," Toran announced, showing off his new gauntlets.

Colren barely glanced at them, much to my surprise. "I'm glad to hear it, but there's no time to revel. We need to head out right away; we just got word another world is about to be tainted by the Darkness."

My heart sank. "That's awful."

His expression was one of someone who'd already experienced loss too many times to feel it anymore. "It's another chance to extract someone," he said.

Toran's eyes widened. "Oh. I'd thought it would just be us."

"This is a large task for three people alone. The more we can add to your numbers, the greater your chance of success."

I didn't necessarily agree with the commander's logic. Sometimes, more people complicated a situation rather than helping it. "How does it work?" I asked.

"We need to jump to the world. You can watch the extraction procedure, if you like—assuming we are able to lock onto anyone."

I looked at my comrades. "I'm curious to see what happened to me from an observer's vantage."

"Yeah, I skipped the others, but I'm curious, too," Kaiden said.

Toran nodded.

"Very well," the commander said. "Get to your jump pods. I'll meet you when we arrive at the world."

12

AFTER ANOTHER STOMACH-CHURNING jump, we gathered in the room where I'd first woken up.

The bioprinter pod was situated near the interior bulkhead, next to a control workstation. On the opposite wall, the shade over the exterior viewport was drawn. Colren directed us to stand along the forward wall to observe the extraction, a position where we'd be out of sight of the newcomer when they first awoke. With the disorientation of waking up still fresh in my mind, I appreciated his concern.

"How does it work?" I asked Colren, who was seated at the workstation adjacent to the pod.

He glanced up from the monitor. "The technical specifications are beyond me. Suffice to say that the alien tech is able to isolate a single hyperdimensional consciousness. Someone who's been altered by exposure to the Darkness has a unique signature. The equipment tries to snare a candidate and draw them in. When it does, it reverse engineers a physical form based on the image in the candidate's thoughts."

Kaiden crossed his arms. "It's strange to think of a person

in a way other than their body."

Colren smiled. "We could spend years debating the nature of existence. But right now, we need to try to get someone out of limbo."

"How do you pick which candidate to extract, or is there only one option?" Toran asked.

"We focus on whichever signal is the strongest," the commander replied. "But there isn't someone receptive on every planet."

"And now?" I asked.

He nodded. "We have three candidates, and hopefully we can coax one of them here."

We watched him work in silence, not wanting to compromise the procedure. I couldn't decide which discipline I hoped we got to add to the team. Maybe it was the immediacy effect from our recent mission, but Toran's toughness was coming in handy with our engagements.

"Okay, trying to draw the consciousness here now," Colren said. He pressed a control switch, and the lights turned off in the room. Only the faint glow from his monitor offered any illumination.

The bioprinting pod whirred to life. In the faint light, I saw it lay the foundation for a new form with long, slim limbs. Frosted glass around the torso obscured the details as it filled out the blank, but I could make out the general shape of curvy hips and breasts.

"I think we're getting another girl," I whispered to Kaiden next to me.

"I noticed that."

When most of the body was formed, Colren rose from his workstation and approached the pod to begin the syncing sequence. "Are you a boy or a girl?" he asked.

The young woman blinked, but her eyes stared blankly ahead. "A girl," she replied in a high, lilting voice.

"What is your name?"

"Maris."

The bioprinter added the final layer of details to her body, caramel skin, dark hair, and hazel eyes. She looked to be a year or two older than me—though, as we'd discovered with Toran, that didn't necessarily mean anything. When the physical features were complete, a white jumpsuit appeared around her.

Colren activated the holographic projector inside the pod, displaying the sword, shield, and wand icons. "What is your strength?" he asked.

"The wand," Maris answered after several seconds.

"Are you sure?" Colren asked.

"Yes."

The bioprinter had completed its work, but Maris arched her back like something had just been done to her. Then, a pendant just like Kaiden's appeared around her neck.

Thinking back to my own experience, I realized that I'd felt different after making the final selection, too. Maybe there *was* something to the alien tech being tantamount to magic.

"You are a caster. Use your power well," Colren stated as he stepped back. The door on the pod swung open. "Welcome."

The young woman took an unsteady step, smoothing her hands down her white jumpsuit. "Where am I?"

"You're on board the *Evangiel*, a Hegemony ship. I'm Commander Alastair Colren."

"Wha...?" She looked around. "I don't understand."

"I know this is disorienting," Colren soothed her. "Come, sit down." He beckoned to the table where I'd had my first conversation with him.

She noticed us standing along the wall and took a rapid step in the opposite direction. "What's going on? Who are you people?"

"It's okay, I went through this two days ago," I told her. "I'm Elle."

"Went through *what*?" Her tone was downright shrill now that she was agitated.

"Your world was infected by a Darkness. We extracted your consciousness to a new body designed to your specifications," the commander explained.

The look on Maris' face was probably just like the one I must have had when I was told the same thing. "This is insane," she said.

"I know it's a lot to process." Colren gave her an abbreviated overview of the details he'd shared with us over the past two days.

By the end of the explanation, Maris looked like she was about to cry. "I didn't ask for any of this."

"You have strength of spirit or you wouldn't be here," Colren said. "Now that you are, we need your help."

She tucked a length of her long dark, hair behind her right ear. "Can't you just send me back?"

"Doesn't work that way," Kaiden said. "But hey, at least you'll have people to show you the ropes."

"Heh, we did some great literal rope work earlier," I said.

Maris tilted her head. "Was that a euphemism?" She glanced between Kaiden and me.

"No!" Kaiden hastily replied. "We were fighting a rock titan."

"For an artifact," Toran added.

"Artifact?"

I sighed. "We have some more catching up to do."

"I'll leave you to get acquainted," Colren said. "The jump

drive is recharging, but we'll jump in forty minutes to the planet with the next artifact."

"We agreed to go after the Valor item next," Kaiden said.

The commander frowned. "With a new caster on your team, I suggest you retrieve the Spirit artifact next."

Kaiden looked to us. "Do you care?"

"I'm fine waiting for mine," I replied. "I don't feel like I've really tapped into my latent skills yet."

Toran nodded. "If you're comfortable, Kaiden, I will support whatever decision."

He took a deep breath. "Okay, Spirit artifact next, I guess."

The commander inclined his head. "I'll arrange the jump. Prepare to depart as soon as we arrive." He left the room.

Maris stared at the three of us with a knit brow. "Does anything you just said actually make sense?"

I laughed. "It does sound like gibberish, doesn't it?"

The new woman looked all of us over from head to foot, and she took a step back when she evaluated Toran. "I don't know what kind of cult you're running—"

"Whoa! No." I held up my hands. "I know this all sounds crazy, but there's a perfectly reasonable explanation for everything. Well, *mostly* reasonable."

"Ninety percent sensical," Kaiden agreed.

Maris paled. "You're all completely out of your minds."

"We're not. It's the universe that has gone crazy," Toran said in as soft a tone as his bass voice allowed.

"I want to go home," Maris whined.

"Not an option." Kaiden walked over to the viewport and activated the shutter.

The covering opened, revealing a view of a blue planet. Except, there were dark tendrils weaving around the world, slowly consuming it.

"Stars! What *is* that?" Maris took a sharp breath, her face twisted with horror.

"That's the Darkness," Toran stated. "This world has been corrupted. You can't go back there."

She crossed her arms. "Colren said that we're immune. Are we or aren't we?"

I was all geared up for a defensive response against her constant objections, but I caught myself. She brought up a very good point. The commander had insisted that it had to be *us* to accomplish the tasks because we had a special immunity to the Darkness due to our partial exposure, yet all of his statements were about where we *couldn't* go.

Kaiden and Toran appeared to have the same revelation. We exchanged glances.

"I suppose we haven't actually tried," Kaiden admitted.

"Okay, so let's go," she said.

Toran shook his head. "It's not worth the risk."

"If anything you've been told is true, there shouldn't *be* a risk," Maris insisted.

"Fine, then what's the *benefit*?" I countered. "We were in the middle of something before this detour to come pick you up. Is there something valuable on the planet we should retrieve?"

Maris worked her mouth. "I don't know. I just... I want to go back to Yantu."

"Look at it." Kaiden pointed at the Darkness, which was continuing to spread around the world. "That's no place to be right now. Wouldn't you rather help find a solution to return your world to how it was?"

She nodded slowly. "But what can we do?"

Kaiden gave her a reassuring smile. "Let's go over some basics and get you geared up," he said. "You'll get to learn the rest in the field."

We started explaining the artifacts and what we'd learned about the clues to open the Master Archive while we walked Maris down to get prepped for our upcoming mission. We had just reached the equipment room door when we finished going over the most relevant details.

She shook her head. "I don't like it."

"What do you mean?" I asked.

"I dunno, just sounds like a lot of tedious work. I'll pass."

I glanced at Kaiden and Toran. "You're in this now, like it or not."

"This is the best way you can help your world," Toran said.

Maris threw up her hands. "But I'm no one! I can't imagine taking out a giant the way you did."

"You may surprise yourself," Kaiden told her. "You haven't even *tried* to use your new abilities."

She hesitated. "I don't know where to start."

"Not here," Toran cautioned. "We don't need any more close calls."

Maris tilted her head questioningly.

"I maybe accidently almost punched a hole through the hull with a fireball when I was trying to show off to Toran when we first met," Kaiden admitted.

I smirked. "Oh, *that's* what happened."

Kaiden flushed slightly. "Ancient history now. But, at any rate, we have a rule for no significant magic use on the ship."

"Why don't we get your equipment and you can come with us on this next mission?" I suggested. "You can play around with your new abilities and get to know us a little better. If you still don't want to participate, you don't have to come on the next one."

Maris searched my face. "Why are you being so nice to

me?"

"Why wouldn't we be?" I asked.

"I called you crazy."

The three of us laughed.

"We'd think *you* were if you didn't," Kaiden said. "I mean, we can cast magic now. That's wild."

"I won't believe it until I see it," she replied.

"Soon enough," I told her. "Let's get you some proper clothes and a weapon in the meantime."

She wrinkled her nose. "I don't like weapons."

I stepped toward the door to the equipment room and it opened automatically. "Believe me, you'll want something if a rock lizard comes after you, or a golem."

"They aren't friendly," Kaiden agreed. "I hope we don't get into a lot of fights, but you need to be prepared just in case." He followed me inside.

Toran beckoned for Maris to enter the room. "You'll find you have new skills. Actions will come naturally for things you never would have thought you could do."

She stepped inside the equipment room. "If you say so."

"Step onto the scanner," the synthesized female voice stated.

Maris jumped. "Wha—"

The illuminated ring appeared on the floor.

"Oh." Cautiously, Maris stepped forward.

The scanning ring took its readings of her, and then the holographic mesh appeared around her body and the menu popped up.

"Whoa," she murmured.

"Starting with the armor seems like it's easiest," I suggested.

Maris selected that option from the menu, and the

different clothing options appeared. "What do I pick?"

"Our white onesies make a good protective base layer, we were told," I replied. "Beyond that, it looks like we're locked out of the cool stuff like powered armor. You should be able to find something in the civilian catalog with ballistic fabric."

She turned around, her face draining. "Ballistic-rated clothing? What are we going up against?"

"These textiles are a trifecta of awesome," Kaiden jumped in. "Projectile, magic, and slash resistance. Just take our word for it—it will come in handy."

She eyed his cape. "Is that so?"

"You're living in adventure-land now, Maris. Embrace it," I advised.

She returned her attention to the holographic menu and began making selections. In the end, she picked out an armored corset that accented her chest way more than seemed appropriate for proper armor, tight pants, and a knee-length hooded cape in a deep maroon shade. The accompanying heeled boots seemed entirely impractical, but clearly we had different definitions of 'battle gear' given her other choices.

"You've come around to the pro-cape camp, I see," Kaiden commented.

She smiled at him. "Looks good on you."

I fought the impulse to roll my eyes. "Still need to pick out a weapon."

"Do I need a wand for casting?" she asked.

"No, I think these crystals focus our power," Kaiden replied, touching the pendant on his neck.

"Why the staff, then?"

He held it horizontal and thrust it forward. "Makes a good stabby and blocky thing."

Maris flipped through the options in the weapons menu,

pausing on a set of throwing daggers. "I still don't like the idea of having to attack anything."

"Then go with something like that where you can keep your distance," Toran said.

She nodded. "All right, I'll give it a try. You're right, it's better to have something and not need it than the other way around."

She locked in the selections, and the 3D printer got to work preparing her specified items.

While we waited, we found out that she was twenty years old and had been working as a bartender. I wanted to ask if the skimpy outfits or the work gig came first, but I thought better of it.

"I like taking care of people," she explained. "I never intended to make it a career, but I enjoy it."

"Don't think we'll have much chance for mixology, I'm afraid," Kaiden said. "But you can clearly multitask and are coordinated, so that will come in handy."

A chime sounded when Maris' items were finished printing, and she crossed the room to retrieve them. The items layered nicely, following a color scheme of black and maroon with the occasional silver accent.

When the corset was in place, it was even more accentuating than it had appeared in the holographic preview. Kaiden and Toran, to a lesser extent, had clearly noticed, as well.

"Looks good," Kaiden commented, his gaze lingering on certain parts of her more than I wished it had.

After reminding myself that I wasn't in high school anymore and she could wear whatever she wanted, I forced a smile. "All right, ready for your first mission?"

13

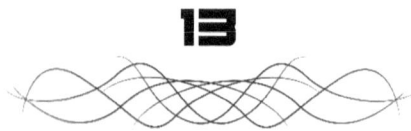

AS IT TURNED out, Maris didn't seem ready at all. I couldn't blame her. The process of waking up on a spaceship with no sense of grounding would throw off even the most level-headed person. Unfortunately, my first impression of her was that she was on the opposite end of the spectrum.

"What is it we're supposed to do, exactly?" she asked while we walked up to the room containing our jump pods.

"We go to the planet and wander around until we find the thing that we need—but we won't know what that is until we find it. Then we come back here and go for the next thing," I replied.

She scrunched up her nose. "How do you know that you got the right thing if you don't know what you're looking for?"

"It just kinda makes sense when we find it," Kaiden replied.

"But, you had to fight that giant before you even knew you were going after the gauntlets. What if you'd gone through the fight but it wasn't actually connected to the artifact?" Maris pressed.

"But it *was*," Toran said.

She shook her head. "I don't know. It seems like a lot of work for not knowing if you're doing the right thing."

"We never said this would be easy," Toran responded. "In fact, I believe we have only indicated quite the opposite."

"I still don't understand why you were all so willing to go along with what the Hegemony is asking. They should have specialists to take care of this, not rely on recruiting random people."

"They don't understand the enemy," I said. "I think they tried other things first, but we're a Plan B that was launched when nothing else worked."

Maris sighed. "They should just do a master reset and purge the Darkness from the worlds."

"Is that even possible?" I asked. I'd heard about resets happening on multiple worlds simultaneously, but my understanding was that those were independent, coordinated resets. If it was possible to do a universal reset, it had certainly never happened in my lifetime.

"I heard rumors from some of the engineers at work," Toran revealed. "Opinions were very divided about whether or not it could be done."

Kaiden shook his head. "I don't see how it could, personally. When talking about an interplanetary reset or something on a universal scale, what would be the locus of the event? A reset needs a point to serve as the constant from which everything else is synced."

"That's the biggest argument against it," Toran replied. "Plus, the slew issues concerning the capacity of the crystalline network."

"It *would* be pretty handy if we could reset to four months ago, or so," I mused.

"The problem is, even if the crystalline network could

reconcile that much data through the hyperdimensional links—which I don't think it can, based on what I know—none of our society's backup systems are designed to handle that scale of reset," Toran continued. "The servers in the Capitol don't have an external backup point."

"Not to mention, the Darkness came from *somewhere*," Kaiden added. "Even if we reset to four months ago, it would still come a month later. We'd need to locate where it's coming from and eliminate the root cause."

"Which we'll probably have to do anyway," I pointed out.

Maris sighed. "This just keeps getting better and better."

I cast her a sidelong glance. "I, for one, would rather be taking action rather than sitting at home helpless while my world falls apart around me."

"As much as I never thought of myself as having a hero complex, I have to agree," Kaiden said.

Maris thought a moment. "Yeah, I guess you do have a point."

"And the universe is far from falling apart yet," Toran stated. "We already have one of the artifacts, and soon we'll have a second."

"That's the spirit." I pumped my arm with exaggerated enthusiasm I wasn't feeling at the moment, especially since we'd reached the room containing the jump pods.

"Like I said, we can see how things go on the next planet," Kaiden reiterated while entering the chamber.

Maris nodded. "Okay."

"Jump in T-minus five minutes," the announcer stated over the comms.

I headed to what had become my usual pod and started stripping down.

"Where are our sedatives?" Maris asked.

"We don't use them here," Toran replied.

"But—"

"Better get in the pod. We don't have a lot of time," Kaiden interrupted. He'd already stripped down to his white base layer and was climbing into his pod.

Maris frowned at the restraint system. "How do you strap in?"

Kaiden stepped back out of his pod. "Get in." He motioned to her pod.

Maris hopped inside and reclined.

"This goes up here and this down here." Kaiden arranged the harnesses. "Buckle in and cinch it tight."

"Okay, thanks."

While I lay down in my own, I saw her smiling up at him as he leaned over her pod.

"T-minus two minutes," the announcer stated.

There were several rapid footsteps followed by clips and fabric rustling as Kaiden got situated in his pod.

The final countdown sounded, and then I was once again in the uncomfortable altered reality of hyperspace.

I listened to my heartbeat and breathing throughout the duration of the jump, just like I'd found was helpful on the last two legs. Now that I knew what to expect, it was much more tolerable than it had been the first time around.

The jump didn't seem to last as long as the others, so I was surprised when my sense of weight diminished and my internal organs felt like they were in their proper places again.

I sat up and stretched as soon as I'd unbuckled my restraints after the pod opened.

Not surprisingly, Maris had yet to emerge.

I exchanged glances with Kaiden as he sat up in his own, and he vaulted out of his pod to go check on her.

"Maris?" He crouched over her.

I came up behind him.

Maris was unconscious and looked pale despite her naturally tanned skin. I reached down to touch the back of my hand to her forehead. It was cold and clammy. "I think she might be in shock."

"Let's get her up." Kaiden reached in and hoisted her torso, I grabbed her feet to keep them from hitting the lip of the pod's lid.

"Should we bring her to Medical?" Toran asked.

"Maybe. Let's give her a minute. Grab my cloak." Kaiden nodded toward his bundle of clothes in the locker behind his pod.

Toran gathered the cloak and spread it on the deck.

I gently set down Maris' legs and Kaiden lowered her the rest of the way.

Her face scrunched up and she moaned.

"Maris, wake up," Kaiden urged. "We're here. The jump is over."

He brushed Maris' hair back from her face. The color began to return to her cheeks. Slowly, her eyes fluttered open.

"Wha— What happened?" she stammered.

"You decided to implement your own sedative," I said from her other side.

She frowned. "Huh?"

"You passed out," Toran clarified. "Do you feel okay?"

Maris placed a hand on her stomach. "A little queasy. Feels like a bad hangover."

"That'll pass." Kaiden held out his hand to help her to her feet.

She wobbled as she found her footing, and Kaiden supported her with one arm.

"How long was I out?" she asked, her voice faint.

"We just got here. Do you remember any of the jump?" he replied.

Maris shook her head. "Just the sensation of being slammed against the bottom of the pod."

"Yeah, that initial acceleration is really disorienting." He loosened his grip on her as she stabilized. "Doing okay?"

"Yes, thank you." She took a deep breath. "Getting better every second."

Kaiden stepped away. "Get dressed. We need to figure out where to go on the planet."

We each donned our outerwear and sheathed our weapons. By the time we were dressed, the color had fully returned to Maris' face and she was looking more confident.

We went down the hall to the room where Toran had set up his device for our ongoing magic locating needs.

Kaiden removed his pendant and placed it in the cradle. "Let's see what this planet's deal is."

The device hummed as it activated, and the crystal glowed soft blue. The touch-surface desktop displayed the waveform of a single contact point.

"Hmm," Toran mused. "That seems surprisingly straightforward."

Kaiden frowned. "I don't believe it."

"What's wrong?" Maris asked.

"Last time, we had four contact points—those three crystals we needed to activate," I explained. "After that complication, this just seems way too easy."

She tilted her head. "But easy is good, right?"

"I suspect the complicating factor will come in a different form," Kaiden said with a sigh. "Let's check it out."

We headed down to the hangar. Workers were huddled

around our shuttle when we arrived, as usual. There were also four backpacks waiting by the entrance ramp.

Tami stepped forward to greet us. "You must be the newest member of the team. Welcome." She smiled. "I'm Tami, the lead tech specialist around here."

"Hi," Maris replied with a faint smile.

"Here's a comm for you." Tami held out a case containing a single micro earpiece.

"Fair warning, it's not going to feel great going in, but it doesn't last long," Kaiden warned.

"I'm sure I can handle it." She took the earpiece and placed it in her left ear. She winced as the comm embedded but otherwise made no indication of the discomfort. Maybe she had a tough streak in her, after all.

"I took the liberty of preparing packs for each of you," Tami continued. "This world appears to have some challenging terrain, so it seemed prudent to offer provisions for a longer stay planetside."

"Thanks." I grabbed one of the packs—heavy, but manageable with my new augmented strength and functioning shoulder. I'd never done well with heavy packs after my injury, so it was liberating to no longer have weight be a concern.

I scaled the ramp and dropped the pack in the far corner of the common room, with the others following suit close behind me.

As soon as we were all inside, I was penned on the far side of the common room and needed to wait for the others to go down the corridor to the bridge. As they filed in, Maris made a direct line for the seat at the front where I'd been sitting in the shuttle.

Not wanting to seem petty, I kept my mouth shut and headed for one of the passenger chairs in the back across from

Toran.

"Actually, that's Elle's spot," Kaiden said on my behalf.

Maris looked between him and me, then shrugged. "Sorry, I didn't realize there was assigned seating."

"It's not, exactly, but we've kind of got our groove going," he said.

She held up her hands and stepped back. "Don't let me intrude."

While I really didn't like judging people before I got to know them, Maris wasn't making a great first impression. I was sympathetic to the situation—being thrown into unknowns with a ton of pressure to deliver—but the mixture of self-centeredness and sense of entitlement was getting to me.

As I took my usual seat in the shuttle, I snuck a glance toward Kaiden. He took a slow, deep breath and gave me a subtle nod.

Okay, so it wasn't just me.

At least, I hoped that's what he was indicating. It was possible he was just telling me to chillax because I was clearly on edge. I decided to just strap in, cross my arms, and stay quiet. However, even that simple plan proved to be overly optimistic in Maris' presence.

"Is this going to take long?" she asked. "What did that Tami woman mean about a longer stay?"

"It will take as long as it takes," Toran replied.

She frowned. "What will we have to do?"

"We'll figure that out when we get down there have a lay of the land," Kaiden said while activating the autopilot to take the shuttle out of the hangar.

"Will we need to fight another rock titan?"

"I imagine this will be a different challenge fitting of the Spirit discipline," Toran told her.

The shuttle glided through the electrostatic shield into the void. It arced and glided the length of the *Evangiel* before beginning the descent to the brown planet.

Following the automated flight path toward the target Toran had identified, we descended through the cloud cover—nowhere near as thick as on Crystallis, but enough to hamper visibility—until we reached an elevation of three kilometers. The clouds cleared, revealing a flat expanse of marshland. According to the map, the target was right up ahead.

The marshes gave way to a lake of murky blue-green water. In the middle was a tiny island with a crystal monument at its center.

"Is that it?" I asked.

Kaiden took manual control of the shuttle and looped it around, making multiple passes over the island.

The crystal hanging around his neck glowed more intensely the closer we got to the crystal monument.

"Yeah, looks like it," Kaiden concluded. "Well, there's that complication we knew was coming."

I frowned. "Everywhere around it is marsh. We have to be at least ten kilometers from solid land."

"Not to mention, how are we supposed to get to the island once we make it to the edge of the lake?" Kaiden sighed.

I scanned the area around the island. "Wait, is that a pathway?" I pointed to the northeast.

He directed the shuttle toward where I was pointing. Almost invisible against the dark water was a stone pathway—only, it appeared to be below the water's surface.

"Hmm, maybe there's a way to raise it up?" Kaiden suggested.

"Likely. Either way, it looks like we should try to land in a place with access to this side of the lake."

He sighed. "This is going to be a long day."

"Looks like we might need to break out those bedrolls," Toran said.

Maris gasped. "You never said anything about camping!"

"We do what the mission dictates," I responded. "If that's where we need to go, then we'll need to hike in."

"This isn't what I agreed to."

I glanced at her. "You're here now. Best make the most of it."

"Can't you bring me back to the ship?" she asked.

"And explain to the commander why we wasted valuable time and fuel? No." I knew the statement was terse, but a person could only listen to so much complaining before it got to be too much.

Maris scoffed and crossed her arms. "Way to show a little compassion."

That was officially all I could handle. I turned around in my seat as much as I could with my harness secured. "Maris, *all* of us were pulled away from our lives and thrown together. Whatever sense of entitlement you think you have, you don't. We're all trying to save our homes. We can either work together and get that done, or complain and moan about not getting our way. So, what do you say that you buck up and try rather than playing the victim card?"

Kaiden cast me an appreciative glance and nodded slightly.

Maris gaped at me. "You want me to pretend everything is okay? I was just ripped from my world and told that everything I took for granted about my reality may be because of some crazy alien tech no one understands. And you think I'm playing a *victim* card?"

"Hey," Toran soothed, "let's just—"

"We're not each other's enemies here," Kaiden cut in.

"What we're up against is bigger than all of us. We need to work together, not be divided."

"Well, way to make me feel part of the team," Maris snapped.

Kaiden scoffed. "Because I won't take you back? No, the only way we're ever going to learn to work together is by going through the motions. If you want to quit after this, fine, but you promised to make a genuine attempt to learn about your abilities before you decide whether to help us or not."

She slouched in her seat. "Fine."

I turned to face forward, drawing a slow, deep breath. Kaiden's and my eyes met for a moment, setting me at ease. I appreciated him having my back.

Given Maris' reaction, it seemed like maybe the criteria for who to extract needed a little refining. Thinking along those lines made me question my own selection, however, so I dismissed the idea. If I was worthy, so was Maris—she just needed to find the part of herself where she could come into her power. Getting upset with her didn't help either of us. Maybe I could use an attitude adjustment of my own.

With our spat resolved, Kaiden consulted the map overlaid on the front viewport.

"I think this is as close as we'll be able to get." He pointed to a patch of solid land just over ten kilometers from the lake.

"We'll make it work," I said.

He nodded. "We don't have another choice."

"LET'S START WALKING," I said, hoisting the backpack containing extra supplies onto my shoulders.

We'd loaded a map of our destination onto a handheld device—one of the new additions in the packs Tami prepared for us—and we were facing a challenging journey across narrow strips of land through ten kilometers of bogs. The path reminded me of the kind of circuitous route we'd take through the boulder fields in the hills back home, only this was much longer and had a lot more opportunity for dead ends.

Fortunately, we'd recorded aerial footage on the fly over to our landing site. The image was loaded onto the handheld along with an optimized path through to the edge of the lake where the underwater path led.

Kaiden lifted his own pack. "Everyone have everything? Double check."

I nodded. "I'm good."

Maris groaned as she picked up her pack. "Do I really need all of this?"

"We don't know what we may find out there, and we'll be

a long way from resources," Toran stated. "Unless you want to potentially find yourself hungry and sleeping on the bare ground, having the contents of that pack on hand is in your best interest."

"Or, you can stay here in the shuttle by yourself for however long we're gone," I muttered.

Maris only flipped her hair out of her face in response.

"I'm ready," Toran said in response to Kaiden's original question.

"Okay, then let's head out." Kaiden set off along the specified path.

After a quarter of a kilometer, the first signs of the marshlands appeared. The ground softened underfoot, and the air took on a faint aroma of decay. Shallow puddles of water popped up in our path. As we went deeper, the puddles multiplied and merged into waterways.

The solid ground on the path we were following was, in reality, only firm when compared to the standing water around it. Covered in short reedy grass, my boots sunk in at least three centimeters with each step, making for an exhausting slog through the maze of relatively dry pathways. Some areas were six or seven meters wide and the four of us could comfortably walk abreast, but in the other places, the pathway narrowed to a meter and we'd have to hop over to another landmass.

After an hour of walking and jumping, my pack was digging into my shoulders. To distract myself, I kept an eye on the water for any signs of life.

The water was still in most areas, but as we got deeper into the marsh, I started to see the occasional flutter of water out of the corner of my eye. Whenever I turned toward the movement, there was only a telltale ripple on the surface, which could easily have been caused by a gust of wind. The appearances were too random and numerous, though, for me to believe that was the only explanation. Something was out there.

"Hey, have you noticed anything in the water?" I asked when I was certain the sightings weren't in my imagination.

"Yeah, I've been watching that, too," Kaiden replied. "I can't tell what it is."

"Wait, is there something stalking us?" Panic pitched Maris' tone even higher than normal.

"It's probably just fish or frogs or something," I said.

Kaiden nodded. "This water isn't very deep. It can't be a large creature."

I hoped that was true. Frankly, it was impossible to tell how deep the water went. It *looked* like it would be shallow, given the pattern of dry land, but for each of the larger areas of land, there were twice as many broad patches of open water. It was possible a creature of substantial size was lurking in the depths. My hope was that we were seeing evidence of multiple, smaller animals rather than one, large creature tailing us for the last kilometer.

Given Maris' predisposition to theatrics, I thought it best to keep that thought to myself. Based on how Toran was keeping a watchful eye on our surroundings, though, I suspected he may have had similar thoughts.

We continued forward in silence.

While traversing one of the narrower land segments, only two meters wide, a distinctive splash sounded to my left. My hand instinctively went to my sword hilt.

"Did you see it?" Kaiden asked.

I shook my head. "No."

Another splash sounded on my other side and I spun around. This time, I caught the back of a creature with dark, green-brown skin slipping beneath the water. It had to be at least a meter long, based on what little I saw.

I swallowed. "We're not alone."

We pivoted to stand back-to-back, with Kaiden and Maris facing one direction and Toran and me the other.

"Looks like you'll get your first chance to use magic," Kaiden said to Maris.

"What do I do?"

"My first time, I just thought about what I wanted to happen, and then it did."

"I don't want to accidently blow you guys up."

He chuckled. "That's not going to happen."

I drew my sabre from its scabbard. With any luck, we wouldn't have any more rock-creatures and the blade would do its job.

Something dark broke the surface of the water and lunged for me. I brought up my sword to block the creature from striking my neck, seeing no more than a dark blur hurtling toward me.

My blade sliced into tough flesh, and the creature shrieked. It flopped to the ground at my feet.

Just over a meter long, it had six stubby legs with webbed feet, and the oblong body tapered into a flat tail. Its head was as broad as its shoulders, with jaws the entire width. Dark eyes positioned near the top of its head were covered in an iridescent film. It was gazing up at me with what I took to be a mixture of confusion and bloodlust. The gash from my sword ran for five centimeters along its left shoulder, and it was favoring the nearest leg.

I held my attack, waiting for it to make the next move. If it went on its way, I saw no reason to harm it further.

The marsh monster shrieked again and wrapped its jaws

around my right ankle before I even saw it move.

I felt pressure around my leg, but my boots did their job to halt its bite. The marsh monster thrashed and tried to roll.

"You had your chance." I stabbed my sword into the base of its neck.

The creature gurgled as viscous, dark blood oozed from the wound and trickled from its mouth.

"Good job, Elle," Toran said next to me.

After twitching for five seconds, the creature fell still.

Two shrieks sounded behind me, and another to my right. Then, a deeper roar chimed in.

My heartrate spiked. "Stars! How many are there?"

"Watch each other's backs!" Kaiden said. "All right, Maris, stay focused. Anything comes near you, think about what you want to do and do it."

"Okay," she acknowledged, a quaver in her voice.

Toran clenched his fists while scanning the dark water for signs of the enemy creatures. "Maybe you scared them off?"

I shook my head. "They're here. I can feel it."

No sooner had I spoken than a black form leaped from the water toward Toran. He batted it to the side with one of his powerful fists.

From behind, the crackle of electrical energy filled the air as Kaiden launched his initial assault. "Attack them!" he urged Maris

"I'm trying!" she cried. "I'm thinking about fire, but nothing is happening."

Another marsh monster leaped from the water toward me, somehow rocketing from the water high enough to snap at my neck. The scent of rotten fish and decaying vegetation assaulted my nose. I elbowed the creature as it approached my face. It flopped to the ground and slipped back into the water before I could attack.

"These things are so quick!" I groaned.

Next to me, Toran tried to smash a creature mid-leap as it charged for his knee, but it recoiled mid-lunged and disappeared into the water in a split second.

Splashes sounded on the other side of the land as Kaiden's energy balls struck the water.

"They're dodging," he said with obvious frustration. "How did you get that first one?"

"I don't know. Maybe I caught it by surprise?" I replied.

A different marsh monster leaped for me, and I slashed at it with my sword. Like Toran's experience, the creature somehow pivoted midair and evaded my swing.

"We need to move faster somehow," Maris said.

A foreign tingling sensation washed over me, and the world took on an orange hue.

The surface of the water broke. One of the creatures emerged, leaping toward me—but, somehow, in slow motion.

I assessed how to make the best intercept strike. When the creature was in range, I plunged my sword into its abdomen and ripped the blade sideways. My movements felt fluid and natural even though my surroundings had slowed to a crawl. The creature slowly dropped to the ground.

Toran was watching the engagement with wide eyes next to me. His own movements appeared to be normal, like mine.

"What ha—" I cut off as a wave of the creatures leaped from the water—seven of them, all charging the two of us.

"Shit! There's too many of them!" Kaiden exclaimed behind me.

We were surrounded.

I slashed and stabbed my way through the mass of marsh monsters. Their bodies dropped to the ground, dark blood hardly distinguishable from the mud.

Toran punched at the creatures nearest him, while blasts from Kaiden sounded behind me. When all of the creatures had fallen, everything was still. The orange glow faded as quickly as it had emerged.

"What was that?" I asked.

"That was incredible!" Maris exclaimed. "You were moving at super-speed."

"Really?" Kaiden asked.

"Yeah, your movements were a blur, then everything dropped dead. It must have only been three seconds."

My mouth fell open. "That last attack only lasted for *three seconds*?"

Maris shrugged. "Or something. I wasn't timing it."

"Did you do this?" Kaiden asked her.

She scoffed. "I was just standing here. All I said was that we needed to move faster."

The tingling sensation washed over me again as the world tinted orange.

Toran rolled his eyes, and Kaiden's lips parted with surprise. Maris, however, was shrugging in slow motion.

"Huh." I nodded with satisfaction.

"So she can speed up our movements," Kaiden commented. "Haste magic will come in handy."

"Indeed it will." Toran looked out over the water. His heavy brow lowered. "Sooner than later."

I shifted my attention in the direction he was looking and saw a new creature emerge from the water. This one was four times the size of the others, and it looked pissed.

15

THE GIANT MARSH monster lumbered toward us—movements that would be a blur in real-time, but were now a slow plod thanks to Maris' haste magic.

"Is this the thing we need to fight for the artifact?" Toran questioned, his fists raised and poised for a fight.

Kaiden turned around to join our line. He glanced down at his crystal pendant; it wasn't emitting any light. "No, we're still too far from the lake island. This is something else."

"Great." I adjusted my grip on my sword.

The new marsh monster was nearly four meters long and stood two meters tall at its shoulder. Its broad head and jaws were a meter wide, and tusks poked up from its inky lower lips. As it loped forward, the front two of its six legs cleared the water, revealing sharp nails at the end of its webbed toes.

While it wasn't a rock titan, the thing was still a formidable foe.

Kaiden made the first move, blasting a ball of electrical energy toward its face. The creature bucked and snorted, but it continued its forward charge.

Toran and I exchanged nods. When the marsh monster was within striking distance, Toran and I simultaneously struck it—my blade stabbing into the side of its neck at the base of the skull and Toran punching it beneath its eyes.

It roared in response, tossing its head back. The creature shifted its weight sideways, aiming its tusks for Toran.

One of the boney points struck him in his left shoulder beneath the pauldron. Toran winced as it made contact, but he took another swing with his right fist.

The punch spurred the creature to buck its head, driving the tusk deeper into Toran's shoulder. When it dropped its head, the bloodied tusk pulled out from the wound. The creature started to align its head for another gore.

I gripped my sword with both hands and drove it into the underside of the marsh monster's throat, twisting as I thrust.

It gasped, opening its jaws wide.

I gagged on the stench of rotten fish, holding my breath as I dragged the blade sideways to open the wound. The creature stumbled, and I ripped the blade out, staggering backward.

As soon as I was clear, Kaiden blasted the monster with an electrified orb, followed by a column of flames cast from the end of his staff.

With a shriek and gurgle, the creature collapsed to the ground and was still.

I took a deep breath, laughing a little. "All right, then."

Toran grunted. "I hope we don't meet more of those." He examined his injured left shoulder; blood trickled from the wound.

I quickly flicked my blade clean and then wiped the creature's remaining blood off my blade using its hide, then sheathed the sword. "Are you okay, Toran?"

"Yeah, it's minor," he replied, wincing as he moved.

"We should clean it out and patch you up," I said.

"This place might not be safe," Kaiden cautioned.

I looked around at the corpses. "I dunno. If I was one of those things, I think I'd steer clear."

"Fair point," he conceded.

The world shifted back to standard color, motion returning to normal.

"Stars, not again!" Maris exclaimed.

Kaiden smiled. "We'll need to work on your casting for yourself, too."

She frowned, seeing that Toran was injured. "What happened?"

I gestured to the slain creature. "Battle wound."

Maris stepped forward. "Maybe I can help."

Kaiden nodded. "Not sure if healing magic is a thing, but I didn't think haste magic was, either."

"I'll try," she said. She approached Toran and placed her right hand over his wound while gripping her crystal pendant in her left. Closing her eyes, she continued to take slow, steady breaths.

A soft green glow appeared beneath her hand, glowing and sparkling as ribbons of light traced around Toran's shoulder. He jumped with surprise when he saw it, then remained still—though his gaze kept darting to the side.

After thirty seconds, the glow faded and Maris opened her eyes. "How was that?"

Toran rotated his shoulder. "The pain is gone." He dropped his backpack to the ground, then unclipped the front of his armor and the shoulder pauldron to inspect the injury. When he bared his flesh, there was only a faint pink mark of new skin. "Amazing," he murmured.

Maris beamed. "I did that?"

Kaiden patted her on the back. "Well done."

"Have any other neat tricks?" I asked.

"Let me see if I can do something for the rest of you." She closed her eyes again.

A wave of renewing energy washed over me—like I'd just slept for six hours and then downed a packet of pure sugar. "All right, yep. That'll do it!"

Okay, so she'd found her niche on our team.

"Why do I suddenly feel like I could climb a mountain?" Kaiden commented.

Toran nodded. "I could get used to this restorative magic."

Maris grinned. "I didn't know this kind of magic existed."

"I'm not sure it did before us," Kaiden replied. "Well, at least not since the ancient times when the crystals were created. The magic of the crystals was always a given in our lives, but nothing like casting."

"The mythology of it has always been there," I pointed out. "There was never a doubt in my mind when I saw the wand icon that is denoted magic."

Kaiden nodded. "I guess now we know that those cultural cues came from the ancients—and that magic is very much a real thing."

"And that the power is more mysterious than we initially realized—the ability to injure but also to heal," Toran added.

"When you described everything to me before, it was all about fireballs and stuff," Maris said. "While that's impressive, and all, it's not really *me*. I enjoy helping people, like I said."

"Hey, I'm all for having a medic on our team," I said.

She smiled. "You know, I was actually planning to go to school to be a nurse."

Kaiden chuckled. "Congratulations! You just got fast-tracked to a degree at Magic University. The curriculum is entirely self-taught, but you're guaranteed to graduate in record time."

Maris laughed. "I'll try to be a model student." She tucked her hair behind her ear while looking him over.

"Well, we should get going!" I said resuming my trek along the path.

"Yeah." Kaiden cleared his throat. "We're almost halfway there."

We picked our way through the narrow strips of land snaking through the swamp. Following the adrenaline rush of the fight, it was nice to walk in relative silence with only the squish of our footsteps.

A kilometer from where the creatures attacked us, I started to see signs of movement in the water again. "Guys, I think more of them have come to say hello."

"Ugh, I really don't want to deal with more of those things," Maris groaned.

"Maybe this is a good opportunity to get in some additional practicing before we go for the artifact," Kaiden suggested.

Maris glanced at Toran and me, then she focused on Kaiden. "What kind of practice?"

"I know you don't want to use offensive magic, but it would be good to get a handle on some basic spells, if you can manage," he explained. "You need to be able to protect yourself."

"Yeah, I guess," she admitted. "I just couldn't get it to work when I tried before."

"Well, there was a lot of pressure then. You can give it a shot now while there isn't something threatening to eat you."

Maris nodded. "Okay, I'll try." She took a deep breath and held out her right hand while gripping her crystal pendant in her left.

I kept an eye on the water and my hand on my sword hilt in case something else decided to attack us.

Toran was equally vigilant. While it wasn't necessarily best for the two people keeping watch to not have any longer-distance attack abilities like Kaiden with his magic, at least we wouldn't be caught off-guard.

After an awkward minute, nothing had happened with Maris' attempted casting.

"This isn't working," she grumbled.

"You're overthinking it." Kaiden placed a hand on her shoulder. "Picture the result like it's already happening."

"I don't know if I can."

"*That's* your problem—you doubt yourself. You control the abilities, not the other way around."

She sighed. "I guess."

"Think about when you were casting haste before, or when you healed us. You just did it without thinking."

"Maybe that's the only kind of magic I *can* cast." Maris shrugged.

Kaiden gave her a stern look. "Not everything will be easy. You'll have to dig deeper and find it."

She tilted her head. "Then why don't *you* learn the curative and support casting, too?"

The question appeared to catch him off-guard. "Well, offensive magic comes easily to me, and the other to you, so—"

"But you want *me* to learn the other kind. Shouldn't that go both ways?"

I had to admit, she did bring up a valid point. "You know, if we had *two* casters giving us extra bonus skills…"

"Okay, I'll work on it," Kaiden conceded. "But my bigger

concern right now is making sure you can defend yourse—"

A dark creature burst from beneath the water, heading straight for Kaiden.

Maris yelped, her hand still outstretched for the practice. As soon as the creature's shoulders cleared the water, a column of flames shot from her hand and enveloped the marsh monster.

Its shriek pierced the silence, only lasting a moment before fading out. It dropped back into the water and lie still at the shore, its rubbery flesh charred.

I let out a relieved chuckle, my eyes wide with surprise. "That's one way to take care of things."

Kaiden grinned at Maris. "See? You're a natural."

"Still nowhere as good as you." She giggled.

I tried to suppress an eye-roll. I don't think I was successful, but she didn't seem to be paying attention.

"All right, so now we know Maris can get badass with the offensive magic in a pinch. But shouldn't we keep moving? You can practice more while we walk," I said.

"I concur. We still have a ways to go," Toran added.

"Right, yeah. We'll keep working on it," Kaiden acknowledged.

We set out again at our same brisk pace. A fireball or electrical blast occasionally shot out behind me while Kaiden and Maris practiced casting. It would have been annoying were it not for Maris' restorative spells thrown into the mix, which helped mitigate my weariness from slogging through the mud for hours.

Our path was true for most of the trek, with the exception of two times we needed to backtrack when we discovered that what had looked like land on the aerial image was actually exceptionally murky water. On the second backtrack, two of the smaller marsh monsters attempted an ambush, but we quickly dealt with them using quick reflexes and Kaiden's casting skills.

After two and a half hours, the putrid water began to clear. According to our tracking on the downloaded map, we were almost to the lake.

"Nearing the artifact site," Kaiden reported in over the comm to Central Command.

"We've been tracking your progress," Colren said in my ear comm. "It looks like you've logged some combat time. Is everything okay?"

"Yes, nothing we can't handle," I replied.

"All right, keep us updated on your progress. Sunset is coming up on you quickly, so it looks like you won't be able to make it back to the shuttle before nightfall."

I frowned; the notion of trying to traverse the marsh after dark didn't appeal to me, but spending the night on the alien world with hostile creatures didn't have a great ring to it, either.

"We'll be in touch," Kaiden assured him.

A low double-beep sounded as the commlink disconnected.

"Staying here overnight?" Maris moaned.

"I suspected that would be the case as soon as we saw the island, but I'd hoped we at least wouldn't have any predators to deal with," I said.

Kaiden nodded. "It isn't ideal, but we have everything we need to make it through the night."

"We should find a campsite and set up before we lose daylight," Toran suggested.

"Yeah," I agreed. "Let's find that stone bridge. Maybe there's something paved around there."

"Good thinking." Toran took the lead.

"This will be my first night sleeping outside," Maris said while we walked.

"Total 'city girl', huh?" I asked.

She chuckled. "Yeah, I guess you could say that. Yantu, my homeworld, was pretty focused on interplanetary business. Most of my customers at the bar either worked for the Hegemony as administrators or were in middle management or executives for private industry."

I cocked my head and glanced back at her. "Ever overhear any juicy gossip?"

She smiled. "All the time! You know that you can convert pericol into tridarium holdings then cash it out and avoid the import taxes?"

"I have no idea what you just said."

"Ugh, commodities trading," Kaiden groaned. "I spent way too much time dealing with that for my parents' grain transport business."

"That's way more important than anything I heard about," Maris said. "You were helping to feed people; all of my customers just wanted to make money so they could retire somewhere on a beach far away."

"Can't say that's a bad aspiration," I admitted.

"No, but a little *too* aspirational, given our present circumstances. I'm more focused on *not dying* right now than my future earnings prospects," she replied.

I looped my thumbs behind the shoulder straps of my backpack. "You know, that's a good point. What's going to happen after this is over?"

"We are operating on behalf of the Hegemony. I'd hope they would compensate us as independent contractors," Toran chimed in.

"Seriously, guys?" Kaiden raised an eyebrow. "We're

tromping through a bog on an alien world and you're wondering if we're going to get paid for saving known civilization?"

I smiled at him. "Well, when you put it that way, it would be ridiculous for them *not* to give us all the money for being the bestest heroes ever."

He narrowed his eyes. "I can't quite tell if you're joking or not."

"Probably because you recognize I bring up a valid point."

"It *does* seem like we should get something for going to all of this trouble," Maris interjected.

"I could see getting an endorsement deal," Toran said. "Pretty sure there's a fitness company that would want to get in on this." He flexed his arms to model his sculpted torso.

"You've all lost your minds," Kaiden muttered.

"Probably swamp gas," I quipped.

He sighed. "And here I thought I'd get to finish out my last term of school in solitude charting the growth patterns of new hybrid alfalfa strains."

I turned back toward him. "Kaiden, I'm not gonna lie, that sounds really lonely."

"Okay, granted, it wasn't the best. I was attracted to the agro angle because I thought I could be part of a community. Turns out it wasn't quite what I thought."

"Do you regret it?" I asked.

"No." He paused. "Maybe. I don't know. I just wanted to have a sense of grounding that I never got growing up."

"You know, sometimes it's about the people you're around more than the place," I said.

"Yeah, I've heard that, too." He sighed. "I have a feeling that this whole experience is going to upend my plans. I'll see how it shakes out in the end."

"I'm never going to be able to look at things the same way again," Toran murmured.

"Wow, that conversation took a turn for the deep and introspective." Maris chuckled.

"I guess being faced with mortality and the fate of one's world can do that to a person," I said.

She took a deep breath. "Yeah, I have a lot to think about, too."

"Like, I mean, the whole *magic* thing is a game-changer," Kaiden said.

"That is very true. It complements being a nurse, but this would be different," replied Maris.

I nodded. "Tough to know how the established medical community will respond to the notion of magical healing."

"Can't argue with the results, though." Kaiden pointed out.

"The very confirmation of magic will change many perceptions," Toran mused. "I could see us becoming the subject of many studies."

"No, there have to be others, right?" Maris asked. "We're not the only casters."

"Have you ever heard of a genuine magic user?" I questioned. "I haven't. I was familiar with the idea, and I was taught that magic was commonplace during the time the crystals were created, but those were the last known instances of true magic, as far as I know."

"That's what I learned growing up, too," Kaiden said. "When I saw the wand, it called to the fanciful dreams I had as a kid. I never imagined... this." He cupped a flame in his palm.

"There's a lot to worry about before we think about returning to our normal lives," Toran stated. "Let's focus on the Spirit artifact."

"To that end, I suspect it's somewhere over there." Kaiden

pointed to the west.

A shimmering expanse of blue-green water was now distinct from the surrounding marshy landscape. At its center, the small island rose a few meters above the water's surface and measured approximately ten meters in diameter. The crystal at the summit of the island's rise shone with soft blue light, beckoning us to approach.

However, the sun was getting low in the sky, and nighttime would be upon us within the hour. We'd have to wait to tackle the island in the morning.

We continued toward the lake, the last half-kilometer going faster as the ground transitioned from sticky mud to drier, plant-covered clay.

As we approached the lakefront, I kept an eye out for any signs of a road or bridge, which might connect to the underwater pathway to the island.

"I wonder if there's a magical switch," I mused aloud.

"What, now?" Kaiden asked.

"You know, the bridge," I clarified.

"Oh that, yeah." He nodded. "I'm hesitant to try anything tonight, since it may trigger another battle like that one with the giant. I *really* don't want to attempt a magic fight in the dark."

"Might actually be easier than a physical fight in the dark, though," I pointed out.

He took a deep breath. "The intent of that statement was *any* nighttime battle equals bad."

"I can't argue with that."

Toran squinted. "Is that the entry to the bridge up ahead?"

I diverted my attention from Kaiden to where Toran was pointing at two horizontal stones along the water's edge.

"That does look promising," I agreed.

"Let's get a closer look." Kaiden picked up his pace.

We slowed on the final approach, instinct taking over to warn us that we might be walking into a trap.

"I don't feel any active magical presence," Kaiden said.

"Me either," Maris agreed. "Not that I know what that is, exactly, but nothing stands out as this being different than any other stone."

"Assuming this is the trigger for the bridge, let's not wake it up just yet," Kaiden cautioned.

"Yeah, no." Maris shook her head.

Toran gazed thoughtfully at the strip of land to which the bridge connected. "I believe this will make a suitable campsite."

The low, horizontal stones formed walls along a sloped ramp leading into the lake. The walls would make for reasonable seating, and a flat, paved area between them would serve for a relatively dry campsite to lie down with our blankets and tend a fire.

"I like it," I said. "We should get a fire going. That tends to deter most creatures."

Toran nodded. "I had a similar thought."

"What are we going to burn?" Maris asked.

"No trees, no wood," I realized.

"Those reeds and bushes?" Maris suggested.

Kaiden shook his head. "Good tinder, but there's no staying power to the burn on something like that."

She frowned. "Then what?"

"Peat," I said. "We used to bring bricks of it camping with us."

"Uh, Elle, if you haven't noticed, everything is wet here," Kaiden countered. "We can't burn anything from the ground here."

"All that you need to prepare it is pressure and heat." I

gestured to Toran and Kaiden. "This ground is packed biomass. It'll make the perfect long-burn fuel with a little preparation."

Toran nodded slowly. "You may be onto something there. Don't know until we try it." He shrugged.

"How do we get it out of the ground?" Kaiden asked.

Maris scowled. "What are you even talking about?"

"You know, peat." I stamped my foot on the ground.

She tilted her head. "Who's Pete?"

I sighed. "Just watch." I dropped my pack on the stone ledge and rooted around inside. We weren't lucky enough to have a shovel in our collection of random useful things, but I did have my sword, a plate, and a bunch of tape; I always loved improvising.

My makeshift 'shovel' was slightly horrifying to behold, but when I gave it a test-scoop in the ground, it worked surprisingly well. While Maris watched with crossed arms and a bemused expression, I scooped out a dozen chunks of the ground from near the water's edge where the reeds grew. It had the right kind of fibrous look I recognized from untreated peat back home, so I was hopeful it would fulfill our needs.

"All right, let's make this into something that will burn," I said.

With Kaiden and Toran's help—Maris didn't want to get her hands dirty—we relocated the chunks of wet biomass to the paved stone area and stomped on it as a first pass to get out the moisture. Then, I removed the plate from my sword and Toran also got out his. He pressed the chunks between the plates until they were relatively dry pucks. We then set the pucks on the stone pathway, and Kaiden held a flame in his hand—enough to heat the pucks without igniting them.

As the last of the sun dipped below the horizon, the pucks

appeared to be about as dry as they'd get.

"Let's see how this burns," I said.

Kaiden nodded. "All right."

We located a suitable spot in the center of the stone ramp to use as a fire pit, and Kaiden focused a low-intensity flame on the puck. It sputtered at first, then ignited in a warm, golden glow.

We laughed with relief and glee; our efforts had paid off.

"Now *that's* how you improvise a fire," I said.

"Huh." Maris nodded. "So, did Pete invent this, or—"

"Different spelling," I cut in, holding up one of the pucks. "P-e-*a*-t. Apparently, they don't teach you *everything* in the city."

She crossed her arms, accentuating her figure even more in the firelight. "Yeah, we didn't burn a lot—not even candles."

"I barely knew about the material, myself," Toran admitted.

"Fire can be fun," Kaiden interjected.

I smiled. "You were a total pyro as a kid, weren't you?"

He looked off to the side. "Well, let's just say it's not surprising that a fireball was the first thing I cast."

With the immediate needs of warmth and animal deterrent tended to, we got settled into our campsite for the night. We had thin sleeping pads and thermal blankets in our inventory, along with half a week's rations, a water filter, and various other gadgets.

The horizontal walls to either side weren't ideal for sitting on, but at least it would be a dry place to sit off of the ground. I selected a spot on one of the mossier sections to get some extra insulation from the stone. Across the campsite, Kaiden noticed me getting settled and started to head over. Before he could sit next to me, however, Toran plopped down.

"I bet it gets cold at night," the large man commented.

"Yeah, we'll need to get cozy." Maris grabbed Kaiden's arm and tugged him to toward the wall across from me.

He sat down next to her, seeming a little reluctant, but I wasn't sure if that was only in my head.

As the temperature dropped, we found ourselves scooting closer together and leaning in toward the fire to gather as much warmth as we could. True to Tami's statement, the base layer of our clothing *did* regulate temperature well, but even with that, the chill crept in.

We ate a simple meal around the fire, admiring the starry sky as the last of the light faded. To my relief, there was no sound of animal activity around us.

"You know, maybe spending a night outside won't be so bad, after all," Maris said, breaking the intervening silence. "It's peaceful out here."

"See? Told you." Kaiden nudged her gently with his shoulder as they sat side by side.

An unwanted wave of jealously rose in my chest. He wasn't actually warming up to her, was he?

Like I was one to talk—even I wasn't finding her as annoying now that her unique magic skills were coming into play. And, aside from the 'Pete' incident and occasional whining, I was probably overreacting to her attitude. I could see how anyone could be drawn in by her perfect figure and desire to nurture.

Meanwhile, I had never considered myself anything special to look at, I had a tendency to slash things with my sword when they upset me, and snark was my go-to mode of communication. When evaluating girlfriend potential, I may as well admit defeat in a competition I didn't want to have in the first place.

I did my best to suppress the thoughts. Petty distractions. But, seeing Kaiden sitting next to Maris, I knew ignoring my feelings wasn't going to be that easy.

I rose from the wall and plopped down on my bedroll. The ground was hard, even with the pad, but I'd have to tough it out. "We should get some rest."

Kaiden drew away from Maris to head for his own sleeping pad. "Yeah, sleep well. We'll cross to the island at daybreak."

I HAD A restless night on the cold ground under the stars. I'd always enjoyed camping as a kid, but being on an alien world knowing that creatures who wanted to eat me might only be a dozen meters away didn't make for restful sleep.

As the first golden light peeked over the horizon, I sat up and stretched.

The last of our peat bricks were now smoking ash, but they'd served their purpose and gotten us through the night.

Maris, surprisingly, was the next to stir. Somehow, her hair was still perfectly styled despite spending a night on the ground with no pillow.

I ran my fingers through my own tangled mess of fuchsia hair, making a mental note to pack a comb for our next outing.

Kaiden stretched on his pad, then cracked open an eye. "Morning already?" He rubbed his eyes.

Toran startled awake. "Toast?" He looked around. "Oh, right."

I chuckled. "Everything okay over there?"

"Yes, just thinking about my family," he replied.

"Breakfast, anyone?"

My heart dropped as I thought about my own family and how nice it had always been to wake up to the scent of baking muffins on the weekends. "Yeah, sounds great."

We ate more of the bland rations identical to our meal the night before, then packed up our simple camp.

When everything was stowed in our backpacks, Kaiden took a deep breath and turned toward the island. "Now we need to figure out how to get over *there*."

I had no idea what to suggest. The previous locations we'd visited to access the artifacts had columns or some other indicator to mark what we were supposed to do. This, however, was a flooded bridge, a crystal on an island, and a whole lot of nothing everywhere around us.

"Do we have to swim over?" Toran asked.

Kaiden approached the water's edge. "That doesn't seem right. But this water is definitely too deep for us to wade across the bridge."

"Maybe the landscape has changed over time," I suggested. "It's possible everything flooded. Who knows when all of this was built—a lot can change in a few hundred or thousand years."

"That's a good point." Kaiden turned around and looked at the paved area we were standing on. "What do you think this was?"

I took a step back and examined the area more objectively in proper lighting. At first glance, it reminded me of a boat ramp, though I knew that was unlikely.

Then, it hit me. "What if all of the ground settled and the columns fell over?"

"These walls we were sitting on?" Kaiden returned to our campsite and rubbed the layer of sediment and moss off of a top segment to expose the stone underneath. "This *does* look like the stone that was around the crystals on the other planet."

"I touched the crystal to activate the stones on the other world," Toran pointed out.

"Doesn't mean it will work the same way here." Kaiden nodded toward the other stone wall. "Maris, try touching that one. Maybe they need to be activated by casters at the same time."

"Wouldn't the system be designed to work with one person?" I asked.

Kaiden stretched out his hands toward each column, falling a meter short to either side. "Definitely can't reach both of these at the same time. I guess it's possible that someone is supposed to cast magic at them from a distance—or maybe they fell down farther apart than they were when standing."

Maris glanced at the column and then at Kaiden. "So, do you want me to touch it or not?"

Kaiden looked to me and Toran.

I shrugged. "This is your discipline. Follow your instincts."

He nodded. "You're right—this is different from the other one, but that could be done by one person so this should be, too. Must be related to casting."

"Makes sense," Toran concurred.

"Stand back." Kaiden raised his hands.

I cleared the vicinity and stood with Toran and Maris four meters to the side of the stones.

Kaiden took a deep breath and extended his hands, holding his staff in his right. A warm glow danced across his fingertips and to the end of the staff, and then a dazzling tendril of yellow light snaked through the air toward the stones.

The stones emitted a blue glow in response to the magic, which radiated through the ground toward the water. Blue light traced all the way to the island at the center of the lake. The light intensified as the ground began to tremble.

I broadened my stance to keep my balance in the shaking. "That seems to be doing *something*."

The water above the path through the lake churned as the stones beneath began to rise. The ramp leading down to the water leveled out to meet with the newly raised path, and when the stones were on the same plane, the trembling ceased.

Kaiden lowered his hands and the magical ribbons dissipated. "Well, that wasn't so hard."

"Neither was activating the other columns," Toran replied. "There is likely still a trial ahead."

"Walking through that bog wasn't enough of a trial?" Maris sighed.

"Tolerance for wet feet isn't the test." Kaiden looked at the puddles on the stones along the path to the island. "Despite all evidence to the contrary."

"Well, my feet are toasty and dry in these boots," I said, heading for the path. "Are we going to do this or what?"

Kaiden pointed his staff ahead. "Let's go."

I followed him onto the stone walkway with Toran and Maris close behind. The rock was slick from algae growth, so I had to keep my hands outstretched for balance, since my weight was thrown off by the heavy pack.

It was just over two hundred meters to the island. The crystal at its center gleamed in the early morning sun, and for a minute, I could almost convince myself that it would be a straightforward task to retrieve whatever artifact awaited us.

As we approached the island, I focused on the crystal with the hope of seeing what kind of artifact it may be; nothing obvious was placed inside the crystal, as with Toran's gauntlets. By the time we were almost to the land, however, I could discern a faint shape within the four-meter-tall crystal.

"Is that the artifact?" I asked.

"I think so," Kaiden replied, "but I can't make out what it is."

We reached the land and walked up the gradual incline to the crest of the hill. Standing in front of the crystal, I realized that the object embedded inside it was a silver circlet, which explained why its delicate shape hadn't been visible from a distance.

"You get to be king?" I joked.

Kaiden grinned back at me. "Only a prince."

I drew my sword.

"And you're... staging a revolt?" Kaiden questioned me.

I laughed. "No. Just have a feeling that the moment you touch that crystal, this is going to turn into a battle zone."

He nodded. "Well, it started out as a nice, quiet morning."

"Those never last." I turned so I could see both the crystal and the lake, taking a defensive stance.

Maris and Toran took up mirror positions on Kaiden's other side.

"Okay, here it goes." Kaiden extended his hand toward the crystal.

A singular chime sounded, as though a bell had been struck. But, rather than fading, the sound intensified. The ground began to tremble underfoot again, this time agitating the entire lake. Water surged toward the island, a solid wave moving as one from all directions around the island.

Panic set in. I dropped my backpack, bracing for the water to hit. I wondered if I should ditch my coat, too, to have a better chance at swimming. But, when the mini tsunami reached the island's shoreline, the water shot straight up for ten meters and then arched overhead to form an aquatic dome.

I looked at my comrades with confusion. "Wasn't expecting that."

"We're trapped in here," Toran stated the obvious.

"What do we do?" Maris asked, more than a hint of concern in her tone.

Kaiden glanced down at his pendant; it was glowing brightly. "There's something here."

Maris' pendant was glowing, as well. "I feel it," she murmured.

My spine tingled and a pressure filled the back of my mind. I hadn't sensed anything like that around the rock giant, but this was a different artifact guardian with its own unique properties—that is, assuming it was its presence I was feeling. I couldn't see anything in the water beyond faint light shining through the thin dome overhead.

"Where are you?" Kaiden called out. "I'm here to claim the artifact."

The water swirled in response, a distinct wave rippling around the circumference of the island. When it had completed the circuit, the wall of water swelled in front of us, taking on a lighter iridescent sheen compared to the darker water surrounding it.

"You think you are worthy?" a musical voice spoke all around us, as though coming from the water itself.

I swallowed and tightened the grip on my sword—like that would do any good against a wall of water.

"I hope to prove that I am," Kaiden replied.

"Your companions are driven by might, but that will not win you your prize."

"I will meet any challenge you present me."

In response, an arm of water reached out from the wall and knocked Kaiden to the side. His staff flew from his hand and clattered to the stones at the shore.

"And you call yourself worthy!" the voice taunted. "This lake will become your grave."

The wall swelled inward to envelop Kaiden where he stood.

"No!" he bellowed. "I am here to prove myself." He raised his hands. In the direction he pointed, the water froze to ice. The ice crystals shattered and dropped to the rock like chimes.

I'd only seen fire and lightening before, but if there was any time for him to add a new spell to his arsenal, this was it.

"How can we help?" I asked.

"I don't know," Kaiden shook his head. "I haven't figured out what it wants me to do yet."

A blob of water launched from the wall and landed two meters from Kaiden, standing as an oblong column on the ground.

"Uh... what?" I scowled at it.

Kaiden shook his head. "I have no idea."

The blob shuffled toward him.

"Ideas?" Kaiden asked.

"Smash it," Toran suggested.

Kaiden frowned. "Pretty sure that's *not* it."

"Casting. This whole challenge is about Spirit, right?" Maris said.

"But casting *what*?" Kaiden stared down the blob. "What do you want me to do?"

The blob leaped forward and dropped down onto Kaiden's shoulders, completely enveloping his head.

His eyes widened with obvious panic. He clawed at the water, but it flexed around his fingers and it couldn't get any purchase.

"Maris, do something!" I shouted.

"I can't fight *that*!" she exclaimed.

Kaiden gasped, a flurry of air bubbles escaping his mouth.

"He's going to drown." I dropped my sword and ran to him, not sure what relief I could offer, but I needed to try *something.*

His eyes pleaded to me.

"This is a test," I told him. "There's a way out using your magic. You can do this."

He shoved me back from him and brought his hands to his face once more. This time, they glowed red and the water vaporized where he touched it.

The blob around his head burst, drenching him.

Kaiden took a gasping breath, coughing and sputtering.

"Are you okay?" I asked while bending down to pick up my sword.

He nodded, though he was still coughing. "What was that?"

"You were just attacked by a blob of water," I replied.

"Yeah, I got that. But... *what* was it?"

I shrugged. "Angry water?"

He rolled his eyes. "I have no clue what we're supposed to do here."

"I liked the rock giant," Toran interjected. "We just had to smash it."

"That was a lot more straightforward," I agreed. "But only after we found it. There was a lot of sciencing to locate the correct location."

"That's true," Toran replied. "We wouldn't have been able to find it so quickly if I didn't have my engineering background."

I nodded. "Maybe there's more to these challenges than the main engagement itself."

"Either way, I feel like I'm missing something really

obvious here," Kaiden said.

Another blob emerged from the wall and landed near Kaiden. It scooched toward him.

"Oh, no. You're not going to try to drown me again!" Kaiden blasted the blob with a fireball. The water vaporized.

"Progress, maybe?" I shrugged again.

A moment later, another blob appeared.

"This is going to get old really fast," Kaiden muttered.

"Maybe a different spell?" Maris suggested.

Kaiden conjured an orb of electrical energy in his palm and lobbed it at the new blob. The pillar of water burst apart, leaving only a puddle behind.

I placed my sword tip-down on the ground and crossed my hands on the butt of the hilt. "Okay... Not sure where this is going, exactly."

"That makes two of us," Kaiden huffed.

Another blob leaped from the wall and formed a column of water near Kaiden.

He rolled his eyes. "You have to be kidding!"

"Have any other spells you've been meaning to share?" I asked.

Kaiden took a deep breath. "It doesn't work like that. Things just... come to me sometimes."

"Like the ice earlier?"

"Yeah." He examined the blob. "I guess I could try that one again." He held up his hand, and the water column turned to ice crystals. It shattered.

"Well, looks like you have that one down now," I commented.

"It's toying with you," Toran said. "Maybe we need to try to break down the wall."

In response, the walls and domed roof began swirling and

crashing as the enclosure turned into a turbulent whirlpool.

"I don't think it likes that idea," I observed.

Three water blobs launched from the frenzy and landed as glistening columns in front of Kaiden.

"Okay, that's new." Kaiden launched three fireballs in rapid succession.

The columns vaporized, but the water became more frenzied.

Another three blobs emerged from the wall.

Kaiden shook his head. "Was that the wrong spell?" He tried freezing them instead.

The swirling water rose to a roar.

The three blobs appeared again.

"The three appeared after you'd cast three different types of magic," I observed. "Maybe you need to hit each of these with something different?"

Kaiden stared at the blobs. "I think you're onto something." He frozen the first, cast a bolt of electrical energy at the second, and vaporized the third with a fireball. Then, a new, solitary blob appeared.

"What do I do with this one?" Kaiden asked.

"Does the pattern start over?" I wondered.

He shook his head. "No, that doesn't feel right."

"The other side of yourself," Maris suggested. "You have destroyed, now you must heal."

Understanding passed over Kaiden's face. "Yes, that's it. But I've never used that kind of magic."

He stepped closer to the blob. Though featureless, I couldn't help but get the impression it was looking up at him with a kind of helpless innocence, wondering if it was about to be helped or destroyed.

Kaiden placed his hands to either side of it ten centimeters from the water's surface. He closed his eyes.

A soft green glow appeared between his palms, passing through the water and radiating within it until the entire blob glowed with the green light.

Then, without warning, the blob collapsed into a puddle.

The deafening roar of the waves stopped, and the water stilled.

"You have mastered the challenge," the voice said. "You have shown a balanced spirit worthy of wielding the power bestowed upon you. Use it well."

The wall of water encircling the island dropped back into the lake with a splash, and then all was still.

I took a deep breath, wiping my damp hair back from my eyes. "I think we're getting the hang of this."

Kaiden cracked a smile. "Couldn't have done it without all of you."

The glow of the crystal behind us intensified, and I turned to face it. The light appeared to pulse, beckoning.

Kaiden approached it, transferring his staff to his left hand. With his right, he reached out to place his palm on the smooth crystal.

The light intensified, and with a blinding flash, the crystal shattered into fragments no larger than a grain of sand. The silver circlet within floated to the ground along with the fragments, coming to rest atop the shimmering pile.

As Kaiden reached out toward it, a purple gem affixed in the front of the circlet began to glow. Indigo light flowed from the gem and momentarily wove around Kaiden before it absorbed into him. He picked up the circlet and placed it on his head, the gem resting at his hairline. "Do I look ridiculous?"

I smiled. "Well, you might draw a few strange looks in a bar, but it goes with the whole cloak vibe thing you have going on."

Kaiden beamed. "It's doing something. I feel… stronger."

Toran nodded. "I had a similar experience when I got my own artifact."

"I can't wait to—" I cut off when the ground started to tremble.

Water lapped at the edge of the stone path leading to the island. The stones were sinking.

"Run, hurry!" I shouted. I swung my backpack over my shoulders and dashed toward the mainland.

The stones seemed even slipperier underfoot than the way out, but I did my best to run at top speed. If the path sank before we made it back, it might be impossible to swim the rest of our way with our gear; I didn't want to try to navigate the swamp without a map or weapon.

The water level was up to my ankles by the time I reached the halfway point of my run to safety. I glanced over my shoulder to check on my companions, and I saw Maris struggling on the slick stones while Kaiden tried to help her along using his staff. I ran back.

Toran turned back, as well. I motioned for him to keep going, and he complied after a moment's hesitation.

"Go, Elle!" Kaiden urged. "We'll catch up."

"No, we need to balance together," I insisted, wrapping my hand around Maris' other side.

The three of us splashed down the path as the water reached our knees. It was as cold as it was dark, chilling me. With water sloshing over the top of my boots and pooling inside, each step was heavier and more difficult than the last.

Only a dozen meters to go. The water eddied around my thighs, and I was soaked past my waist from the splashing.

"We might have to swim it," I said.

"No." Kaiden stopped suddenly, gripping his staff.

My skin tingled as a strange energy surrounded me. The crashing water crystalized to either side of the path, and I quickly jumped up on it before my feet were frozen in position. Maris scampered up next to me, and we steadied each other on the slick ground.

The purple gem on Kaiden's circlet was glowing brightly as he joined us on the strip of ice. "Hurry!" he shouted.

Taking each other's hands for balance, we ran toward the shore as the frozen water slowly turned to mush underfoot. With a final surge of speed, we made it to the ramp's upward incline just as the final ice remnants melted away.

I released Maris' and Kaiden's hands then leaned against the fallen column. "That's a neat new skill."

"I like this new circlet," Kaiden said with a weary smile. The glow in the purple stone had faded; it looked like the more powerful magic had taken a lot out of him.

"Glad you're okay," Toran said. "That was quite a feat freezing part of the lake."

"I'll need to play around to figure out what other new abilities I have thanks to the artifact," Kaiden replied. He brushed his fingertips along the silver circlet.

Maris took several panting breaths. "Lesson learned. As soon as we get back to the *Evangiel*, I'm getting some shoes with better traction."

I laughed. "The things you don't think about, right?"

Toran gazed out at the island slowly sinking into the lake. "What caused the path to fall apart?"

"I think whatever magic allowed us to raise the stones vanished as soon as the Spirit artifact was claimed," I said. "Without that magic to hold it in place, everything returned to how it would naturally be."

"Pretty incredible to think about," Kaiden said, taking one

final look at the lake.

Maris nodded. "We get to control a piece of that ancient power."

"And we have a lot we need to do with it." Kaiden tore his gaze away from the water. "Come on. We should get back to the ship."

17

WE MADE GOOD time on our slog back to the shuttle, now that we had a better sense of how to navigate the waterways with minimal backtracking. Plus, since we were already wet, we waded through some channels that we would have otherwise found a way around.

I felt grimy and sensed that I probably smelled like rotten fish by the time we made it to the shuttle. The craft was one of the most welcome sights I could imagine after the miserable ten kilometer hike.

"First order of business when we get back is a shower," I announced as we approached the shuttle.

"Definitely," Kaiden agreed.

We tried to clean off our mucky boots as best we could before boarding, but we tracked muddy footprints up the ramp despite our efforts.

I sighed. "So much for Tami warming up to us."

"In all fairness, it's probably *more* unusual that we brought it back last time clean and intact," Kaiden said.

"May as well set reasonable expectations," Toran agreed.

We climbed aboard the shuttle and dropped our dirty bags in the common room. As I feared, as soon as we were in the enclosed space, a decidedly fishy smell filled the cabin.

Kaiden wrinkled his nose. "I'm really glad it's not a long flight."

"Please, let's get out of here." I rushed to the bridge.

We went through pre-flight checks as quickly as possible, then strapped in and were on our way. By the time the *Evangiel* came into view, I no longer noticed the scent, but I had no reason to believe it had diminished.

We made it to the ship and slipped through the electrostatic field into the hangar. As soon as the shuttle had come to a rest, we filed into the common room to retrieve our bags. Toran dropped the ramp.

Breathing in the filtered air of the hangar, I realized how foul an atmosphere we'd been in for the last day.

Tami rounded the shuttle, then quickly brought up a hand to cover her nose and mouth when she saw us. "Stars! What happened?"

I sighed. "Marsh monsters."

She lowered her hand, but her nose remained wrinkled. "If I didn't know better, I'd think you'd spent the last month in a bio reclamation tank."

"Oh, I'm sure the swap was on par with a decades-old waste bin," Kaiden replied. He rubbed his shoes together and some of the drying mud flaked off in a clump on the deck.

Tami frowned. "Maybe you should strip down before you go through the ship."

I looked down at my own filthy self. "Solid plan."

We removed everything but our white base layers, which were now closer to a light taupe, and left the other soiled items piled on the deck.

"I'll reach out to the maintenance crew and get all this cleaned up for you," Tami told us.

I flushed. "Sorry about the mess."

Tami shrugged. "I think I have it easy compared to you, considering what you must have gone through to end up looking like that."

We thanked her again and then headed up to our respective quarters—pausing to acquaint Maris with her own room in line with ours.

I'd never experienced such a glorious shower in my entire life. While I'd spent plenty of time playing in the dirt as a kid, most of Erusan was dry, so dust was our biggest problem. This mud was sticky, and the scent of decay lingered even after two thorough scrub-downs. If I never had to traverse another bog in my life, I'd be happy.

As I exited the shower, I realized that I'd neglected to check for clean clothes; there was no way I was putting on my old shipsuit until it had been thoroughly laundered.

I wrapped a towel around myself and went to investigate the wardrobe. Inside, to my relief, were three white suits and undergarments. It was generic sizing, unlike my other custom-fitted suit, but I'd take anything clean and dry at that point.

After dressing, I exited my cabin and wandered down the hall to the room we'd designated as our combination hang out, planning, and rendezvous place. Toran was the only one present, and he appeared to be absorbed in an inspection of his magical signature locator device. With only a generic shipsuit at his own disposal, he had the top portion of the suit folded over with the arms tied around his waist.

"Hey," I greeted when he didn't appear to notice me enter. "Looks like a trip to the equipment room is in order."

"Oh, hello, Elle." He looked down at his bare chest. "Yes.

Feeling better?"

"Much." I moseyed over to him. "What are you working on?"

Toran set down the device and frowned at it. "I was wondering if there might be a way to have the device tap into a nearby signature rather than needing direct physical contact, so Kaiden or Maris wouldn't need to remove their pendant each time."

"That would be handy."

"Unfortunately, I don't see a way to make any quick modifications." He sighed.

"Well, bright side is that we only have one more world to visit to get the remaining artifact."

"Yes, very true. We can always work on it more depending on what our future missions entail."

I leaned my hip against the table and crossed my arms. "I still can't believe they want *us* to go up against the Darkness."

"It would be like any other task—break it up into steps and take actions that progress toward that end."

"This isn't just a random project. We're talking about maybe dealing with advanced alien tech here. *You* at least have training. I don't know how much I can offer."

Toran smiled. "Don't sell yourself short, Elle. You've held your own quite well. I seem to recall many of our successful ideas coming from you."

I dropped my gaze, blushing. "Maybe."

"Feeling better?" Kaiden asked from the doorway, stepping inside.

"Much, aside from a draft," Toran replied, running one hand down his other exposed arm. "I was just telling Elle that she has no reason to doubt her worth on our team."

"Oh, stars no!" Kaiden exclaimed. "Using peat in place of

firewood was a stroke of genius."

My lips parted in a bashful smile. "Thanks."

"Not to mention, you're getting pretty good with that sword," he added.

"That part is weird," I admitted. "I haven't really practiced with it, but these new forms just come to me in my mind, and it's like I have muscle memory of doing things I've never done before."

"I think it might have something to do with how our bodies were re-formed," Kaiden said. "It's like that with the magic, too."

"Same." Toran leaned against the table next to me. "I'm thankful for the help, wherever it came from."

"Yeah, no kidding." I sighed.

"Speaking of help, what are you working on there?" Kaiden asked Toran, gesturing to the device the other man had been fiddling with.

"Nothing that matters at the moment—"

Toran cut off when an announcement sounded on the central comm. "Jump in T-minus ten minutes."

I pushed off the table. "Back at it again."

"So much for getting a night's rest in our own beds." Kaiden headed for the door.

"The only consistency is that nothing is predictable," I commented while following him out of the room.

"I don't expect that to change any time soon," he replied.

"There you are!" Maris exclaimed from down the hall as soon as we left the room. She ran over.

"Hi," I greeted.

Her dark hair was still damp from a shower, and she fluffed it with her fingertips. "Jumping again already?"

"Final artifact world," Kaiden replied.

She looked to me. "This one's for you?"

I nodded. "That's the plan."

"Then back to the Archive." Kaiden continued toward the pod room to get prepped for the impending jump.

As much as I hated jumps, the thought of this one didn't bother me nearly as much knowing that the end was in sight—at least, I told myself it was. I recognized that the situation with the Darkness wouldn't be resolved when we sealed the Archive, but at least I would have a sense of security once a backup of my world was safely sealed.

We strapped into our usual pods and endured the stomach-churning jump. When it was complete, I sat up in my pod eager to face our next challenge. This one would be on me, but I was ready to prove myself.

"Ugh, I hate jumps," Maris moaned across the room. She popped up above the lip of the pod then lie back down.

"You all right?" Kaiden asked.

"Yeah," she said, though her tone indicated otherwise. "Just gimme a minute."

"Any bets on what the Valor trial might be?" I asked the group while her stomach settled.

"Hmm." Toran got a ponderous expression. "Something requiring strength and courage."

"Um, yeah—" I stopped when I noticed him smirking. "You don't say?" I finished, smiling back.

"It's probably fair to assume something will try to crush, suffocate, or eat you," Kaiden chimed in.

I grinned. "It will be sorely disappointed when I disembowel it instead."

"Let's get a look at the world," Kaiden suggested.

Maris was just hauling herself out of her pod. "I'll be right there."

We left her to finish getting her bearings and headed down the corridor to our staging room. Kaiden removed his pendant and placed it on the device.

"I hope finding this location is as straightforward as the last," Toran murmured while he activated the device.

The characteristic soft blue light illuminated in the pendant. After a moment, readings appeared on the touch-surface tabletop.

Toran frowned. "That's strange."

"What?" I asked.

"This isn't showing anything."

"Like, no magical signatures?"

"No, as in *nothing*," Toran clarified. "It's like there isn't a proper planet here."

My brow furrowed as I looked out the viewport, but there was only a typical starscape. That didn't mean anything, since the room was often orientated away from any planet we may be orbiting. "Did we jump to the right place?"

Kaiden backed away from the table. He pressed behind his ear. "Commander, we—"

"Please come to Central Command," Colren replied over the general channel through the comms in our ears.

"We'll be right there." Kaiden ended the link. "I don't like the way this is going."

"Yes, agreed." Toran removed the pendant from the device and handed it to Kaiden.

The three of us returned to the hall. Maris was still in the pod room as we passed by on our way to the lift.

I poked my head through the door. "Maris, did you hear that? We need to go to the bridge."

"Yeah. Is something wrong?" she asked.

"The planet is giving some weird readings. We need to get

a visual on it," Kaiden replied.

Maris frowned. "What about getting back the rest of our clothes? I feel naked in just this shipsuit."

"It'll have to wait," I said, though I could relate to how she was feeling. Before she could protest further, I strode toward Central Command.

We were buzzed inside, and Colren greeted us in the center of the bridge. "I trust you tried to use your device to examine the planet?"

"Yes. Are you having difficulty getting readings, as well?" Toran asked.

The commander gave a grave nod. "We hadn't prepared for this contingency."

"What contingency?" I questioned. My stomach twisted. Things were just started to go in our favor; it figured something would go wrong now.

The commander beckoned us closer to the viewscreen on the forward wall. I gazed out at the beautiful spacescape, drawn in by the stars, but then I noticed something at the bottom of the view. There was a planet there, except it was dark.

The tension in my gut spread to my entire chest. "Wait, is that…?"

"This world has already been consumed by the Darkness," Colren stated. "We're too late."

"TOO LATE FOR *what*?" I asked, though I already knew the answer. If the planet had been consumed by the Darkness, that meant the final artifact we needed to open the Master Archive was now beyond our reach. We had failed our mission.

Kaiden's brow furrowed. "Is that it? There's nothing we can do?"

"Perhaps there is an alternative way to seal the Archive," the commander suggested. "We need to explore every available option."

"But, why can't we just go down to the planet?" Maris asked.

"Look at it! It's been almost completely consumed," I said, pointing at the depressing image on the screen.

The reddish world was crisscrossed with dark smoke-like lines, and the tendrils were continuing to expand. I had no idea how long it took a world to be overrun, but based on what little I'd seen, we only missed our window by hours. If we had been able to land closer to the Spirit icon and hadn't lost a day, or if we hadn't slept, then maybe—

I stopped myself. Thinking in those terms wouldn't change what we were facing now. It's not like we could reset across multiple star systems and do it over again.

"But, that doesn't matter, right?" Maris continued.

"Of course it does," Kaiden said. "That's a dead planet now."

"No, we talked about this before," Maris insisted. "We're supposed to be immune to the Darkness, right? We can go there."

I stood in silence, my gaze flitting between my companions and the commander. "What *happens* to a world when it's consumed?" I asked tentatively.

"We don't know," Colren admitted. "When we first encountered the Darkness, we sent in teams to investigate and they didn't come back."

I eyed him. "You said we're different—that we should have an immunity. How do you know that?"

The commander shook his head. "That isn't important."

"I don't know, seems pretty relevant to me." Kaiden crossed his arms.

"Commander, if you would like our continued cooperation, being forthcoming with us will get you the best results," Toran stated. Despite the soft heart I knew he had on the inside, I had to admit that any firm statement from Toran carried additional weight due to the intimidation factor of his stature.

Colren evaluated us. "All right, come on." He led us to the private conference room, and we stood around the table. "Remember when I told you that the Darkness appeared three months ago? Well, you weren't the first people we extracted."

That wasn't the least bit reassuring. "Who were the others?" I asked.

"We first had the bioprinter ready for the extraction procedure a month ago," he explained. "The details about how it functioned were vague in the ancient records we were referencing, but the technical team was able to piece enough of it together to give it a shot. The first results were... not viable."

My stomach turned over again. "How do you mean?"

He shifted in his seat. "The consciousness never properly knitted with the physical form. That's why we ended up developing the initiation procedure you all experienced."

"Don't need the grisly details, but okay, they died," Kaiden said. "Were you able to make it work with others before us?"

"We did. And that's how we discovered the secondary feature of Darkness exposure resulting in a sort of tolerance for future encounters," the commander continued. "The team— there were three of them—were on a Hegemony world that served as a research post; in fact, it was where the bioprinter was first developed and tested. Due to the sensitive nature of the activities, the data was saved on local servers rather than backed up through the subspace relays to the Hegemony's central data repository. When the Darkness came to the world, the team volunteered to retrieve it. We sent them in with half a dozen armed guards.

"The team was composed of two Spirit casters and a Protector. When the Darkness arrived at the research site, the Protector stayed behind to finish the data upload to this ship. The two Spirit casters proceeded to the extraction site, but they were overrun by the Darkness mid-travel. The guards accompanying them were all frozen, but the two casters were able to make it to a shuttle to escape."

He swallowed. "I suppose it would have been more accurate to say that we believe someone with abilities such as yourselves can withstand *temporary* exposure. We don't know how long they could have lasted; we never wanted to risk sending them back in."

I folded my hands on the desktop. "Okay, if they made it out of that encounter, then where are they?"

"They crashed while trying to land on Crystallis," Colren revealed.

"Hold on, you'd tried to send people down there before us?" Kaiden glared at him.

The commander backed up a little. "We attributed the crash to a legend that only a team representing all of the disciplines could land on the world. So, we set about waiting for you."

"This is insane," I muttered.

Kaiden shook his head slowly. "You lied to us."

"I conveyed what was useful in the moment," Colren corrected. "Based on this reaction, I should have kept those details to myself."

"You use people and move on when they're no longer helpful. That's the kind of behavior I've always actively fought *against*." Kaiden scoffed.

The commander threw up his hands. "What else should we do? Our conventional weapons are useless, our trained soldiers freeze into columns of black soot when they come in contact with the Darkness, and we lost our last two best hopes by what we now realize was just a freak weather-related shuttle crash. We don't have a lot of options here. We need to stop this, and as far as I know, you're the only people who can get close enough to give us any clue what we're dealing with.

"I apologize for keeping the details from you, but it didn't seem like divulging that information would sway you in the direction of helping. I'm only saying anything now because I have nowhere else to turn. We know how important this world was for the mission at hand. I don't know what to suggest."

I was struck by the commander's raw emotion. I'd always thought of military types as being stoic no matter what, but I was reminded in that moment that even the most serious of officers were still people. And *we* weren't trained soldiers. This was an emotional appeal to fellow citizens. Our worlds and our very existence was being threatened, so we needed to join forces to be more than our singular selves. We had to rise to the occasion and become the heroes our people needed.

"If there's a chance we can still retrieve the artifact, then I'll take the risk and go down there," I said.

"Elle," Kaiden started.

"No, I mean it," I shot back. "We didn't ask to be placed in this position, but we're the only ones standing between the Darkness and the total annihilation of everything we love. If there's even a *chance* of saving my family, I'll risk getting turned into a column of soot, or whatever it is that happens when touched by the Darkness."

My new friends sat in stunned silence.

Surprisingly, Maris was the first to speak. "Elle is right. We're already invested this much. We need to do everything we can to see this through."

"I will gladly give my life to this mission, if it comes to it," Toran agreed. "However, I trust whatever technology—or magic—enabled us to escape the Darkness in the first place. I believe we will be able to travel to that world and not be harmed. Well, at least not by the Darkness directly."

"I'm in, too, of course," Kaiden said. "I won't turn my back on that commitment." He cast another glare in Colren's direction. "But in the future, I hope for continued transparency. We need to work together. Secrets won't help get the job done."

The commander nodded. "And you'll have it. I assure you, you now have all of the information we do."

I swallowed. "Okay, so, the original team was able to escape a planet overrun by the Darkness on a shuttle. Does that mean that it doesn't alter manufactured materials?"

Colren shook his head. "Yes and no. Organic matter is the most susceptible, as far as we know, but everything eventually succumbs. In terms of going down to the planet, my suggestion would be for the shuttle to drop you off, and we'll send it to retrieve you once you have the artifact."

"What about our comms?" I asked. "Those are inside us, but not exactly a *part* of us."

"An excellent question to which I don't have an answer. I would hope that it being completely encased in your skin that they would be protected from the Darkness' effects. In the event the electronics become corrupted, we can arrange a rendezvous place and time," the commander stated.

"Right, about that." Toran folded his huge hands on the table. "The device we've been using to locate the artifacts didn't pick up a signal because of the Darkness. We have no idea where to go."

"If the artifact is intact, it will likely still emit a signal," Colren replied. "Perhaps you can adapt the device to interface with the shuttle's sensor suite and do a high-altitude sweep of the planet."

"That could take hours. At the rate the Darkness advances, we may not have that long," Kaiden objected.

The commander shook his head. "I have no other solution to offer you."

"Then let's stop talking and start doing." I stood up. "Even our clothes and equipment might not stand up in that environment. We'll need to move quickly."

"Is it, like, contagious?" Maris asked. "Can we track it back to the ship?"

"As far as we know, no," Colren replied. "However, we'll follow a full decontamination protocol for your return, and the shuttle will drop you off without touching down on the surface. The atmosphere is clearly tainted, as well, but it seems to spread much more quickly on the ground."

"Contact between solid matter, versus the more spread out structure in air," Kaiden hypothesized.

"As reasonable an explanation as any. I'm sure scientists will be seeking answers for years to come." The commander sighed. "But, for now, the Master Archive remains the priority."

I nodded. "We're on it."

"Safe travels, and good luck."

After Toran grabbed his search device and extra tools, we hurried down to the hangar to get our laundered equipment from Tami. While the preflight check was underway, Toran began his modifications to the device so it could interface with the shuttle. Since he was busy, I ran to the equipment room on his behalf to get him a new custom shipsuit from his saved profile, which he graciously accepted. Once we were dressed, the other preparations completed within minutes of each other, and Tami saw us off with well wishes.

Speeding toward the dark world was a decidedly unnerving experience. Every part of me screamed that it was wrong to head toward something which was so obviously tainted.

Next to me, Kaiden's face was drawn with concern. He still sat in the pilot's chair, though the auto-pilot was solely responsible for this voyage.

I tried to set aside my own worries and focused on the

positives. After all, there was still a *chance* that we could get the final artifact. A slim chance, but some hope remained. Too much was riding on it for me to give in to doubts. The certainty that there would be a secure backup of my world was the only thing keeping me moving forward. If I didn't have that… Well, I didn't know *what* I'd do. But the fight wouldn't be there. It just wouldn't be the same if I was only trying to save myself.

The initial descent into the atmosphere was bumpier than usual. It would seem that whatever was causing the Darkness was somehow impacting the air currents and the shuttle's inertial compensators. That made the dark tendrils snaking through the sky even more ominous.

I shuddered. Everything about it was creepy. I couldn't wait to be back on a planet far away from the Darkness' influence.

The shuttle followed a preset flight path designed to optimize our aerial search for a signal using the modified device. Maris handed over her pendant this time, and Toran kept a watch on the readings to double-check the automated search software's findings. At an elevation of thirty kilometers, the shuttle leveled out and began its search pattern above the umber landscape.

"I know what you're thinking, and I hope we don't have to go around the entire planet," Toran stated to break the uncomfortable silence.

"Not that you have much control over the situation," Kaiden replied.

"Actually," Toran countered, "the previous sites were all within a several degree spread to the north of the equator. If that pattern holds, we will have a much smaller search area to cover."

"Here's hoping." I settled deeper into my seat.

Half an hour passed in relative silence.

I propped my feet up on the front console and would have dozed off if it wasn't for the occasional jolt from a shifting air current.

At last, Toran came to attention. "I think I might have something." He used his console to indicate a point on the holographic map overlaid on the front viewport. A red point was highlighted approximately eighty kilometers from our present location. According to the topographical map, it was on top of a steep hill, which offered no easy drop-off point, even without landing—especially due to the wind gusts.

"Let's check it out from the air," Kaiden said. "We don't want to commit to the wrong site." He programmed the destination into the autopilot.

The moment the destination came into view, any doubts about it being the correct location vanished. Whereas the other sites on past planets had been a crystal situated in a predominantly natural landscape, this crystal sat atop an eight-story tower at the summit of a steep hill covered in dark orange grass.

"How in the…" Words escaped me.

"I have no idea," Kaiden murmured. "But look at these wind readings—there's no way we can set down at the summit."

I reviewed the scan data he was pointing to. Gusts of wind as great as eighty kilometers per hour weren't insurmountable, but between the risks of smashing into the tower, touching the ground, and sending us accidentally rolling down the entire length of the hill, it was in our best interest to find an alternative.

"How about we have the shuttle drop us off at the base and we can hike up?" I suggested.

"Except *that* might be a problem." Maris pointed down to the left.

While the hill face was still untouched by the Darkness, one of the sinister tendrils was snaking its way toward the slope from the west. I hadn't been watching it for long enough to get a sense of the time to interception, but my gut told me we didn't have long.

"We'll figure it out. Let's go." I unstrapped from my seat and steadied myself against the wall using my hands as the shuttle rocked in the wind.

In the common room, I removed the mess kit and bedroll from my pack to lighten it but was sure to leave in the rope and flashlight knowing that we had a tower to negotiate. The side ramp didn't make for a reliable midair egress, so I headed to the airlock at the rear of the craft. I opened the interior door and waited for my companions.

They followed my model of removing the items likely to be unnecessary for this mission and then put on their packs.

I kept watch out the side viewport and saw that the shuttle was hovering at a holding elevation, awaiting our final instruction to descend for a quick drop-off.

"Ready?" Kaiden asked with a smile as he joined me in the airlock.

"As I'll ever be." I patted my sword hilt. "I have this."

"Assuming it doesn't disintegrate in your hands."

I frowned. "Wait, what about the artifacts?"

Kaiden hesitated. "I'd really hope that whatever gives us special immunity would apply to them, too."

"But we're organic and were altered by a brush with the Darkness. That has nothing to do with them."

"Yeah, but they were encased in crystal and then floated to the ground. Magic is different. I don't have any logical reason

I can point to, but my gut tells me that it's not an issue."

I nodded. "Considering that I became a blade master overnight, I can't argue with the power of unexplainable knowledge and hunches."

"So, my circlet stays?" Kaiden asked.

I smirked. "Oh, I get it. You just don't want to give up your crown."

"I have no comment."

"Uh huh…" I eyed him suspiciously while Toran and Maris joined us.

When we were all in the tiny chamber, I closed the interior door and cycled the exterior hatch. Kaiden tapped on a control console within the chamber to initiate the next phase of the automated flight sequence for our drop-off.

Wind ripped through the chamber the moment the exterior hatch cracked open. I gripped a handhold to steady myself as we descended. The shuttle stopped just under three meters up from the ground, swaying as it struggled to compensate for the winds ripping down the slope.

Keeping a firm grip on the handhold, I leaned out to spot my landing. Scrubby grass covered the vicinity, so at least we wouldn't be landing on rock.

I took a deep breath. "Here goes!" I leaped.

The ground raced toward me. I bent my knees as I touched down to absorb the impact, then transferred my weight and rolled to a stop. I rose to my feet.

Kaiden and Maris dropped down nearby, following a similar technique. Toran, the last to leap, just took one big jump and landed with both feet like it was nothing.

"How are we going to get back up?" Maris asked.

"I can reach it and haul myself up then help you," Toran said.

She didn't look entirely convinced but nodded anyway.

The shuttle quickly gained elevation and then accelerated back into space.

No longer under the influence of the artificial gravity on the shuttle, I felt lighter. "Is the gravity lower here?"

"I felt the shift, too," Toran said.

"Maybe it's a product of the Darkness," Kaiden suggested. "Or could just be the planet."

"That first notion is deeply unnerving." I took a step and found that my movement was easier, but there wasn't any significant extra bounce.

"Okay, we have six hours until the rendezvous, if we can't get in touch before then," Kaiden stated. He peered in the direction of the approaching Darkness. "But we don't have a lot of time for other reasons."

"No need to tell me twice!" I started jogging up the slope.

The combination of my lighter pack and the reduced gravity made for an easier ascent than I'd anticipated. However, the winds were against us, and I found myself leaning up the hill to maintain a good equilibrium.

From a distance, the slope had seemed relatively featureless aside from some orange foliage, but as we trekked up the open exposure, I spotted the openings to caves mixed in among rock outcroppings.

"Think anything lives here?" I asked.

"Maybe, but potentially not for long."

My heart sank. "I hadn't thought about that part. I've been thinking about the people on the infected worlds, but all of the wildlife…"

"Don't go there, Elle," Kaiden cautioned. "We're already actively pursuing the best—and maybe only—way we can help them."

"Yeah, I know." I took a deep breath.

Another cave was up ahead. As we approached it, movement drew my attention. I tensed. "Uh oh. I think there's something in that one."

KAIDEN READIED HIS staff and Maris grabbed a dagger from a sheath at her hip, apparently not yet ready to rely on offensive magic alone.

I drew my own blade. Whatever was in the cave might be dangerous, and I wasn't about to take any chances after our most recent encounters. I altered my path to dip to the left so we'd have better coverage of the cave mouth.

Scuffles and tapping sounded within the shadowed recess. My muscles tensed as I prepared for a beast to leap out.

When I was four meters from the cave opening, I caught a flash of gold as a tiny, scaled head poked out from the shadows.

Brilliant green eyes that reminded me of my own looked at me with curiosity, and the creature tilted its head. It crept forward, revealing a long neck that flared into a scaled body with four legs, folded webbed wings, and taloned feet. Dorsal spikes ran the length of the creature from the crest of its head to the tip of its slim, scaled tail. Its belly was a lighter shade than the top, and it had a glowing orange patch at the base of its throat.

"Uh, guys… is that a dragon?" I felt ridiculous asking, but there it was staring at me.

"Those are just a legend, aren't they?" Maris asked.

I raised an eyebrow. "Like magic?"

Kaiden examined the creature. "I mean, it *looks* like I'd expect a dragon to look, but isn't it a bit small?"

The cute little thing *was* tiny, no more than seventy centimeters from nose to tail. I got a sudden impulse to pick it up and bring it with us. "It's not bothering us. Let's let it be," I said instead.

No sooner had the words left my mouth than four more heads appeared—blue, green, red, and black. They all had the same vibrant green eyes.

The red dragon squawked and jumped on the blue one, and the two tumbled off of the rock ledge onto the grassy hillside.

"Aww, they're playing!" Maris squealed.

"I think these might be babies," Toran conjectured.

"They're adorable, I won't try to deny it, but we don't have the luxury of playtime right now." Kaiden glanced down the hill at the advancing Darkness.

"No, we don't." I smiled at the baby dragons and then took a brisk pace up the slope.

After fifteen minutes, we reached the brow of the hill. The relatively flat area around the base of the tower was only four meters wide, and it was as windy as the shuttle's sensors had indicated.

My hair kept smacking me in the face, so I quickly bundled it into a braid and tucked it inside the back of my coat to keep it out of the way.

Kaiden's cloak beat around him in the wind. "I don't see an entrance to the tower on this side."

I inspected the smooth stone face. We could probably find a way up using the rope in our packs, but I really hoped it wouldn't come to that.

"Let's walk the perimeter." I set off to the left.

The winds remained strong as we rounded the northern side of the structure. There were no windows in the stone face, as far as I could see, and the ground level had no ingress points along the first half of the building's circumference.

Finally, rounding the east side of the tower, a three-meter-tall reinforced metal door sealed an arched entryway. I grabbed the door handle and gave it a good tug. Nothing happened.

"Locked?" Kaiden asked.

"Or magically sealed. Who knows?" I frowned at the door.

"May I?" Toran asked.

I held out my hand. "Please."

The large man gripped the door handle and pulled. Unlike with my attempt, the metal groaned, but it still didn't budge.

"I can try to force it," he said.

It was a tempting offer, but I wasn't sure that was the best move. All of the tasks to retrieve artifacts on the other worlds hadn't involved forcing open a doorway. Yes, we'd needed to engage in fights, but the built structures had all responded to the touch of someone aligned with the corresponding discipline. If that pattern followed, then I needed to be the one to open the door.

I motioned Toran aside. "Let me try again."

The question was, why hadn't it opened the first time I tried?

I thought back to our previous challenges. Toran had activated the columns with his bare hands, which is also how he fought. Likewise, Kaiden had had to cast magic at the stone pillars to activate the pathway to the island. Since I fought with a sword, maybe...

I drew my blade. In one swift motion, I slashed the steel across the metal door, leaving a golden streak where it scratched. The golden line glowed brightly for a second, and then the door dissolved before my eyes.

Kaiden smirked. "Well, that's one way to open a door."

"I do love to make a showy entrance." I smiled back.

Inside, the tower was dark beyond the shallow pool of light cast from the doorway. I cautiously peered inside.

"Help me," a woman murmured from the shadows in a voice so faint and cracked the words were barely intelligible.

"Stars!" I ran into the chamber.

Kaiden was a step behind me. He ignited a ball of light in his palm, illuminating the room.

The woman was chained to the far wall. Seated on the floor with her legs outstretched, her hands were cuffed at head level and she looked as though she'd been dragged across the ground and beaten.

Anger swelled in my chest thinking about what kind of horrible person would do that to her. "It's okay, we're friends." I approached her slowly, checking for signs of a trap.

"We'll get you out of there," Maris said, rushing up behind me.

"Maris, wait." I held her back.

"Why?" she glared at me.

I don't know why I hesitated. It sickened me to see the woman suffering, yet something didn't feel right about the situation. She could be dangerous, for all we knew.

"You have to assume this is part of the test," Toran interjected. "Who is this woman and why is she here?"

"Exactly." I stopped three meters from her. It was too suspicious that anyone would be chained inside a tower on the top of a hill in the middle of nowhere—especially considering that there were no nearby signs of civilization aside from this singular structure.

"Why are you here?" I asked the woman, as much as I wanted to free her from her shackles and heal her. Just looking at her battered face made my own skin throb.

"Please. Release me. Before they come back," she whispered.

I couched down. "Who put you here? Why?"

She shook her head, the motion jangling the chains binding her wrists.

"Look, I hate seeing you like this. I *want* to help you, but trust should be earned."

The woman scoffed. "You wouldn't trust a poor woman chained to a wall?"

"No one deserves to be treated that way, but that's also something people don't often do to others without reason—however misguided the action may be." I looked her in the eyes. "Now, how did you come to be here?"

She cracked a smile, some vitality seeming to return to her. "Do you always question innocents?"

"How do I know if you're innocent? If you've been wrongfully imprisoned, then you should at least have a story to tell. But you keep dodging my questions."

"It takes wisdom to know when to act and when to observe," the woman continued. Her voice was definitely getting stronger; there was no mistaking it now. Even her skin appeared more vibrant.

"Who are you?" I asked again.

She looked me square in the eyes—her intense, luminescent emerald irises now far different from the vacant appearance she'd had only moments before when we entered.

"The more important question is, who are *you*?"

In the blink of an eye, she vanished, leaving behind no trace of the chains or her presence.

I took an unsteady breath. "That was weird."

"Man, I thought were we just going to attack stuff. I wasn't planning on mind games again," Kaiden said.

"Shouldn't expect anything to be so straightforward," I replied.

"I thought maybe the encroaching Darkness was complication enough."

"Whoever set up these trials didn't know that would be the case."

He shrugged. "Maybe they did, maybe they didn't."

I massaged my eyes with one hand. "I'm too on edge to think about records of events that haven't happened yet."

"Or maybe they *have* happened and we don't know," Toran cut in.

"Nope, not gonna think about it." I shook my head.

"Help!" another voice called from the story above.

"Stars, not again." I jogged toward the stairs.

"Elle, it's not real," Toran said.

"That doesn't mean ignoring it is the right thing to do. It's a test, and we need to participate if we're going to get that artifact." I bounded up the stone stairs two at a time.

The staircase curved around the outer wall of the tower, passing through a hole in the floor at the second level. With no windows, it was too dark for me to make out any details until Kaiden came up behind me with the light floating above his palm.

"Flashlight time," I muttered, stopping to retrieve it from my backpack. I clicked it on as my companions all made it to the second story.

The space was relatively plain, with only a stone bench along the outer wall and a single, low stone column in the center of the room. What made it strange, however, was there was no sign of the woman who'd cried out for help, nor did there appear to be a way upward in the tower.

"Help, please!" the woman cried again.

"Where are we supposed to go?" I mused aloud. With nothing else appearing out of place, I approached the stone column at the center of the thirty-meter-wide room.

Upon closer inspection, the meter-tall column was a pedestal table sporting a broad, flat top engraved with foreign characters. The language was familiar, however.

"Hey, Kaiden, is this Laeric?" I asked.

He walked up beside me to examine the marks. "Yes, it is, but I don't know what to make of it." He swung his backpack around so it was hanging on one shoulder to his front and rummaged around in bag. After several seconds, he located an electronic handheld device. He smiled. "Translator. We're getting better at this 'planning ahead' thing."

I smiled back. "Please, enlighten me."

Kaiden held the device over the top of the pedestal, and a screen on the back displayed a translation of the ancient words. There were six wedges, each labeled in order: *Vengeance*, *Conceit*, *Valor*, *Humility*, *Cowardice*, and *Duty*.

"No idea what to make of that." I frowned at the translation. "Except, Valor is the name of this discipline, so maybe that means something?"

"Of those options, that seems like the one to pick," Kaiden agreed.

Toran raised his fists defensively. "Why do I feel like a fight is coming?"

Maris drew a dagger. "I don't like this."

"Has to be done," I replied. I pressed the stone labeled *Valor* with my right hand.

Nothing happened.

"Maybe you have to use a sword like with the door?" Kaiden suggested. He took a step back from the pedestal.

"Could be." I started to draw my blade.

No more than two centimeters were exposed when the tower began to tremble. The walls opened up on all sides, revealing six identical stairwells leading into darkness. The stairs extended far beyond the outer walls of the tower, yet they were completely enclosed.

"Oookay, this is officially weirding me out," I admitted.

"This one is all you, Elle. Where does your gut tell you we should go?" Kaiden asked.

Valor was again the obvious choice, being the namesake of this discipline. However, just like something had told me to hold back from helping the woman, I had a feel that wasn't the correct answer.

Assuming the staircases were representative of paths—not a stretch, since it was pretty literal—*Vengeance, Conceit,* and *Cowardice* were all obvious rejects. *Humility* and *Duty,* though, had appeal. After all, strength could easily be misdirected if it wasn't balanced out by humility, and even otherwise vicious acts could be honorable when performed in the line of duty. Still, I wasn't sure if the straightforward answer of *Valor* was the way to go or if I should pick one of those supporting components.

I stared at the pedestal, frozen by indecision. "I don't know what to do."

"Pick something," Kaiden urged.

"Help!" the unseen woman cried again from all directions.

"Elle, not to rush you, but the Darkness—"

I held up my hand to cut Toran off. "I know. I'm thinking."

None of the singular paths felt right to me. There was more to heroic acts than a one-dimensional characterization.

Without thinking, I slammed my hands down on the pedestal, pressing *Valor* and *Humility* with one and *Duty* with the other while holding the flashlight.

The stairways blurred as they merged into a singular path leading in the direction across from *Valor*.

Toran nodded. "A bold choice."

"Looks like it paid off," Kaiden added.

"Come on. There's no telling what we'll find up there." I jogged toward the stairs.

The stairwell wove around the outside of the tower, despite having appeared to go straight outward from my vantage inside the second-story chamber. It spiraled for another six stories at a steep angle until it reached the tower's roof.

I shut off my flashlight as we stepped out into daylight. I expected to get a spectacular view of the surrounding landscape, but instead I was surprised to see that the tower was surrounded by a strange mist. The light filtered through like it was a clear day, but everything beyond fifty meters away was blurred like looking through an out of focus camera.

"What's with this place?" I murmured.

"I don't know, but let's get out of here fast," Kaiden replied.

The focal point of the rooftop was the crystal monument we'd seen from the shuttle. It radiated a soft blue light like all of the others we'd come across, and I was relieved to see that it wasn't yet clouded by the Darkness spreading throughout the rest of the land.

Floating in its center was a slim sword with a slight curve to the blade. The sabre beckoned to me, drawing me toward the monument at the center of the rooftop. I reached out toward it.

"Are you sure you want to do that?" a woman asked from behind me.

I pivoted toward the voice.

Standing before me was the same woman who'd been chained in the basement, but she was now dressed in a regal crimson gown and her golden hair was styled in ringlets. Her red lips were curled into a knowing smile and she evaluated me with her piercing green eyes.

"I'm here for the artifact," I stated.

She nodded. "You have passed the first test. You desire to help, but you have learned since your youth that actions have consequences."

"Don't pretend to know what's in my mind," I replied.

"I needn't pretend. I *do* know." She clasped her hands in front of her, and I noticed she wore golden finger caps, which ended in sharp points.

My eyes narrowed. "Who are you?" I asked once more, though I didn't expect an answer.

"A better question may be about *what* I am." She began to walk slowly toward us. "And the answer to that is that I am a guardian created out of necessity. For all of the powers the ancients mastered, they were not immortal. I, and the two others like me, were created to pass on the knowledge that all others would forget, so that the worlds could be saved in the time of their greatest need."

The woman gazed to her left, and for a moment, the mist parted around tower and the encroaching Darkness was visible below. "You have been chosen, but that doesn't necessarily make you worthy."

"Then let me prove myself, as my companions have," I replied.

"If you fail, then this place will be locked to you. Are you sure you're ready?" The woman tilted her head.

"This place will be inaccessible, anyway, once the Darkness reaches it," I replied.

"There are forces stronger than the Darkness."

I came to attention. "There are? There's a way to stop it?"

The woman smiled. "You haven't answered my question. Are you ready to face the challenge?"

"Yes. I'll do anything I need to in order to stop the Darkness."

The woman inclined her head. "Very well. Prepare to face your challenge."

She dissolved into scarlet mist, which flowed over the stone railing behind where she had been standing.

I placed my hand on my sword hilt.

Behind me, Kaiden, Toran, and Maris tensed.

A roar echoed from somewhere below the tower, followed by a concussive whoosh of massive wings beating. My heart skipped a beat as a red, scaled head with jaws two meters wide came into view.

The massive beast roared again and thrust its wings, creating a strong enough gust to almost knock me off my feet. It flew past the tower on the side and a patch on its throat glowed bright orange. It opened its jaws, releasing a plume of fire.

I squinted against the heat of the flames. "I think we found those baby dragons' mom."

I BACKED AWAY from the stone railing. Setting aside the surprising revelation that dragons were real, the part about them being able to turn into mist and take the form of a human was definitely a new one. "How did it…?"

"Doesn't matter." Kaiden hoisted his staff. "Just need to fight it."

My heart sank. "It doesn't feel right to kill it." A dragon… a creature that was by all accounts mythical. And it had babies…

Kaiden nodded. "Then you better find some other way to make it say that we won so we can get that artifact."

Toran rushed up next to me. "We will follow your lead, Elle."

The crimson dragon roared again and then disappeared into the mist. I gulped as I stared in the direction that the creature had gone; it would undoubtedly return in any second. "Okay, aim to disable."

Despite giving the order, I had no idea what I meant by it. The dragon was fifteen meters long and breathed fire. I had no clue how to disable a creature of that size without killing it—or even how to kill it, for that matter. But, I couldn't admit to my friends that I thought we were doomed.

I dropped my backpack on the ground and drew my sword. "Maris, can you figure out some sort of protection spell for us?"

She looked unsure, but nodded. "I'll see what I can do."

The others set down their packs, as well, and held their weapons at the ready.

While I stood poised for the dragon's return, Maris clutched her crystal pendant in one hand. A shell of purple light appeared around me.

"If that did what I wanted it to, we should now have some fire resistance," Maris said.

"Hey, I'll take anything." I looked to Kaiden next. "Going along with the plan to not kill the dragon, maybe some ice attacks would be helpful against the flames?"

He nodded. "I'll give it a shot."

"How would you like me to proceed, Elle?" Toran asked.

"I don't think punches will be deadly against a creature that size. Hit it as hard as you can, and hopefully we can stun it," I replied.

He inclined his head. "I'll try."

"Say we do stun it. Then what?" questioned Kaiden.

I checked to make sure the dragon wasn't back in sight, then set down my sword to access my backpack. I retrieved my restocked length of rope.

"Tie it up? Seriously?" Kaiden raised an eyebrow skeptically.

"I know, I know. But if we can demonstrate dominance and mercy, maybe it will declare it a win."

Kaiden's gaze alternated between the rope and me. "If you

say so."

A roar drew our attention to the sky overhead. The dragon was diving from above.

"Kaiden, hit it!" I shouted.

A ray of frost streamed from his staff, striking the dragon square in the face. It blinked as the ice made contact, then shook its head slightly like it hadn't even been bothered. To my horror, the patch on its throat glowed brightly again and it opened its jaws.

The flash of heat was too intense to look at. I was convinced I must be burning alive, but as I diverted my gaze to the stone rooftop, I saw the flames curving around the purple protective bubble.

The onslaught subsided, and the dragon flapped away into the mist to make a loop back toward us.

"Way to go with that shell!" I cheered to Maris.

She grinned. "I think I'm getting the hang of this."

The brief exposure to the intense heat had wiped me out, but a sparking green wave washed over me and I felt a surge of energy.

Maris smiled. "Figured you could use a pick-me-up."

"You read my mind."

Toran and Kaiden also appeared to be recharged.

"We need to lure it in close," Toran said. "I will try to stun it."

My mind raced as I thought about how we might be able to get it to land. Suddenly, I wished I'd brought a goat to sacrifice. Dragons liked goats, right?

I returned my thoughts to the present and what I had at my disposal.

"I'm going to offer myself to it," I stated before I could second-guess the idea. Granted, rethinking the action was probably *exactly* what I should have been doing.

"Elle, no," Kaiden said, firm.

The protective barrier is up, I'll be fine. I really don't think we're supposed to slay it. I need to show that I want to work with it."

"I don't like that plan, either," Toran said.

"This is what we're doing," I replied. "This is my discipline and you said you'd follow my lead."

The large man released a slow breath. "Very well."

"I'm going to have an ice ball ready in the event it tries to eat you," Kaiden said.

"Thanks."

Another roar sounded to my right as the dragon returned from the mist. I lowered my sword and ran to the stone railing on the far side of the roof away from my friends, wanting to distance myself to keep them out of danger as much as possible. "What do you want me to do?" I shouted.

The crimson dragon tilted its head. If I didn't know better, I'd think it was smiling at me.

It dove lower, but this time made no sign of breathing fire. Only four meters above me, it broke from its collision course dive, flapping its enormous wings to pull up.

I lost my footing in the gust, falling backward. My back struck the railing, and the momentum carried me over the lip.

My sword hand flailed as my torso dipped over the railing. Time seemed to slow down for me, even without a spell from Maris. I knew I had only a moment to act. I could drop my sword and catch myself, or hold onto the sword and likely fall to my death.

As poor form it seemed for a Valor challenge, I opted to ditch the sword.

In one motion, I released the weapon and managed to snag

the inside lip of the stone railing with my index finger—a sole digit keeping me from toppling over the edge. As the sword plummeted down the side of the tower, I tried to secure my grip with my other hand, but the awkward semi-sideways angle had pinned my other arm underneath me.

I was terrified to move. My finger was slipping, and any attempt to swing my legs to shift my weight back toward the roof caused me to slip further.

This wasn't how I pictured the end.

A strong hand gripped my wrist. "I've got you."

I breathed a sigh of relief as Kaiden pulled me up. I shimmied my hips back to the proper side of the railing and slid to my feet. "Thanks."

There was genuine concern in his eyes—the kind I'd seen from my father while my mom talked about a particularly bad day at work. Even with a dragon looping back toward us, he set me at ease.

"That didn't look like it went to plan," he said.

"Yeah, no, not really."

"Maybe more working together and less using yourself as bait?"

"Yeah, we've got this." I gave him a confident smile and he nodded back.

Together, we turned to face the dragon as it came for another pass.

With my hands empty, I'd be next to useless in a fight. But, I was still determined to end the engagement peacefully.

"There is no honor in senseless killing," I shouted, stepping forward with my hands held wide. "I wish to protect others, not take the lives of innocents."

The dragon halted its descent, flapping its wings to hover above me.

"There are times to fight, but this isn't it," I continued. "We have bigger concerns." I pointed in the direction of the plains below which I knew were being consumed by the Darkness. "I'd rather help save you and the rest of your kind."

The dragon planted its taloned feet on the rooftop, crumbling the stones beneath it. It gazed at me with its brilliant green eyes, somehow seeming to see inside and through me.

Twenty intense seconds passed in silence as it stared at me unblinkingly. It took all of my willpower to stand with my hands at my sides, completely at its mercy.

Just when I felt like I could take it no more, the dragon bowed its head. As quickly as it had taken shape, the dragon dissolved into red mist. It swirled in the air for a moment and then reformed as the regal woman.

"You have shown both duty and humility in your actions today. A virtuous leader knows what the true fight is." She bowed her head.

"How can we help you and your babies?" I asked.

"Do not worry about us," the woman replied. "Our magic is more ancient than even the crystals. We have withstood greater calamities. All will be restored in due time."

I hesitated. "What of us and our worlds?"

"You will soon have what you need to face the menace. But that is something you must discover for yourself. Good fortune until we meet again." The woman faded into mist.

A tingling wave passed through me, and I was left with a renewed sense of strength and focus. The call of the crystal at the center of the roof was even stronger.

I turned toward it. "Is that it? Is that all I had to do?"

Toran nodded. "Not every victory requires a fight. You proved that today."

"Final artifact, Elle. It's yours," Kaiden said.

I stepped forward. A pace from the crystal, I stretched out my hand.

An electric tingle spread from my fingertips up my arm and throughout my entire body. The crystal shattered into glassy sand and fell to the ground. Before me, the sword hovered in the air for a second before slowly drifting onto the mound of crystal fragments.

I bent down and gripped the hilt in my hand. Another tingle ran up my arm, almost like the sword was an extension of myself. When it was fully in my grasp, a blue flame ignited along the length of the blade.

"Whoa!" I almost dropped it in surprise.

Maris crossed her arms. "Gotta say, guys, Elle gets the award for the coolest artifact."

I grinned. "No argument here."

Kaiden adjusted his circlet. "Yeah, whatever."

"We should get back," Toran advised.

"Yes, we got what we came for." I tested the blade in the scabbard from my old sword and found that it was a close enough fit to work temporarily, though it would be better to get one custom made once we got back to the *Evangiel*.

"I'll call the shuttle to come pick us up," Kaiden said.

With my sword stowed, I retrieved my backpack from where I'd dropped it and headed for the stairwell while the others gathered their gear.

When Kaiden had completed the call, we jogged down the steps to the bottom of the tower. As we rounded the final curve to the ground floor, it seemed far darker than it should. I slowed my pace.

"Does anyone else feel that?" I asked.

"Yeah, and I don't like it," Maris replied.

Toran nodded. "We shouldn't be on the world any longer."

We reached the ground and headed for the door.

I froze the moment I caught my first glimpse of the world beyond the tower. Gone was the orange-tinted landscape of rolling foothills. Now, there was only black—and something was moving within the Darkness.

21

"STARS! WHAT'S DOWN there?" My heart pounded in my ears as I stepped outside on the windy hilltop outside the tower.

"I don't know, but it's standing between us and our pickup point." Kaiden's eyes were hard and his face was lined with worry.

The Darkness had almost reached the hill's summit and was continuing to advance. The strange movements in the shadow were still at a distance beyond the base of the hill, but it was headed in our direction.

Toran took a slow breath. "I had hoped we wouldn't need to test our supposed immunity to the Darkness."

"Yeah, no kidding." I sighed, then tapped behind my ear. The comm chirped, and I opened the link with my team and Central Command. "Commander, we have the artifact, but this area has been overtaken by the Darkness."

He didn't reply at first. "The shuttle is already on its way."

"What do we—"

"Get to the pickup point."

"But—"

"Fight your way out if you have to. Just get there." He ended the commlink.

"That wasn't the least bit helpful," I said.

"No, it wasn't." Toran evaluated the Darkness swirling below.

"We only need to make it twenty minutes," Kaiden encouraged. "We can do this."

I nodded. "Okay." I took off down the slope and the others followed my lead.

A hundred meters down the hill from the tower, we reached the first patch of ground tainted by the Darkness.

I hesitated. "I really don't want to touch this stuff."

"We don't have a choice. There's nowhere for the shuttle to retrieve us up here," Kaiden said. He continued forward, though his movements were cautious.

Watching his steps, he passed over the threshold to the tainted ground. The blacked grass crunched underfoot, the blades disintegrating into black dust when disturbed.

"I don't understand how it could have advanced so quickly," Maris said. "We weren't in there for long at all."

"There was some strange magic in that place. Maybe time perception was different," I hypothesized.

"Yes, whatever was going on with the pathways and rooftop, I do not believe we were perceiving the reality that we experience out here," Toran agreed.

"I'm looking forward to getting back to a place that isn't infected like this world." Kaiden continued forward. "Are you coming?"

"Yeah, sorry." I jogged forward, trying not to think about what I was walking on.

Seeing it in person, I realized that the moniker of 'Darkness' was more a term of convenience than an accurate description of what it had done to the world. Everything *had* turned black in color, but it wasn't pitch black in the sense of there being a lack of light. Rather, it was like smoke blanketed the land and mini cyclones had ravaged trees and other once-living things that now looked like they had been turned to charcoal in a fire.

The upper expanse of the hill was only short grass, but I cringed when I saw up close what the Darkness had done to larger foliage. Bushes that had been covered in orange leaves on our way up were now black, and the slightest brush up against them caused the entire structure to fall apart into what looked like a pile of soot.

My stomach turned over. "Is this what happened to our worlds?"

Despite his tough exterior, Toran appeared to be on the verge of tears. "That's why protecting the Master Archive is so important."

I hadn't really understood until that moment. In my head, my family was frozen in time—Colren had been careful in his phrasing to give that impression. I had pictured them standing in the town square right where I'd left them, concerned expressions on their faces and the members of our town around them. If I'd visited, I'd imagined I could walk around them and give my parents a hug, even if they didn't know I was there.

But now, seeing what happened to a world that had been consumed, I realized the truth was very different. The planet was lost—as destroyed as it would be if it had been hit by an asteroid. The inhabitants and all other life were dead, but their backups lived on in storage. What that meant for their consciousness, I didn't know. Resets were only supposed to take a moment. Were all the people who had been on those worlds now floating in perpetual darkness, their consciousness searching for a physical form that no longer existed? Or was their hyperdimensional consciousness roaming freely outside of spacetime unaware of the body they once had?

No matter the case, I hoped they were at peace. If anyone had awareness of what was happening to their world, I couldn't imagine they'd ever be able to psychologically recover. I had a feeling my mom would agree if she'd been there to comment.

The pressure in my chest swelled, making it difficult to breathe. I just wanted to know they were going to be okay— that when we could restore our world, things could go back to how they were.

But I knew that was impossible. I'd already been through too much. Even if *they* were all the same, *I* wouldn't be.

I caught Kaiden's gaze as I ran up next to him on the journey down the hill. He was off somewhere distant in his own mind, even though he looked right at me.

"I know," I murmured. "I didn't get it until now, either."

There wasn't a family for me to go back to—as of right now, they were gone. The only hope was to perform a global reset to restore the world.

He nodded solemnly. "We'll figure out what's causing this and stop it. We'll get them back."

"I won't stop trying until we do," I affirmed.

We were almost to the cave where we'd encountered the baby dragons. I braced myself for the horrific sight of their tiny bodies turned to black soot, but instead, a perfect dome surrounded the cave and everything within it was like we'd seen it before—the grass still vibrant orange and it even seemed to be lighter inside the dome.

The baby dragons stood on the stone outcropping outside the cave mouth, concern in their mesmerizing green eyes.

When they caught sight of us, the red one bound across the grass toward the perimeter, stopping half a meter short from the invisible barrier. It tilted its head questioningly.

"We'll get you your world back," I told it as we rushed by. "I don't know how, but we'll figure it out."

I couldn't tell if it understood me, or maybe it just picked up on my positive intentions, but it bounded back toward its siblings while making a chittering sound.

The other baby dragons joined in the chittering, and the blue one flapped its wings as it started hopping.

I wished we could stay to watch them, but we had to keep moving. I tore my gaze away so I could watch my footing.

"I think they like you," Kaiden said.

"I'm glad their mom decided to cooperate."

"Assuming they're even related."

That hadn't occurred to me. "You think there might be other dragons on this world?"

"If there are, I hope they've been able to make other sanctuaries like this—" Kaiden cut off. "What was that?"

"What was what?" I'd been looking down at where I was stepping, but I snapped my head up to look ahead.

"That movement we saw when we were up above," he said. "I think the creatures are almost here."

The shadows had only seemed like tiny specks from our previous vantage, but the top of the hill was a long way away. Up close, the creatures coming into view through the dark, approaching mist were two meters tall and three long. I couldn't get a clear view of the dark beasts against the black backdrop, but they seemed to slink like a cat despite being sized like a horse.

I drew my new sword, and the flame instantly ignited along the blade. "Keep moving forward. Get to the pickup site and watch each other's backs."

"Time for the Dark Sentinels to finally fight the dark," Toran said.

I had to think for a second. "Oh, yeah! Team name."

"What?" Maris asked.

"Our intrepid trio at the time nicknamed ourselves the Dark Sentinels," I explained. "Seemed fitting."

She nodded. "The trio is now a quartet, but I like the branding."

I smiled. "Glad you approve."

My pleased expression only lasted for a second. One of the black creatures bounded forward through the dark mist, heading directly for me.

I brought my new sword up in one swift motion, ready to cut down the loping beast.

However, as it cleared the mist, I hesitated—its skin was rippling like something underneath it was trying to break through. I stared at the bizarre sight of what appeared to be hands and limbs pressed against the skin from the inside. It didn't seem possible for the creature to be functioning.

Despite my disbelief, it was almost on top of me.

At the last second, I leaped to the side and flourished my sword. The flaming blade sliced the creature's sleek side. But rather than blood and innards, six small, black bodies burst through the wound. The original creature turned to black dust around them.

I recoiled with horror. "Stars! What—"

"Not going to wait to find out." Kaiden launched a fireball from my right side.

The blast struck the front two of the meter-long creatures. They let out high-pitched shrieks and bared a double row of needle-sharp teeth.

"How did that not take them out?!" I shouted.

Kaiden paled. "What *are* they?"

I had no answer for him. Their four limbs and a head were within my frame of reference, but their movement seamlessly alternated between using two and four feet as they undulated across the ground, their chalky, black skin hiding the details of their physique. Coupled with their tiny fangs and the lack of visible eyes, they were the most alien creatures I had ever seen—not that I'd been on other worlds before four days ago.

Kaiden's magic had been ineffective, but my sword worked better. I rushed the two beasts he'd hit with the fireball, swinging my new blade like a scythe at neck-level.

One of the creatures ducked. The blade struck true with the other, severing its head.

I braced for another wave of even tinier creatures to leap out of the body, but there was only thick, dark blood.

The five other creatures hissed in unison.

My skin tingled as a purple barrier appeared around me, presumably cast by Maris. As soon as the spell was in place, Toran rushed forward to punch the creature closest to us that was still standing.

It yelped as the blow collided, knocking it to the ground. The four others condensed their bodies then pounced, launching themselves a meter or more into the air to grip Toran with their paws.

"Gah! Why did you do that?" I ran forward so I could attempt to help him tear the creatures off.

They snarled at us and tried to snap at my fingers.

Toran was able to pry one off of his chest using his metal gauntlets, and I beheaded it the moment it was on the ground.

He managed to fling another to the side, out of my reach.

Kaiden concentrated a beam of electrical energy on it with

his staff, and the creature fell motionless.

We tore the two remaining creatures free, and I sliced one while Toran stomped on the other.

The one remaining creature, which had managed to survive Kaiden's first fireball and Toran's attack, made one final attempt to sink its teeth into my thigh. I kicked it back and then buried my blade in its chest.

"What are these things?" I asked no one in particular.

"I don't know, but I think more are coming." Kaiden gulped. A herd of the larger creatures were advancing—too many to count.

I tightened my grip on my sword, heart racing. "When is that shuttle going to get here?"

"Two minutes," he replied.

Toran evaluated the approaching herd. "We might not make it that long."

"Not with a scattershot approach like what we just did," I agreed. "Backs together! Maris, can you bolster that protection spell?"

"I'll try," she said.

"Toran, hang back on this one," I continued. "We need to keep them at bay with ranged attacks. I'll slice 'em if they get too close; get any behind me."

"Got it." He spun around to face the opposite direction.

Kaiden came in close on my right and Maris to my left.

Maris held up her hands and a second purple dome shimmered around us only seconds before the first wave of large creatures broke through the dark mist.

They charged forward, seemingly unaware of the barrier. When the first of them struck it, the beast stopped cold with a yelp like it has run into a wall.

Kaiden took the opportunity to blast it with a concentrated

beam of electricity, like what had been effective on the other. Energy crackled around the creature until the beast collapsed to the ground, then it arced to another coming up from behind. When a third beast neared, the beam split.

"That's it!" I cheered, thrilled with the increased strength of Kaiden's spells since he got the circlet.

I glanced at Kaiden and saw the strain on his face—he wouldn't be able to keep it up for long, artifact or not.

Another beast looped around our protective ring and pressed against it. The barrier stretched at the pressure points, threatening to tear.

I stepped forward from my place in the ring to impale it through the neck. As I pulled my blade back to drive it home, the snarls from the creatures outside stopped as a descending engine roared overhead.

"That's our ride!" Kaiden shouted over the rumble.

"How are we supposed to get up there with all these creatures around?" Maris asked.

"I don't know if my original plan to jump up and pull you inside is feasible anymore," Toran said.

"Don't have another choice," I replied. "You'll have to make it quick."

"Can you make the barrier bigger, Maris?" Kaiden asked.

She laughed. "I don't even know how I'm making this one!"

I glanced at her over my shoulder. "Not helpful."

"Just being honest." She shook her head. "I already feel pretty drained. I don't think I can do the big, grand thing you're after."

My mind raced. "Okay, Toran, get Maris inside. She can maintain the shield from in there, and then Kaiden and I will follow."

"But—" Toran cut off his protest as the shuttle made its final descent.

"Just go!" I shouted, barely able to hear my own voice over the engine. Loose strands of fuchsia hair whacked against my face from the turbulence.

The creatures appeared to be over their initial shock from the shuttle's arrival, and they crowded in around the perimeter of the protective sphere.

Out of the corner of my squinted eyes, I saw Toran hoisting Maris into the shuttle. As she grabbed hold of the airlock handles, the protective shell started to flicker.

"Hold it!" I shouted, but my voice was lost.

The barrier collapsed.

Creatures rushed in from all sides, a black mass moving as one. Each of their bodies contorted with the same pressing of limbs and heads inside. It was only a matter of time before the smaller creatures broke free, even if I didn't cut them out to speed up the process.

One of the large beasts reared in front of me, flailing hooved feet. I slashed my sword across its legs; amazingly the flaming blade sliced clean through the bone.

The creature toppled to the side, its undulating torso still intact.

Two more came for me. I swept my blade without thinking, twisting and bobbing through the creatures as they advanced.

I lost track of how many there were or how much time had passed—it was just me and my sword. It found its mark every time. I was entranced by it. With my old sword, I had been using a weapon. Now, I felt like the sword was an extension of my own being.

The creatures kept coming. I leaped over the bodies of the

disabled creatures to fight the new wave. My friends needed to get to safety; that was the most important thing. I had to give them time.

I ducked to avoid a hoof and then spun around to de-limb the creature. The wounded beasts writhed around me. The abdomens of the first to fall looked like they were about to burst.

"Elle!"

I didn't hear the voice at first, thinking it a phantom in the wind.

"Elle!" the shout came again.

I snapped to attention.

The bodies. There were so many of the felled creatures around me—dozens. Had I really done all of that myself?

"Take my hand!" Toran shouted at me. He was up above, leaning down with his right arm extended.

"Kaiden—" I started to ask, looking around for him.

"He's inside. Come on!" Toran shouted back.

The abdomen of one of the felled beasts ripped open and six vicious creatures jumped out.

Without hesitation, I sheathed my weapon and then leaped up to grab Toran's arm with both hands. His fingers wrapped around my right wrist.

"Go!" he yelled.

The shuttle quickly gained elevation.

Toran heaved me into the airlock. It was just the two of us, and the interior door was closed.

He hit the control panel and the outside door cycled shut.

I realized I was shaking. My heart pounded in my ears and I could barely fill my lungs.

Toran placed a hand on my shoulder. "You're okay, Elle. Breathe."

Closing my eyes, I took several slow, labored breaths. My pulse slowed and my breathing came more easily.

"What happened?" I asked when I felt able to speak. My voice trembled.

"I don't know, it was like you were in a trance," Toran replied. "I got Maris up and then climbed inside, myself. When I bent down to get Kaiden, you were slashing your way through anything that moved. We both shouted at you to come inside, but you didn't seem to hear us. Kaiden and Maris went in to take manual control of the shuttle, and I kept shouting your name until you responded."

"What?" I leaned against the wall, shaking my head. "How long was it?"

"A few minutes? I don't know."

"I…" It had only seemed like seconds, *maybe* a minute, tops. How could I have zoned out like that?

"We all made it out. That's the important thing," Toran said. "That was some good fighting down there."

"It's all a blur," I murmured.

"And it looked it from up here, too, even without Maris' special spell."

"What's happening to me?"

Toran shrugged. "These artifacts have special properties. Beyond that, I can't say." He opened the internal airlock door.

I slowly rose to my feet. "This is going to be a wild ride."

"Speaking of which…" Toran motioned me toward the bridge.

"Right." I jogged toward the nose of the vessel.

In the bridge, Kaiden and Maris were in their customary seats.

"Nice of you to join us," Kaiden said.

"Yeah, sorry." I strapped in.

He glanced at me questioningly, switching the shuttle over to autopilot for the journey back. "What happened back there?"

I shook my head. "Got in the zone, I guess."

He chuckled. "Was there even anything left down there? I think if Toran hadn't pulled me up, I may have met a swift end by your blade."

"No, of course I wouldn't hurt you."

"I dunno, you seemed like you were somewhere else."

I crossed my arms and slumped in my chair. "It was weird. I remember it, but it's like it was a dream."

"More like a nightmare," Maris interjected. "What were those things, anyway? Native to the world, or were they part of the Darkness?"

Kaiden shrugged. "There aren't any records of the lifeforms on this world—it's not in the database, which is probably why it was such a safe place to store the artifact."

"Until this Darkness," I murmured. Or maybe the artifact had been sealed away because it caused the user to go into a murderous trance. After what just happened, I wasn't about to rule out any possibility.

"Considering the state of the other organic matter, I'd hypothesize that the creatures were somehow born of the Darkness," Toran chimed in.

Maris drew into herself. "Where did they come from?"

"Who knows?" I shook my head. "And I hate to say it, but there might be a lot more of those things. We'll need to figure out the most effective attack against them."

"Unfortunately, that will require proximity," Toran said, "and I'm not looking forward to being anywhere near them."

"We can deal with that later," Kaiden said. "As long as Crystallis hasn't been overrun, we shouldn't need to face any more of them in the near term."

"And if the planet already *is* infected, we have bigger problems," I added.

"Exactly."

The shuttle traversed the remaining distance to the *Evangiel*. As it spun around to dock, I caught a glimpse of the planet we'd just left. It was now almost entirely dull black.

I shook my head slowly. "Why do this to a world? Is it deliberate or just some awful disease?"

"I can't imagine this happened on its own," Kaiden said.

"If it's caused by an enemy, then where are they?" Toran asked.

Maris shuddered. "I don't want to meet whoever could do this."

"With you there, but we likely won't have a choice," I said.

The shuttle passed through the electrostatic field into the hangar, but rather than its typical docking location, it instead taxied to an open area away from the other craft. Crew members in hazsuits ran to meet us.

"What a lovely welcome," I said.

"Can't say I blame them for the precaution," Toran replied.

We walked to the shuttle's common area and dropped the ramp. Workers were securing a tent around the shuttle.

Tami, dressed in a hazsuit, approached the base of the ramp through a temporary tunnel. "Strip to your base layer. Leave everything else here and head straight to the decontamination booths." She pointed to a marked tent ten meters away at the end of the tunnel.

"Even the artifacts?" I asked.

She nodded. "Trust me, Elle, we all want you to complete this mission. Everything is safe with us."

I nodded and did as I had been instructed.

The decontamination process was as unpleasant as its name suggested, but within fifteen minutes the chemical scrub was complete. Afterward, I had to admit I felt really, really clean—the ultimate full-body exfoliation. A fresh shipsuit and undergarments were waiting for me in my stall, and I dressed.

Kaiden stepped out from his booth moments after me. He grinned. "You look radiant."

I smiled back. "So do you. I guess having an outer layer of skin burned off will do that to a person."

"Good times." He crossed his arms. "Can we get out of here?"

I shrugged. "I assume so, since no one is telling us to stay."

Toran stepped out from his booth. Based on the way he exited the door sideways, I could only imagine how tight of a squeeze it had been for him to maneuver inside. "We should jump back to Crystallis as soon as possible."

"Yeah," I agreed. "Let's go check in with the commander."

22

COLREN RELEASED ME from an awkward bear hug. I was a little stunned by that reaction to our story, but I guess successes had been in short supply for the past three months.

"Well done," he said for the seventh time.

"Thank you. Just doing our part," I replied as a variation on my previous acknowledgements.

While we'd given him a recap of the events on the surface, he'd listened even more attentively than during our previous meetings. When we got to the part about the black creatures, he'd seemed particularly intrigued.

"This information about the lifeforms is invaluable. We've never known if there was anything on the surface before now," he continued. "This is the evidence we've needed."

"Evidence of *what*?" Kaiden asked.

The commander took a deep breath and leaned his hip against the conference table. "We've suspected this was an attack, but we never knew for sure. Now that there's a lifeform involved, it supports that this was by design."

"Those were a far cry from an intelligent invasion force," I replied. "Seemed like mindless beasts to me."

"Maybe, maybe not," Toran interjected. "Watching you at the end, they were coordinated. Granted, many wild animals also use coordinated attacks, but that gets into a whole other matter of instinct versus intellect."

I crossed my arms. "Even if they're 'smart', there's a big difference between being an effective killing machine and being able to design tech that can blanket a world in Darkness. Those things down there don't strike me as the scientist type."

"But, it sounds like they *were* very well designed for their task," Colren cut in. "And the Darkness is, as well."

"That sounds like a leap in logic. There's no evidence that those creatures were designed to do anything; it might just be a side-effect of the Darkness infection. We don't know if they originated on that planet or not."

The commander sighed. "Perhaps I am just trying to see connections where there are none. It's been so many months with no answers."

Kaiden pursed his lips. "Say that they *were* designed, though. Why have such a creature when the native population has already been turned into a pile of soot?"

"We don't yet have enough information to even hazard a guess," Colren replied with a dejected shake of his head. He gathered himself. "Let's just get you back to the Archive. That's one part in all of this we *can* control." He rose from the table and smoothed his black uniform jacket.

"We'll be ready to head out right away," I said.

"It'll be at least another three hours before we can jump," he replied. "They're still tending to the shuttle. We don't want to leave anything to chance, and we can't jump until the crew is finished and can go to their pods."

Kaiden cracked a smile. "A little R&R, then?"

I nodded. "I could certainly use it. And a stop by the equipment room to get a new scabbard."

"Tend to your business. We'll announce the jump time when the maintenance crew is nearing completion."

"Thank you, Commander. We'll see you on the other side," Kaiden acknowledged.

We departed the conference room in Central Command and nodded to the crew on our way out. There were smiles on their faces and their eyes were alight with hope that hadn't been there when I'd first met them.

Though I didn't feel like we'd accomplished much, we were delivering on the promise we'd made to *try*, and that counted for something. I wouldn't feel better until the Master Archive was sealed—the artifacts were next to meaningless without that step.

"I'm going to see if my sword has been cleaned yet so I can size a new scabbard for it," I said once we were out in the main corridor.

Kaiden nodded. "I'd like to browse through the equipment inventory again now that we've been through a few fights. Mind if I join you?"

"Of course not."

"Well, *I'm* going to relax," Maris stated, not shocking me in the least.

"I could use some down time, myself," Toran admitted. "I'll be in our common room."

"Okay, see you there later," I said.

Kaiden and I headed for the lift.

"Are you feeling better?" he asked me when we were alone. "You seemed pretty shaken up after that fight."

"Yeah, I'm fine."

He didn't say anything else for the lift ride down, only

casting me the occasional sidelong glance. When we reached the lower deck, we strolled down to the hangar. Tami and the crew were out of their hazsuits, and we found them arranging our equipment near where our shuttle was typically berthed.

"What can I do for you?" Tami asked when she saw us approaching.

"I was hoping to get my new sword," I said. "I need a scabbard for it."

"Ah. Well, it's all cleaned up," she replied with a frown. "Looks like things got messy down there."

"It's been quite an eventful day or three." I forced a smile.

"We'll be back to the Archive soon, as I understand it," she said.

Kaiden nodded. "Not sure what will happen after that, but we're making progress."

"And we're grateful for it," the engineer responded. She paused. "Well, help yourself to your things. Holler if you need anything else."

"Thanks."

I grabbed my sword and Kaiden took his circlet.

"I *knew* it!" I teased. "You're addicted to your crown."

"It's not a—" He sighed, shaking his head.

I nudged him. "Come on, let's go see if any new items are available to us now that we have some combat experience.

We traced the corridor back to the equipment room with the 3D printer.

As soon as we were inside the privacy of the room, Kaiden stopped and looked me in the eyes. "Elle, are you sure everything is okay? You've seemed a little... off since Maris joined the team."

"We've had a lot going on," I replied.

He crossed his arms. "Don't be evasive. I can tell something is bothering you."

"I don't think you've known me for long enough to be able to read my mind."

"Who says I'm not telepathic?"

My mouth fell open a little, and my pulse spiked as I recounted some of the things I'd thought over the last several days. "I—"

He laughed and reached out his hand to place it reassuringly on my shoulder. "Relax, I'm just messing with you. But seriously, what's wrong—aside from everything?"

I took a deep breath and looked down. His touch on my shoulder was warm and comforting, and I fought the impulse to go in for a hug. So much had happened over the past few days, I could feel myself fraying around the edges. But the group dynamic was already strained as it was, and the last thing I needed was for him to react awkwardly about it. It was better to keep my concerns to myself and let my emotions fall back in line on their own.

"We had our trio thing going, and it worked. Now, the balance is weird," I replied, trying to sound diplomatic.

"Yeah, that addition caught me by surprise, too."

"And, if I'm being honest, it bothers me that she'll just kind of give up midway through. A moment of brilliance followed by 'I can't' rather than trying to push through."

He dropped his hand from my shoulder and shook his head. "Yeah, she's an odd one, isn't she?"

I eyed him. "What do you think of her?"

"A little too high maintenance for my taste. You and Toran have taken everything in stride, and she... hasn't. Then again, you seem more resilient than most."

"I thought maybe I was just being petty."

He nodded. "No, I hear you. I do think she's starting to get it, though."

"I'm..." I hesitated. "I'm concerned about you with her—"

Kaiden raised an eyebrow. "Oh, *really*?"

My cheeks flushed. "You cut me off! I'm concerned about her as a fellow caster—being your backup for an offensive spell. I worry that she could freeze while we're in the Archive when the pressure is really on."

"That could happen to any of us, Elle. Are you *sure* that's the only thing on your mind?"

I sighed.

"Come on, if we can't be honest with each other, then how are we supposed to work together?"

"Well," I mumbled, "I've seen the way she looks at you. You haven't exactly stopped her."

"Ah."

I crossed my arms. "What I mean is, this isn't remotely the right situation to be having those kind of thoughts. We can't afford distractions."

"Is it bad of me to point out that you're distracted by worrying about potential distractions?"

I glared at him.

"Sorry." Kaiden cracked a smile. "In all seriousness, though," he continued, "there's too much going on right now to have attention divided. Yeah, Maris puts on a show, but that's just how she is. It doesn't change what's important— what we're trying to do here."

"Yeah, you're right."

Kaiden dropped his voice to a whisper and looked me in the eyes. "Besides, Elle, if anyone had a chance of distracting me in that way, it wouldn't be her."

My heart warmed with the words—the kind of fulfilling flutter my friends had described but I'd never experienced for myself. I stayed focused on his intent gaze and I gave him a coy smile. "That's good to know."

He returned the smile. "You shouldn't have had any doubts."

"I have a bad tendency of overthinking things."

Kaiden brushed his hand down my arm. "Don't. We should probably focus on getting through this Archive sealing before... whatever might happen happens."

I nodded. "Getting all happening-y..." I bit my tongue. "Sorry, that went better in my head."

He chuckled. "It's fine. You're just overthinking it again."

"I'm bad at this stuff."

"Clearly I am, too, if you genuinely thought I had a thing for Maris."

"Okay, maybe not *that* much," I admitted.

"Still, I could have handled things better so you'd never have doubted my interest in you."

"It's only been a few days. I wasn't expecting anything."

Kaiden searched my face. "But it's been plenty of time to form an impression."

"That can happen in a moment."

"I know that feeling." He took half a step closer to me. "Any thoughts you'd like to share?"

There was a lot I wanted to say, though I knew I shouldn't... How at first I'd been drawn in by his looks, then questioned the attraction when his initial cavalier attitude came to light. But then I'd gotten to know his intelligence and heart, and it was clear he cared—not just about what we were doing, but those around him. And the more I learned, the more I liked what I saw.

We hadn't known each other for long enough to gauge how our viewpoints aligned on all matters, but there was no denying that a spark had been there from the beginning. I'd ignored it at times and misinterpreted it at others, but standing centimeters apart now, it was the most certain thing amid the present chaos.

I swallowed. "Didn't we *just* say what bad timing this is?"

"I'm also bad at listening to my own advice."

"Hey, we have that in common." I smiled.

He leaned closer to me the slightest measure. "I mean, if a distraction is there anyway, it might be better to get it out in the open."

I ran my fingers through the ends of my hair, suddenly feeling exposed with only my white shipsuit on. "Won't it be weird for the others if we…"

"You can only spend so much time worrying about other people before you go crazy."

"That's true." My heart pounded in my chest.

He brushed my hair away from my face with his index finger. "What would make the next trials easier for *you*? You don't have to ignore your own needs while looking after others."

"I don't know." A tingle spread throughout me, radiating from his touch. I wasn't sure exactly what I wanted to happen next, but I knew I wanted more.

His eyes locked on mine. "Well, *I'd* like—"

The door slid open, breaking the moment.

Maris barged in, and Kaiden and I instantly took a step back from each other.

"I decided I really need more practical sho—" She cut off when she saw us standing away from the scanner. "Sorry, am I interrupting?"

"Not at all. New shoes are always top priority," I replied, hoping the dim lighting in the room hid the flush in my face.

Whatever had almost happened, she didn't need to know about it.

She gestured to the scanner. "Have you already…?"

"No, go ahead," I told her.

Maris looked us over again but wisely said nothing.

When she turned her back, Kaiden cast me a knowing glance and subtle smile, which I returned.

I didn't have much experience in relationships of the romantic nature, but I did know that a solid friendship was the foundation of any worthwhile partnership. If nothing else, the challenges ahead would be very informative about what kind of future we could possibly have together; if this madness didn't test a bond, nothing would.

Maris stepped into the scanner and made her new footwear selection while we waited. She picked a pair of boots with only a slight heel, not too dissimilar from mine. I wanted to make a snide 'I-told-you-so' comment about her original footwear, but I didn't since I knew it wouldn't be helpful—especially since I hadn't cautioned against it before when I had the chance.

She sent the production request to the 3D printer. "All yours. Thanks for letting me jump ahead."

"Yeah, no problem," Kaiden acknowledged. "Elle, you want to get set up?"

"Sure."

While Maris waited for her new boots to print, I held up my sword in the holographic scanner and used the interface to customize a scabbard for it using one of the base designs.

"May as well see if anything else catches your eye," Kaiden suggested when I'd sent the scabbard to the printer.

"You don't mind?"

"That's all I came down here to do. I'll watch for anything that looks interesting."

A chime at the back of the room beeped and the panel slid open to expose Maris' new black boots.

"These will do," she murmured, admiring them. She scooped them up in her arms. "Have fun with your shopping. See you upstairs."

"See ya," I bid her as she left the room.

I waited for the door to close. "Browsing the inventory is the *only* thing you came down here to do?" I asked Kaiden.

"Well, I did also want to make sure you were doing okay."

"Then the conversation kind of took a turn."

"It did." He paused. "Should I finish saying what I was about to when Maris showed up?"

Almost every part of me wanted to shout a resounding 'yes', but the logic part of my brain had had a chance to regain a foothold. "I want to see where this can go, but we'll be at the Archive in a few hours. We can resume this after it's sealed."

He nodded. "Okay."

I sensed his disappointment, but it was the kind that came from accepting a harsh truth. And, realistically, we were only hitting pause for a day. If we couldn't exhibit that measure of self-control, then we had no business getting involved in the first place.

With the tension temporarily diffused, I turned my attention to the holographic menu system. I was content with my present clothing, so I decided to focus on potential accessories.

Most of the items were useless for our mission, but a glove caught my eye. It was classified as an accessory, but the description struck me as a weapon.

"Is this right?" I questioned. "Can it really fire a blast capable of knocking an enemy back?"

Kaiden read the description from next to me. "Certainly

makes it sound that way."

The rendering of the glove was dark gray in color with teal accents along the fingers and knuckles. Its palm contained a white patch ringed in the same teal accent color.

"I don't get how *that* could produce a physical blast," I insisted.

"Maybe it has something to do with your abilities? This magic-tech likes to bend the rules."

"That it does." I shrugged. "Well, only one way to find out if it works, right?"

"Very true," Kaiden agreed.

I sent the item to the printer.

"All right, let me take a quick look to see if there's anything else open to me that wasn't showing up for you." Kaiden took my place on the platform and started browsing through the inventory to see what was available for the skills in his discipline.

"Huh, that's weird," he said after a minute.

"What?"

"That glove you got is marked in my menu as being only for casters."

"Really?" I walked up behind him. "That can't be right."

"Take a look." He pointed to it.

There was no mistaking the notation. My brow knit. "Then why did it let me select it?"

"That's a very good question."

OUR RELAXATION TIME was short-lived before the jump, but I was eager for us to get back to the Archive. I tried to nap as much as possible during our time in hyperspace in my pod; though it was next to impossible to sleep unless one was passed out, I at least managed to clear my mind.

We were about to enter the final push. There could be anything waiting for us in the Archive—a single button to push, an endless string of monsters, a labyrinth. I wasn't about to rule out any possibility after what we'd been through over the past several days.

I was also happy to have the time to reflect on my conversation with Kaiden. After thinking it through, I decided it was ultimately a good thing Maris had shown up when she did. As curious as I was to explore our growing connection, this *really* wasn't the time to test that out; after all, if we decided we hated each other, it'd make for a pretty awkward trek through whatever caves or fields we might find ourselves traversing in the future. Still, I looked forward to a time when we were settled enough to give a relationship a chance.

When the *Evangiel* arrived at Crystallis, we exited our pods and began dressing in our clean gear, which we'd retrieved before the jump. In the case of my boots, however, apparently the treads had been so caked in guts from the alien creatures that the crew had deemed it easier to manufacture a new pair using my saved template rather than clean them.

I wiggled my toes in the replacement shoes. "Damn, I'd *just* gotten the other ones properly broken in."

Kaiden buckled his belt. "I'm sure these will be seasoned in no time."

"Please tell me there isn't another ten kilometer hike in our future," Maris moaned.

I slipped my coat over my white base layer. "Oh, come now! Don't you want to test out your new boots?"

"I can do that quite successfully by staying within a reasonable distance from the shuttle," she replied.

"We can land close to the cave," Toran said as he secured his pauldrons. "However, we have no idea how deep we'll need to go inside."

"Great." She sighed. "The only thing better than going on a long hike is going on a long hike into a creepy cave."

"I wouldn't call it creepy, per se," I interjected. "More… mysterious, perhaps?"

"Yeah, let's go with that," Kaiden agreed.

"Creepy, mysterious, whatever it is, I don't like confined places," Maris said.

"It'll be fine," I tried to assure her. "I'm sure we'll be in and out in no time."

We finished dressing and then headed for the hangar. Our bags were waiting for us at the base of the shuttle's ramp, and we gathered them.

"Good luck down there," Tami said to us. "We made some

upgrades to the shuttle's sensor suite, which should help with your landing. We'll be cheering you on from here."

I placed my hand on my sword's hilt. "Thanks. We'll see you— Oh!"

"Forget something?" the engineer asked.

"Yeah, the monument. We were going to bring cleaning supplies to get it back to how it should be."

Kaiden shook his head. "Elle, I have to say that I'm impressed. After everything we've done over the past week, you still care about scrubbing some sealant off of an old stone."

"It's a *crystal*," I corrected, "and it's connected to an ancient artifact. We should be respectful."

He smiled. "I appreciate that you care."

"Sealant, you said?" Tami frowned. "That stuff is a pain to get off, but I have something that should do the trick." She motioned to one of her maintenance techs and gave instructions about what to bring back.

A minute later, the tech returned with a container of cleaning solution, some wipes, and gloves.

"This should get it off." She handed it to me.

"Thank you. We'll see you soon."

I dropped my bag and the cleaning supplies in the common room and then went to the bridge to assume my usual seat.

A somber mood settled in the bridge while we strapped in.

"Do we need a pep talk?" I asked while the shuttle taxied out of the hangar.

"This does seem like one of those times for a speech," Toran replied.

"I think you just volunteered yourself, Elle." Kaiden smiled at me.

I sighed. Giving speeches wasn't typically my thing, but I

was feeling oddly inspired. "Okay, well… I know we haven't known each other for long, but the past week has shown we're here because of a common goal. It has nothing to do with where we're from or what we were before we were called, but what's in our hearts. We will do anything to help our loved ones and the other victims.

"We didn't ask to be chosen for this role, but we were. It hasn't been easy, and I'm sure it won't get easier, but we have each other." My gaze met Kaiden's for a moment. "Everyone is counting on us now, and we need to push forward for them. We're going to go in there and do whatever it takes to seal the Archive, because that's the only way we can be sure our loved ones are safe. I know that won't be the end of it—the Darkness isn't going to go away just because the Archive is sealed—but it's a big step forward. It's a step that shows we can work together and do this.

"We may have started off as strangers, and maybe not all of us wanted to be fighters, but we've all risen to the occasion. I know *I've* done things I never dreamed I could do. Whoever I thought I was going into this, I now know I'm so much more. All that we need to do is try."

The others stared silently at me as I concluded.

"Was it that terrible?" I asked.

Kaiden shook his head. "No, that was actually really good. You sure you didn't prepare that?"

"No, just got all psyched up in the moment." I glanced behind me at Toran and Maris, both of whom still looked stunned. "You know, when someone gives a rousing speech, typically you cheer, or, you know, *react*."

"I was moved by your words," Toran stated matter-of-factly.

I shook my head and slouched in my seat. "I'm definitely

going to dial back my expectations for speech reception in the future."

"Might be the setting," Maris said. "Like, we're not facing each other, and arm-pumping is a little awkward in these harnesses."

"I am not a cheer-er," Toran said.

Kaiden chuckled. "Guys, the Dark Sentinels need to work on our team spirit."

"I'll say." I crossed my arms. "Well, I tried."

After clearing the *Evangiel*, the shuttle began its descent into Crystallis' turbulent atmosphere. Kaiden took manual controls as the clouds thickened outside the viewports.

The shuttle jerked as the first of the winds hit.

"What was that?" Maris asked.

"Oh, did we not mention that part?" I glanced back at her. "This whole planet it a mess. The inertial compensators don't work here for some reason, and we need to go in for a semi-blind landing."

She paled. "You *what*?"

"Nah, it'll be fine with the upgrades, I'm sure," Kaiden assured her. He frowned at the control panel. "Well, I mean, we'll figure it out."

"What's wrong?" I asked.

"The destination won't lock in the nav system," he replied.

"That's not the same issue we had last time, is it?"

"No, before we knew where we were going but couldn't see it. Now we have sensors to see where we are but the destination isn't standing out."

My chest constricted. "We saw something like this before… on the last planet that was touched by the Darkness."

"Shit, you're right." Kaiden paled.

"There's no visual sign of it," Toran stated in an assured

tone, but his drawn face belied his inner concern.

"Maybe the magical signatures are the first to be affected," I hypothesized.

Kaiden nodded. "Let's hope there's an extra layer of protection around the Archive like the dragons had."

"Stars, I hope we're not too late." I sunk as deep into my seat as I could.

"First we have to *get there*," Kaiden said. "I'll head us toward the spot where we entered the valley last time." He entered in our previous stopover location and adjusted the shuttle's course.

I nodded. "We found it once before that way."

We descended through the thick cloud cover, bracing ourselves against the turbulence. Maris moaned most of the way down, but I tuned her out, distracted by thoughts of what we might find at the Archive.

It hadn't occurred to me before that the Darkness might reach Crystallis before we returned. It had felt like we were making good time in our quest to retrieve the artifacts from the other worlds, though, in truth, we had no idea how the interstellar infection was transmitted. The affected worlds followed no clear location pattern or commonalities that were readily apparent. The only reference guide was the information the Hegemony had been able to extract from the Archive, and that was far from complete.

After an uncomfortable ten minutes, the shuttle dropped through the lowest cloud layer, revealing the barren landscape of the world.

I saw no hint of the Darkness, giving me hope that perhaps that wasn't the reason for the navigation issues. In my heart, however, I knew that was wishful thinking; this world was at risk like any other, and its time may have come.

"I think those are the rocks where we fought the lizard things," Toran said while pointing out the front viewport from his seat.

"That's correct based on this nav log," Kaiden confirmed. "Which means the valley should be up this way." He altered the craft's trajectory to head toward the mountain range to the east.

Kaiden followed the readings from the new sensor suite to navigate the shuttle through the foggy mountain pass to the hidden valley.

The cloud cover cleared as if a veil had been lifted, revealing the sheltered valley filled with thousands of crystals. To my relief, there was no sign of the black speckled infection I'd seen on my own world right before the reset. Maybe the Darkness *wasn't* here yet.

"Stars, this is amazing!" Maris gasped.

"Pretty incredible, isn't it?" I agreed.

"I've never seen crystals this size."

Kaiden shook his head. "Didn't even know it was possible before we came here."

"It's no wonder this place is kept hidden. I can only imagine what would happen if the location of this world got out," Toran said.

I nodded. "Regardless of your political opinions, I'm glad the Hegemony has more sense than that."

"They have reverence for the crystalline network, that much is clear," Toran murmured. "Their motivations behind it might be another matter, given what little information they've been willing to share."

"Can you blame them?" Kaiden asked while navigating the shuttle toward the landing site. "We're a bunch of random people they bioprinted after extracting our consciousness from… wherever it is we go between resets. Would you really trust us with your secrets, either?"

I laughed. "When you put it like that, I wouldn't, no."

Toran inclined his head. "We're only here because they were desperate, that's true. Perhaps after we complete this task we will have earned their trust."

"*I* think we've already done a lot for them," Maris stated.

"Well, *we* have," I corrected. "You pretty much just got here."

"Two days after you!"

"That's an eternity in this business." I grinned.

Kaiden landed the shuttle, with only a slight bump to indicate we were on the ground. "We'll all be veterans after we face this. Ready to go to the place no one has been for hundreds of years?"

I unbuckled my harness. "That *does* make it sound even cooler and more exclusive."

"The coolest and most exclusivist." Kaiden smiled back while he powered down the engine.

"I don't believe that's how I'd characterize this mission," Toran said, unbuckling his own harness.

"Just keeping it light, my friend." I patted him on the shoulder while I passed by his seat on my way to the common room.

I was about to put on my backpack but then thought better of it; whatever we might face inside, I wasn't going to need camping gear. I opted to instead grab the flashlight, a length of rope, and a tablet from the pack. I was able to fit the small tablet and flashlight in my coat's pockets, and the rope I slung diagonally over my arm and torso.

By the time I was finished, the others had joined me in the common room and had retrieved select items from their own bags. Only Toran opted for his full backpack.

"I'll bring a med kit," he stated. "May as well be prepared for a fight."

"I can take care of that." Maris replied.

"What if you're the one hurt?"

"Oh, right." She frowned. "I don't want to get hurt."

"I think that's a pretty universal sentiment," I responded.

Kaiden slipped a flashlight into his pants pocket. "We might not even have to fight anything. The artifact guardians may have been the worst of it."

"Hopefully." I didn't believe it for a second.

"Everyone ready?" Kaiden asked.

I checked my pockets. "Yep." I paused. "No, wait." I jogged over to where I'd left the cleaning supplies.

Kaiden sighed. "Elle, I appreciate what you want to do, but can't we deal with that later?"

I smiled. "Just saving us a trip. We can take care of it on the way back out."

"All right," he agreed. "Everyone else good to go?"

Toran and Maris nodded.

"Okay, let's go."

Toran released the exit hatch, and we filed down the ramp into the sand-like ground covering of crushed crystal.

The diffused light through the fog gave the valley a strange purple tint I hadn't noticed on our previous venture, likely because I was distracted by visiting an alien world for the first time. Even having spent the last week in space and on other planets, walking among the giant crystals remained the most awe-inspiring location of all those we'd visited.

We wove our way through the groups of crystals and rock formations toward the slope up to the cave entrance. I was mesmerized by the subtle hum in the air, which seemed to come from the crystals themselves. I was barely paying attention to where I was walking when a snarl from the shadows next to some rocks snapped me back to focus.

The sound was familiar. "Freaking stone lizards," I mutter, drawing my sword from its new scabbard.

Kaiden sighed. "Ugh, I hated those things."

Three of the spiny creatures emerged from the shadows at the base of a giant crystal five meters to our left.

"We really don't have time for this." Kaiden raised his hand, and a fireball shot out from the end of his staff. It divided into three, each headed directly for one of the stone lizards.

The fireballs struck each center mass, and they all but vaporized into ash.

I sheathed my blade. "You've gained some skills since the last time we were here."

"Crazy how far we've come, isn't it?" Kaiden strolled toward the cave's entrance.

When we reached the foot of the incline leading to the cave, we took a running start to get up the scree. The task was more challenging with my hands full of cleaning supplies, but I managed to make it to the top on my first attempt.

At the cave mouth, Kaiden illuminated a light orb in his palm and led the way inside.

We walked in silence on the way down to the inscribed column that had sent us on our hunt for the artifacts. When we arrived, everything was just as we'd left it, with the black sealant still marring the opaque crystal.

I set down the supplies at its base. "We'll get you back to how you should be."

"I don't think it can hear you," Maris said.

"Considering the artifact guardians, some kind of sentient force here wouldn't surprise me, actually," Kaiden said.

"Even if there isn't, good cosmic karma is never a bad thing," I added.

Toran nodded. "Indeed."

Maris sighed. "Okay, whatever."

Kaiden approached the back wall of the cave. "How do you think we get this open?"

"Maybe touch our artifacts to the symbols?" Toran suggested.

"Sounds reasonable." I drew my blade.

Together, Kaiden, Toran, and I extended our respective artifacts toward the stone wall, touching each to its corresponding symbol. I held my breath with anticipation.

Nothing happened.

"Okay, there goes that idea." Kaiden returned his circlet to his head.

I lowered my blade. "Maybe we need to use the items?"

"Punch the wall?" Toran raised an eyebrow.

"I dunno." I shrugged. "All of the other worlds we visited required us to interact with the crystals."

"Hmm, I wonder if that's the problem." Kaiden walked back over to the central column. "Maybe we need to do something with this?" He brushed his hand against the crystal's surface.

The white monolith glowed pale blue in response to his touch.

"I think you're onto something!" I jogged over and placed my hand on the opposite side. The light intensified.

Toran joined us. As soon as his hand touched the crystal, the light flashed blindly bright and then returned to a subtle light blue glow.

"Did that do it?" I wondered.

A moment later, the symbols on the wall started to glow.

To the left, the central crystal that the tunnel wrapped around began to glow, as well. The light took on more definition as the outline of an archway formed in the surface of the crystal wall, then pressed backward through the crystal to form an arched passageway.

I stepped toward it. "Well, shall we?"

24

"YEP, HIDDEN PASSAGEWAYS aren't the *least* bit ominous," Maris muttered when we entered the ethereal crystal corridor.

The walls were as smooth as a plane of glass. I wasn't sure if there had been some sort of camouflage over the entryway or if the pathway had actually formed right before our eyes. Given the transformative feats we'd witnessed over the past week, I was inclined to believe it was the latter.

The corridor sloped downward at a subtle angle, presumably passing underneath the spiraling tunnel we'd entered on the way in. It continued straight for twenty-five meters and then there was only blackness.

Kaiden held up his hand and increased the intensity of the light orb. The illumination cast on our faces got brighter, but the light faded three meters from us.

"Okay, yes, it's a little creepy," I acknowledged.

"Is the space so large that we can't see the walls, or is something actively suppressing the light?" Toran asked.

I looked behind us; the passageway through the crystal was visible, but it was only darkness all around us. "This is going to sound a little weird, but I don't know if here is *here*."

Kaiden spun around to look where I had. "What do you mean?"

"Remember on the last world in the tower where we fought the dragon? The geometry didn't work," I said. "I think there was some kind of magic at play, where reality was... distorted."

"Like, portals?" Toran asked,

"Maybe. Or perhaps distances aren't what they seem." I walked back in the direction of the passageway but stayed to the right. "There's one way to test the idea."

I stretched out my hands in front of me when I neared what should be a wall, but there was only emptiness. I continued forward until I was parallel with the mouth of the passageway; standing next to it, I saw only blackness.

The sight freaked me out, and I hastily stepped backward. "That isn't right."

"What?" Kaiden prompted.

"The corridor is there, but it... isn't." I steeled myself and returned to the parallel position. I extended my hand toward where it should be, feeling nothing. "Okay, if I'm not crazy, this is about to get even weirder."

I turned to my left, directly into where the crystal-lined corridor should be, and walked forward. I took five steps through the darkness, then turned left and continued walking. When I glanced over my shoulder, I saw that I was now on the left side of the passageway.

Kaiden was staring at me, dumbfounded.

"I just walked through—or behind—or whatever that supposedly solid thing we all came through, didn't I?" I questioned.

My companions nodded silently.

I shuddered while I returned to the group. "Okay, yeah,

this place is officially messed up."

Toran frowned. "So, if we're here-but-not-here, then where do we go?"

"That's assuming *here* is a place and not a... *not*-place?" Kaiden's statement ended more like a question.

"In other words, we may no longer be on Crystallis," Toran said with more certainty.

"Or, at least, maybe not the Crystallis we know," I replied. "This could be another reality entirely."

"How are we supposed to seal the Archive if we can't see anything?" Kaiden asked.

"I'd really love a 'how to' guide right around now," I muttered,

Maris wrapped her arms around herself. "I don't like this place."

"You can say that again." I took a few tentative steps deeper into the blackness away from the passageway. To my surprise, the doorway didn't seem to get any further away, though my friends did. "Hey, I think it's okay."

"*Nothing* about this is okay," Kaiden grumbled.

"No, come on. We just have to trust it," I said.

Kaiden eyed me suspiciously. "Did the Darkness get to you on the last world?"

I sighed. "No! The passage is there, even when I move away from it. I think it's a test—'only those willing to take a risk will advance' kind of deal."

"If you say so." Kaiden walked forward to my position. He looked back over his shoulder. "Huh. I see what you mean."

"I'll trust you," Toran said, coming to join us.

"Wait up!" Maris hurried after him.

We continued forward through the blackness for what felt like half a kilometer but it was impossible to tell. The passageway entry remained at a constant distance behind us as we moved forward, and whenever we backtracked, we were able to get to the opening.

I had no explanation for the magic at play, but it was one of the most fascinating things I'd ever witnessed. Had the situation been less dire, I could think of a dozen ways to play around with my friends using the unique properties of the place.

At last, something in the environment changed—so subtle I didn't notice it at first. A breeze was picking up around us, ruffling my long hair.

"Where's that coming from?" I asked.

Kaiden licked his finger and held it up in the air. "That way, I think." He pointed to the left.

"Wind means an opening," I said. "Maybe we should head that way?"

"I'll buy that logic." Toran altered his course to head in the direction Kaiden had indicated.

The arched passage continued to follow us to our left, moving perpendicular to us. As unnerving as it was to have something behave in such an odd fashion, I was thankful for the presence of its subtle white light amid the otherwise oppressive blackness—a lone constant to offer grounding.

After several dozen meters, the wind intensified until it was clearly coming from a specific point.

Kaiden's light didn't illuminate any walls, but I could feel the currents. The wind was coming from what I perceived to be a narrow tunnel.

"Onward?" I asked.

Kaiden nodded. "We've come this far."

"All right." I clicked on my flashlight and led the way inside single-file.

Like the light orb, the beam from my flashlight dissipated after three meters. However, the further I went into the tunnel, the ground began to take on more definition—transitioning from pure blackness to textured, dark stone.

Gradually, the walls began to take shape, as well. They started as an arched corridor and deeper into the tunnel flared outward until a cavern took shape. Behind me, the crystal passageway remained.

"Under any other circumstances, I would totally be freaking out right now," I said.

"I still might," Kaiden murmured. "This is *weird*."

"But fascinating," Toran stated.

"On a positive note, I'm loving my new walking boots," Maris chimed in.

I rolled my eyes. "Thrilled for you."

"Hold up." Kaiden grabbed my shoulder, stopping me.

My heart skipped a beat. Half a dozen paces ahead, the ground dropped out in front of us; I'd become so accustomed to walking through the blackness that I hadn't even noticed. "Thanks."

He came up next to me and smiled. "Gotta have each other's backs. Friends don't let friends walk off of cliffs."

"You never met my friends."

"Right, you and your cliff-jumping for *fun*."

"I would advise that we not recreate those antics here and now," Toran cautioned.

"No argument here." I cautiously approached the lip of the precipice.

There was only blackness below. Looking outward, I could tell the cavern continued, but I couldn't gauge how far back it went.

"Nothing down he—" I cut off as the ground started to

rumble.

I hastily stepped back from the ledge as rock fragments broke off and fell into the depths. "What's happening?"

"Either we did something wrong and the place is falling apart around us, or we're about to be tested again," Kaiden murmured. His orb of light morphed into a fireball.

"That figures." Maris sighed.

A purple protective shell appeared around me. "Thanks, Maris."

She smiled. "Here to help. You guys do… whatever it is you're supposed to do."

"Fight the thing?" Toran speculated.

I drew my sword. "Sure. Let's go with that."

The rumbling intensified, then a series of distinct concussive thumps shook the ground underfoot.

Poised with my sword at the ready, I braced for whatever monster might emerge.

Yellow light illuminated in the dark depths before us, casting a shadow of the creature climbing upward along the rock wall. It appeared to be shaped like a person, only bigger— or maybe that was a trick of the light.

When a hand sporting fingers longer than I was tall cleared the lip of the cliff, it was clear the lighting had not oversold the feature attraction.

Kaiden staggered backward. "Is that a rock titan?"

"It appears to be," Toran concurred.

"Wait, *that's* what you fought before I came?" Maris squeaked.

"Well, maybe one half this size," I replied.

"How… No. No way." She backed away.

"Relax, we probably don't have to actually fight it," Toran said.

Maris stared at him blankly. "What?"

"The other one just required us to demonstrate the principles of the discipline—protecting others," he explained.

The creature's head cleared the cliff and it fixed us in the vacant stare of its glowing yellow eyes.

"Should we skip the slashing and blasting bit?" I asked.

He nodded. "Mind being the bait again?"

"Not at all. I just hope this is right." I sheathed my sword and stepped forward.

"Elle—" Kaiden started to protest, but Toran placed a hand on his shoulder.

"I won't let it harm her," he said.

The titan glared at me as I walked forward until I was two paces from the edge of the cliff. Heart pounding in my ears, I waited.

The giant raised its hand to strike.

I stared into its yellow eyes, glowing with the same light I'd come to associate with ancient power. While I watched intently, waiting for the blow to come, I thought I saw the light flicker—a touch of Darkness clouding the brilliance.

"Did you—"

Before I could ask my question, the hand was rushing down to squash me, and time decelerated.

The hand's motion slowed as the world tinted orange. Toran ran up from behind me and held up his right fist above his head.

The rock titan's palm struck Toran's fist. From the point it made contact, the bonds holding the rest of the titan together disintegrated in a slow-motion wave, and it shattered into dust. The debris rained down around us.

"Well, that was easy," Kaiden said.

Maris looked dumbstruck. "I thought it was going to

smoosh you."

Toran gently patted my back. "I told you that wouldn't happen."

"Good thing you were right." I sighed with relief. "Hey, I don't know if you saw it, but I think I noticed a dark spot in the giant's eyes."

"Like, the Darkness kind of dark?" Kaiden asked.

I shrugged. "It was just a flash. I'm not sure."

The light emanating from the depths beyond the cliff shifted, drawing my attention. The rays consolidated and began to sway. After several seconds, ribbons of spiraling light drifted upward, heading for Toran.

He stood transfixed by the swirling light. The golden ribbons wove around him, then merged into him.

Toran gasped and fell to his knees.

"Are you okay?" I bent down over him.

He stared ahead, terror on his face as he seemed to see something that wasn't there. "The Darkness," he murmured. "It transmits through the crystals. I see it."

"A vision?" Kaiden asked.

Toran staggered to his feet. "Yes, sort of. But it's more like I know things now. It's too much to process at once."

The orange hue in my vision faded as the haste spell wore off.

"Where does the Darkness come from?" Maris asked.

Toran shook his head. "I don't know."

A strong wind ripped through the cavern, almost knocking me off-balance. Light illuminated once more in the dark depths, this time blue.

"Oh, boy. Here we go again." I placed my hand on my sword's hilt but didn't draw it.

"Another repeat of last time?" Kaiden pondered.

"Let's hope so. That was the least kill-y of all of them," I replied.

"It tried to drown me!"

"Only because you did the pattern wrong." I smirked. "You learned the right way real quick after that, didn't you?"

He shook his head. "You're impossible."

"Just speaking the truth."

The sound of rushing water overpowered the wind, and a tidal wave rushed up to form a wall before us, seemingly suspended in midair above the lip of the canyon. It shimmered with soft blue-green light.

"All you." I flourished my hand toward Kaiden.

He stepped toward the water, his staff raised.

A blob of water a meter tall plopped out from the wall and landed on the rocky ground in front of Kaiden.

"Okay, let's hope the pattern holds." He froze the blob into a column of ice and it shattered.

Two more blobs emerged in sequence, which he quickly dispatched with a fireball and lightning bolt, respectively. Then, three blobs appeared together, and he dealt a different elemental blow to each. When they had been dispatched, a fourth blob plopped down. He set down his staff and approached the water column, holding a hand to either side of it.

He stood there for thirty seconds with no magic.

"Uh, Kaiden?" I prompted.

"I'm trying! This healing thing doesn't come naturally."

The blob shuffled forward.

I frowned. "I think it's getting impatient."

"Yes, thank you." Kaiden sighed with obvious frustration.

I walked over to stand next to him and placed my hand on his back. "Hey, you've got this."

He glanced over at me. "Easier said than done."

"Don't overthink it. You did it once. You can do it again."

Kaiden took a slow breath and faced the blob. "Yeah." He closed his eyes.

Green light appeared between his hands, permeating the column of water. It glowed brightly and then lifted from the ground, floating back toward the wall. When it reached the water wall, it merged into it, and the light spread.

The water vaporized, leaving only the light behind.

In the final moments before the water vaporized, I thought I saw a glimpse of Darkness within it. The light was dim, though, so I couldn't be sure.

The ribbons of blue-green light glided toward Kaiden and I stepped back from him. The light wove around him, then seeped inward.

He took a choking breath and doubled over. After a couple of rapid breaths, he straightened. "I saw something," he whispered.

"What?" I asked, wondering if it was the same dark flicker I'd seen.

"It was—" He didn't have time to answer before wind ripped through the cavern once more.

"Talk later. It's dragon time," I said.

"Yeah. I'm a little less clear on the trick with this one," Kaiden said. "As I recall, you almost fell off of the tower."

"I totally had that under control," I lied.

"But what should we do?" he pressed. "Are you going to try to talk it down like you did last time?"

"I mean, the others went down like they did before, right? May as well try," I replied.

Red light lit up the dark depths and a vicious roar echoed through the chamber.

"Yeah, talking to it is a *great* idea," Maris grumbled.

The purple protective shell returned around each of us.

"Watch, we'll be out of here in no time." I drew my sword but kept it angled down in what I hoped was a non-threatening stance.

Another roar cut through the quiet, followed by the flapping of immense wings.

The dragon cleared the cliff, beating its wings to hover five meters above us. This one was darker red, and its scales almost appeared to glow in the scarlet light shining from below.

"We've come to protect the Archive," I shouted. "Please, tell us what we need to do."

The dragon tilted its head questioningly. Then, its brilliant green eyes widened. It spasmed.

"Uh…" I stepped back from the cliff.

"That doesn't seem right," Kaiden murmured.

The giant beast thrashed its wings to stay aloft, writhing in midair. To my horror, its skin began to darken, changing from crimson to inky black. The dark transformation flowed over it like paint until it was completely transformed.

It gained control of its movements and turned its head to face me. The green eyes morphed to black.

"The Darkness!" I started to warn.

A blast of fire surrounded us, with only Maris' protective shields keeping it from scorching us alive. Even through the magical barrier, my skin seared.

"Okay, so maybe no talking!" I gulped.

"Was that supposed to happen?" Kaiden shouted back.

"I think the Darkness has infected it," I replied. "Who knows what this place was supposed to be like."

"Is it too late to seal the Archive?" Toran asked.

"I have to believe it's not. Not everything was corrupted,

just this form. We can still do this." I raised my sword. "Come down and fight us!" I shouted at the dragon.

"Way to invite trouble, Elle." Kaiden readied a ball of ice on his staff, poised to deploy it.

"I'm just reacting to what I'm given," I said.

The dragon swooped down, its talons outstretched.

Toran punched at one of the feet as it passed by overhead, the only part of the creature low enough to reach.

Kaiden blasting a rapid volley of ice balls at it, aiming for the orange fire pouch in its throat. The blasts connected, but the dragon seemed unfazed.

"Another haste spell would be great!" I yelled while jumping and thrusting my blade upward toward the dragon. Being shorter than Toran, the blade only grazed the dragon's foot when I jumped.

"I'm on it," Maris replied.

My surroundings tinted orange again, though it was a subtle difference in the already red light.

The dragon circled around for another assault, now seeming to move in slow motion.

"Toran, boost me up when it comes by," I suggested.

He nodded his understanding and cupped his hands to give me a stirrup.

When the dragon approached again, it was much lower and its talons were extended like it was ready to grab us.

I assessed the timing, and when the moment felt right, I ran toward Toran, planting my foot in his hands. He heaved me upward, and I raised my sword. With the extra height, the blade plunged into the dragon's belly.

It roared and tilted sideways, one of its massive wings dropping toward the ground as the body rotated.

My boost from Toran carried me forward through the air

as the beast fell. I landed on my feet and transitioned into a roll to diffuse my momentum.

When I leaped to my feet and turned around, the dragon was recovering its balance while taking a beating. Toran was administering rapid punches to its side while he had access, Kaiden was lobbing ice balls and electrical charges, and even Maris was slashing at its wing with her dagger.

I ran back to help them.

I'd gone two steps when the orange tint faded and my time perception returned to normal.

The dragon snapped its wing back in one swift motion and slammed it onto my companions. They flew backward and hit the rock wall hard, the protective shell spent. All three of them crumpled to the ground, motionless.

"No!" I ran toward them.

Their chests were moving with breath, to my relief, but they appeared to be out cold. It was just me against the beast.

I stared it down. "Let's end this."

THE DARK DRAGON roared at me, tendrils of smoke rising from its nostrils.

I couldn't hesitate. It was all down to me.

My sword was useless from this distance; I needed a different approach. I ran through a mental inventory of everything I had with me. The rope wouldn't be helpful for me alone, and everything else required being close. Then, I remembered the blaster in the palm of my new glove. I looked at the device and saw that it was now glowing with white light.

In one motion, I dove to the side to distract the dragon from my fallen friends and blasted an energy orb from the new hand device. I expected it to be a little light show, but to my surprise, a blast comparable to one of Kaiden's fireballs shot from it.

The blast struck the dragon beneath its eye, and it rounded on me with a snarl.

I shot another blast, which seemed to do nothing other than annoy the dragon. To take it down, I'd need to hit it in a vulnerable place, and I'd need more than a weapon that only went skin deep.

The orange glow beneath the dragon's jaw caught my eye. Having watched how the creature moved, I could tell it was guarding that part of itself—its one weakness.

But I'd have to get close, and the heat would be a major issue. I hoped my magical blade would be able to withstand it, but my hands would be burned to a crisp before I ever got close enough. I'd need protection, and normal armor wouldn't do.

Toran was only three meters away where he still lay unconscious. I dashed over and grabbed his gauntlets from his hands; the magical items just might be enough to withstand the heat without melting. They were far too big for me, but I could still grip my sword through them.

I was about to turn back to face the dragon when Kaiden caught my eye next to Toran. He was starting to stir.

"Take it," he murmured.

"Are you okay?" I asked, crouching down.

He winced. "Take it," he repeated with a motion toward his head. "The circlet."

"It's useless to me."

Kaiden shook his head. "You're a caster, Elle. I saw what you just did."

My heart skipped a beat. "I am?"

"The three disciplines. That's what this was always about. But not three distinct people—three in one." He managed to remove the circlet from his head. "Take it!"

The dragon roared.

"Stay here." I took the circlet from him and placed it on my head. A surge of energy flowed through me. My hands tingled, and my senses were sharp. I felt like I could tackle anything.

I charged toward the dragon, raising my sword for a strike. Two strides from it, I leaped into the air, jumping higher and faster than I ever had before. I drove the blade into the dragon's throat and used my momentum to rip downward.

The orange fire liquid flowed from the wound, burning the dragon's flesh everywhere it touched.

I fell free of the splatter zone only centimeters from the edge of the cliff.

The dragon sputtered and it fell into the depths.

I panted and it turned into a laugh. "Is that it? Did I do it?"

"I think so." Kaiden staggered to his feet behind me.

Toran and Maris began to rouse.

"What happened?" Maris moaned, gripping her head.

The red light beyond the cliff consolidated and began flowing toward me. I couldn't help tensing as it wrapped around me. It seeped into my skin.

Images flashed before my eyes and my head pounded.

I saw the Darkness snaking its way through a world, permeating everything in its path. The matter morphed to fit the image of the Darkness, becoming twisted to its form. But there was more behind it—not a mindless infection, but design. The beings born from the native wildlife were hybrids, a mutation combined with the genetic makeup of the alien beings behind the Darkness. The worlds weren't being consumed, they were being *transformed.*

My eyes shot open. I realized I was lying on my back on the cold stone. Kaiden was bent over me.

"Are you all right?" he asked.

"Yeah." I sat up, bringing my hand to my head. My gloved fingertips clinked against the circlet. "You can have this back now, thanks." I handed it to him.

"What are you doing with that and my gauntlets?" Toran asked, coming over.

I smiled. "Just saving the day."

Kaiden helped me to my feet. "I think Elle got something of a special treatment when she was formed—a little of everything rather than just one discipline."

Toran's eye widened. "Oh, really?"

I shrugged. "A matter for future investigation. The important thing now is that the dragon is dead."

"What about sealing the Archive?" Maris asked.

"Still trying to figure that part out." I looked around the dark cavern. "There has to be a path, or monument, or something."

"Unless we're too late," Toran said. "I know none of us want to consider that possibility, but we *are* surrounded by darkness right now. Whether it is *the* Darkness, I don't know."

"You're right: I *won't* consider it." I removed the gauntlets and thrust them toward Toran. "There's something here."

I retrieved my flashlight from my pocket and followed the edge of the cliff toward the left and it dead ended in a rock wall. I went the opposite direction and found that it continued. After fifty meters, the ledge narrowed to a two-meter-wide path.

"Elle, where are you going?" Maris asked, running up behind me.

"We're about to find out."

"They certainly make this complicated," Kaiden said.

"Nothing worthwhile is easy," Toran told him. "I only hope our efforts will pay off."

The path widened again after thirty meters to a seven-meter-diameter platform, which was surrounded on all sides by blackness. At the center of the platform was a solitary two-meter-tall crystal.

"Together," I said, motioning to Kaiden and Toran.

We each extended our right hand and touched the crystal.

A soft blue glow rose throughout the cavern. As it got

brighter, the shapes of crystals began to take form. They blanketed every surface for as far as I could see, with no bottom or ceiling in sight.

I took it in, awed. "This is incredible!"

"Wow." Maris shook her head with disbelief next to me.

"Greetings, Chosen," a voice said from all directions in a warm, neutral timbre.

"Hello?" I replied.

"You have made it past the trials and proven you are pure of heart. Why do you journey now to the Master Archive?"

"There's a Darkness spreading. It may already be here, but the Archive needs to be sealed."

"A protocol is in place," the voice replied. "Before the act is complete, you must understand what it means for the worlds connected to the crystalline network. When the Archive is sealed, no new records can be added until it is unsealed. The crystals on the worlds will be useless until then."

I looked to my companions. "Not like they're doing us a lot of good now."

They nodded.

"We understand. Proceed with the sealing."

"Acknowledged."

The crystals flashed briefly, and then the light dimmed to dull gray.

"Sealing complete," the voice stated. "The Archive will remain in this state until the Chosen return."

"All right, so we should probably not die," Kaiden quipped.

I raised an eyebrow. "I would have hoped that was the plan, anyway."

"Is there anything we must know to unseal it?" Toran asked.

"Only purity of intentions," the voice replied.

"What of the Darkness?" I asked. "Can you tell us anything about it? We heard that the Archive might contain information about events that haven't happened yet."

"It is true that this place exists outside of time as you know it. But truths must be discovered in their due course."

"Not even a hint?" Kaiden asked.

"You have already been given the knowledge you need."

"Those visions!" I said. "That was you? I thought the Darkness had infected it."

"The challenge is designed to prey on your fears to test what is in your heart. The Darkness is your greatest threat, and so that is how it manifested. This place is safe, and so it will remain now that you have completed your task."

"Thank you," I said. "Hopefully, next time we meet it will be under better circumstances."

"You will never be far."

The crystal column at the center of the platform flashed, and a shard the size of my thumb flaked off.

"A gift to aid you in the trials ahead," the voice said.

I picked up the shard; it was opaque white and glowed slightly with a soft blue light. I placed it in my pocket. "Thank you."

"Go now. The entry will re-seal behind you."

"All right, Dark Sentinels! Mission number one: accomplished." Kaiden grinned.

"Yeah, I guess so." I expected to feel more excited, but there was still so much ahead. A backup of my world was now safe, but the world itself was lost until we could restore it. We had scored a victory, but it was only the first step.

We walked back single-file along the narrow path.

"Why don't you look happy, Elle?" Maris asked when we reached the wider area near the entry. "It's over."

I shook my head. "It's *not* over. Yes, the Archive is safe now, but the Darkness is still out there and we need to figure out how to stop it."

"About that... I saw things. Right after the Spirit challenge," Kaiden murmured.

"What did you see?"

"Ships," Kaiden replied. "Alien ships. They were traveling to the worlds consumed by the Darkness."

"And I saw the Darkness spreading through the crystals," Toran added. He turned to me. "What about you, Elle?"

"The Darkness was transforming the worlds." I gave them an account of my vision.

"Hmm. So, maybe the Darkness is like some sort of advanced preparation for the aliens?" Kaiden posited. "Transform the world to their specifications."

"And, based on your vision, it would seem that the creatures we encountered may have been transformed by the Darkness," Toran stated.

"If those are hybrids, then what are the beings behind it?" Kaiden wondered aloud.

"Evil, whatever they are," I muttered. "This is a war. A full-on invasion."

"But we did it," Maris said. "We sealed the Archive. It's safe. Our worlds can be restored."

"Not until the threat is gone," Kaiden countered.

I crossed my arms. "Yes, but how do we do that?"

"Not sure, but I suspect it will be up to us to figure out."

"And we won't do that standing here." Toran gestured toward the exit.

We took the doorway to the crystal corridor, which had embedded in the back wall of the cavern, and trudged out of the Archive, exhausted. When we reached the column at the end of the stone tunnel leading from the cave mouth, the cleaning supplies were waiting at the base of the monument.

"I know we're tired, but I think we should put this back how it's supposed to be," I said.

"A few extra minutes won't kill us," Kaiden replied.

"I can help with the tiredness." Maris waved her hand and a rejuvenating wave washed over us.

Kaiden helped me clean off the crystal, returning it to its natural milky white. Though no magical being appeared to thank us for cleaning the ancient artifact, I felt in my heart it was the right thing to do.

When we were finished, the four of us returned to the shuttle.

The mood for the ride back was lighter than it had been in recent days. I suspected that would change as soon as we debriefed with the commander, but it was temporary relief.

We docked on the *Evangiel* in our usual berth.

Tami came to meet us as we exited the shuttle. "Did you do it?"

I grinned. "Archive sealed."

She placed her hand on her chest. "Thank the stars!"

"The Darkness is still out there, but the backups are safe. We'll find a way to restore the worlds," Kaiden said.

The engineer nodded. "I have no doubt you will." She took a shaky breath. "The commander is expecting you."

"We're on our way." Toran headed for the hangar door and we followed.

We took the lift up to the bridge level and walked down the corridor toward Central Command.

When we passed by the entry to an ancillary pod room, Kaiden motioned to me. "Elle, hang back a minute."

Toran looked back questioningly.

"We'll be right there," Kaiden told him.

When the others had gone ahead, and Kaiden motioned me inside the pod room.

"You were amazing today," he said when the door had closed. "I don't mean to say that in private because I wouldn't say it in front of them. It's not that." He stepped closer to me.

"Then why?" I searched his face.

"Because when I was lying there looking up at you, thinking it was all over, all I could think about was that we'd left things at a 'maybe someday'. But we have no idea what's coming tomorrow or a minute from now, so what's the point in waiting?"

"There might always be a 'next mission'."

"Exactly." He continued toward me until we were only centimeters apart. Slowly, he brought one hand up to my shoulder and then gently slid it upward to cup the side of my face.

His touch warmed me, sending an excited tingle to my core. I gazed into his radiant blue eyes. "Then let's not wait."

Our lips met and he wrapped his arms around me. I returned the hug as we shared the tender moment, forgetting our troubles in the universe beyond. We had each other, and in those seconds that was all I wanted.

When we parted, I gave him a bashful grin. "I have to say, that was worth the wait."

"I heartily agree." He gave me another soft kiss.

I wanted nothing more than to lose myself in the bliss, but I knew others were waiting on us. I pulled back slightly and entwined his fingers in mine. "What now?"

He laughed. "I have no idea."

"Should we say something?"

"Seems like a formal announcement would be weird."

"Yeah, so…"

He cupped his other hand around our interlaced fingers. "Maybe we just drop a few subtle hints and let them figure it out for themselves?"

"I like that approach." I placed my free hand over the crystal shard in my pocket. "We should probably go debrief with the Commander."

"Right."

Hand-in-hand, we walked up to the conference room in Central Command.

Our comrades gave us a questioning look when we entered, but we casually dropped our hands to our sides like there was nothing to see.

"So, you did it? The Archive is sealed?" the commander questioned, romance clearly the last thing on his mind.

"Yes, and we learned some things in the process," Kaiden began. He gave a recap of our visions and what we'd been able to piece together, while we interjected anecdotes as seemed appropriate.

Colren shook his head with amazement when we finished. "That explains so much."

"Unfortunately, that doesn't really help us know how to stop the Darkness and whatever beings are behind it," Toran replied.

The commander nodded. "Well, it's a start. And now we know this was a first wave and ships may be coming next. That's more information than we had before."

Maris crossed her arms. "But still, *all* of that and it didn't give us any other hints about what to do next? For a place that supposedly holds all the answers, we didn't get much."

"There was nothing else?" Colren asked.

"Well, there was one other thing," I said, pulling the crystal shard from my pocket.

The commander gingerly took the crystal from me. "Where did you get this?"

"It broke off from a crystal within the Archive," I replied. "The voice said it would aid us in the trials ahead."

"Stars!" Colren exclaimed. "Could it be…?" He stared with wonder at the tiny crystal fragment.

"Does that mean something to you?" I asked.

"If I'm not mistaken," he began, "this might be a shard from a Master Crystal. I didn't think we'd ever get access to one."

I tilted my head. "What is it, exactly?"

"If legend holds, it's connected to the Master Archive," Colren explained. "Such a shard provides a direct tether to the only storage medium that allow backups beyond our inhabited worlds."

Kaiden crossed his arms. "That sounds fancy, but how does that do us any good?"

The commander's eyes lit up. "Oh, it changes *everything*! This gives us a control point."

My heart skipped a beat. "You mean…"

Colren nodded. "This will allow us to access the Master Archive from anywhere." He held up the crystal. "With this, we can perform a universal reset."

"That's great!" Maris exclaimed. "Now you can do a reset and save our worlds."

Toran drooped. "No, having this tool doesn't eliminate the underlying threat."

Colren nodded solemnly. "This gives us hope, but it's not a magical fix." He activated the desktop and brought up a holographic recording of four worlds marred by incremental stages of Darkness infection. The dark clouds swirled around the planets, devoid of any signs of life. "This is what's become of your worlds."

My stomach turned over, realizing that I hadn't even recognized my home of Erusan.

"This is only the beginning," the commander continued. "The aliens will just come back if we do a universal reset now. We need to *stop* them."

Kaiden's gaze hardened. "We have some special abilities, yeah, but how are *we* supposed to go up against *that*?"

"I don't have an answer, but we've exhausted all of our other options," Colren stated. "You may have viewed your last task as a fun adventure, but the real invasion is coming. We currently have no way to stop the aliens' advance. What's happened to your worlds," he motioned to the holograph, "will happen to *every* world in the Hegemony if we don't find a way to fight back. You four are our best hope."

"How long do we have?" Toran asked.

Colren shrugged. "Weeks? A month, maybe? The rate of infection is accelerating. I didn't want to distract you from your task of sealing the Master Archive, but the truth is that we're past desperate. Though I wish I could send you home and say everything is going to be okay, that's not the reality."

I fought back a wave of guilt. I'd spent the last week living a super-charged version of my dream to be a Space Ranger, ignoring the unpleasant facts of my circumstances. The Hegemony was at a critical juncture, and I had the chance to make a difference. I couldn't shirk that responsibility when it mattered the most.

"Whatever's need, I'm in," I declared.

"Me too," Kaiden affirmed, then he whispered just loud enough for me to hear, "I guess you're stuck with me for a little longer."

I smiled back. "I'm okay with that."

"I never turn away from a challenge," Toran said.

Maris drew a deep breath. "Guess I can't lose my nerve now."

The commander gazed at each of us in turn. "We can't afford to lose any more worlds. We don't have any time to waste."

I steeled my resolve. "Tell us what we need to do."

THE STORY CONTINUES IN *A LIGHT IN THE DARK...*

The real invasion is about to begin....

Elle and her friends must venture into the unknown as they try to solve the mystery of the Darkness' origin. With the threat of an alien invasion on the horizon, they are the Hegemony's only hope to stop the insidious menace before every world is consumed.

The shard of the Master Crystal offers them a chance to reverse the damage, but with no knowledge of what a universal reset might entail, its use is a last resort. However, as distant threats turn into brutal realities, no step may be too extreme in the frantic fight for survival.

ALSO BY A.K. DUBOFF

Dark Stars Trilogy
Book 1: Crystalline Space
Book 2: A Light in the Dark
Book 3: Masters of Fate

Cadicle Space Opera Series
Book 1: Rumors of War (Vol. 1-3)
Book 2: Web of Truth (Vol. 4)
Book 3: Crossroads of Fate (Vol. 5)
Book 4: Path of Justice (Vol. 6)
Book 5: Scions of Change (Vol. 7)

Mindspace Series
Book 1: Infiltration
Book 2: Conspiracy
Book 3: Offensive
Book 4: Endgame

Troubled Space
Vol. 1: Brewing Trouble
Vol. 2: Stealing Trouble
Vol. 3: Making Trouble

AUTHOR'S NOTES

Thank you for reading *Crystalline Space*!

I had the idea for this series floating around in my head for a long time, and it wasn't until this year that the timing worked out for me to finally write it.

I first started playing video games in my late-teens—well after many of my peers. For the longest time, I thought games were all Mario-style "platformers" or racing-style games, and I didn't know the genre of role playing games (RPGs) even existed. *Chrono Trigger* was the first RPG I played, and I found it to be like an interactive novel. After I played *Final Fantasy VII* next, I was hooked.

One play mechanic I always found interesting in these games was that when you got a "game over", you could reset and try again with some knowledge of what was coming. With boss battles, in particular, there was almost always a trick to beating them that you could apply from the get-go on subsequent attempts. The *characters* didn't know what was coming, but you as the player did.

I started thinking about how to mimic that precognizance in literary form where the characters were in control of their own destiny without an omniscient player to guide them. And thus, Dark Stars was born.

I couldn't have brought this book to market without the amazing team helping me behind the scenes.

First, a shout-out to fellow author M. D. Cooper for hearing my initial concepts for these series and helping me think through the details. He also organized the *Galactic Genesis* boxset where this book premiered.

My fantastic team of beta readers helped craft this book into what it is today. Kurt, Eric, Pam, Liz, and Randy, you have incredible insights and I love your honest feedback! I appreciate you saying the tough truths and pushing me to bring my writing to the next level.

I also owe huge thanks to my proofing team to add the final polish. Nick, Charlie, John, Diane, Leo, and Jim, thank you for your time and eagle eyes. You are fantastic, and I'm so happy you have my back!

On the personal side, my husband, Nick, has been my greatest cheerleader. He kept me fed and sane during the late nights of working, and I'm forever thankful to him for enabling me to pursue a career writing full-time. He is the best friend and life partner I could ever imagine.

I hope you enjoyed this first installment in the Dark Stars trilogy! Have fun on the rest of the ride :-).

ABOUT THE AUTHOR

A.K. (Amy) DuBoff has always loved science fiction in all its forms—books, movies, shows and games. If it involves outer space, even better!

Now a full-time author, Amy can frequently be found traveling the world. When she's not writing, she enjoys wine tasting, binge-watching TV series, and playing epic strategy board games.

To learn more or connect, visit www.amyduboff.com.